Compelled by circumstances to leave his mother, and sent to live on his grandparent's isolated farm, Jonathan is resentful and hostile towards the change in his lifestyle.

His grandparents, believing their well ordered routine will be disrupted, are not particularly enthusiastic about it either; indeed his grandfather reacts strongly to Jonathan's behaviour, and confrontation is inevitable.

Sometimes hilariously funny, at other times poignant, Jonathan's experiences encompass feelings of joy, sorrow, love, hate, fear and courage. His own emotional development is considerably influenced by these experiences, and his activities ensure that life will never be quite the same again for many people in his environment.

From the mid nineteen thirties, until two years after the outbreak of the Second World War, the story follows those seasonal events which order life in an agricultural community. Jonathan, intentionally or unintentionally, for better or worse, is involved in most of them.

His determination to solve the mystery of a 'missing' uncle results in the disclosure of a family skeleton which nobody knew about, and this has a far reaching effect upon everybody concerned.

Joan Wilkinson

THE DEVIL FOUND SIXPENCE

The Author

It was the beginning of the end of the era of the heavy horses, although they still outnumbered tractors, when John Jarvis began dividing his formative years between agricultural communities in the West Country and East Anglia.

After National Service in the Army, and five years with the N.S.P.C.C., he worked as a Probation Officer in Staffordshire. He then moved up to Yorkshire as a Senior Probation Officer, working in Prison Welfare and Divorce Court Welfare, until early retirement enabled him to find time to write. He also does some Voluntary work, and he and his wife, Betty, try to spend some time with their three grandchildren in the U.S.A.

For his next book, he plans a collection of short stories based on individual characters who appear in 'The Devil Found Sixpence'.

THE DEVIL FOUND SIXPENCE

by John Jarvis

Published by Oakhill Woodstock

First published 1994
by Oakhill Woodstock Publishing
Box No. 91
Doncaster DN2 5TD

John Jarvis 1994
All rights reserved

Printed in England by
Askew Design & Print
Heavens Walk, Ten Pound Walk, Doncaster
Telephone: 0302 323714

British Library
Cataloguing-in-Publication Data
A Catalogue record for this book is available from the British Library

ISBN 0 9521 838 0 3

My grandfather travelled no further than the Norfolk County boundary in his life, and never rode on a train. Notwithstanding this, he may have a footnote in some obscure history book; either because Lloyd George complimented him once, or because of his Shire Horses.

My grandson, by way of contrast, nearly hit the Guinness Book by jetting across the Atlantic five times before his first birthday.

A hundred and eighteen years separate the births of my grandfather and my grandson. Mine falls roughly halfway between them. I am the only person, living or dead, able to claim a close emotional bond with both of them.

I know the feeling of enchantment that comes from being the grandfather of a lively small boy, and I remember the bliss of being a small boy with a fascinating grandfather.

J.J. South Yorkshire 1994

Acknowledgements

It was Bruce Davison's Norfolk dialect which first provoked me into being anecdotal. He and Lenda Brennan and Dave Powell and subsequently my son, Chris, and daughter, Sarah, said: "You should write a book."

Maureen Bartholomew began the typing, Winnie Abbott completed the first full draft, Pauline Croydon and Kath Jackson typed the first full MS. Derek and Carol Farrington, Keith and Pat Burbanks, and Hugh McConnel wrestled with the problems of word processor incompatibility. My wife, Betty, and daughter-in-law, Julia, read the early bits and said 'do it'.

Support and encouragement on the literary side came unstintingly from Andy Thompson, in Oxford, who spent hours putting me through the wringer.

Special thanks to the staff of both Norwich Reference Library and the Eastern Evening News, who, together with members of the Norwich Family History Society, found fascinating people for me to interview.

Contributions in many different guises came from Keri Davey, Pam and Martin Jones, Bob and Midge Littledike and Val and Stuart Coldwell. And from unknown dozens, in village pubs around Norwich, who insisted on rewarding me with beer, for listening to them, when I wanted to reward them with beer for providing me with invaluable anecdotal material.

Recognition must be given to Author Publisher Enterprise, membership of which has been of enormous help.

Finally, because I needed solitude to think about what I was going to write, my thanks to our family Cairn Terrier, Woodstock, who - no doubt from motives of his own - facilitated this by dragging me across vast tracts of unpopulated countryside.

To My Family

Chapter One

"That's Sevres dear," warned Aunt Louise. "Don't touch, there's a good boy."

Jonathan wandered a little further, and came across a pretty little china girl which he picked up and held up to the light.

Aunt Louise jumped out of her chair.

"That's my best Dresden piece," she appealed to his mother. "Really Edith, you must stop him touching my things."

For a while their nerves were on edge, both of them tensing up every time he moved; they only relaxed when he went out to the kitchen to attempt, unsuccessfully, to engage the overfed Persian cat in play.

He had made the effort to be polite to Aunt Louise when they arrived on their visit, despite her austere and forbidding appearance. She strongly resembled some of the photographs of his deceased father; without her brother's black moustache and slightly receding hairline but with the fascinating addition of a huge hair-sprouting mole on the side of her chin, which – Jonathan's mother had become somewhat intense – he must not stare at or comment upon. She had also devoted some time, during the long train journey up from Gloucester, to repeated warnings that he must be on his best behaviour during the visit.

It was to be, essentially, a duty call; contact was limited to an annual visit because his mother sensed some antipathy from Aunt Louise, who somehow managed to continually imply that her brother had married beneath himself in taking to wife the daughter of a smallholding Norfolk farmer. She also offered the opinion, quite frequently, that he had done well to survive the eighteen years until nineteen thirty four with his lung capacity reduced by eighty percent, and that he may have lived even longer without the burden of a wife and child to support.

She was referring, of course, to the fact that he had finally succumbed, three years ago, to the high quality German gas that a capricious breeze had wafted into the already inhospitable Somme trench he had been occupying in nineteen sixteen.

Jonathan – only here now because he had created a scene about an unfulfilled promise to give him a day out in London – had hitherto been excluded from the annual visit because his mother, only too painfully aware of his ability to create havoc, did not want to give his Aunt Louise even further cause for complaint. Observing his fascination with the priceless collection of china marshalled regimentally on most available shelves, she had every reason to dread the realisation of her worst fears.

Having failed to make any headway with the cat, Jonathan decided to steer clear of the china collection in favour of the other curious artefacts on the few remaining surfaces. His mother and aunt were so engrossed in their discussion, they failed to notice him as he mooched around again. He stopped, fascinated, when he reached the sideboard. Resting in a deep silver tray lay the biggest egg he had ever seen. It was almost the size of a rugby football, and quite flawless apart from a tiny hole in each end where the contents had been blown.

"I'll bet it was hard work blowing that," he said, lifting it out of the tray. "I can't hardly blow a wren's egg, let alone one as big as that."

Aunt Louise glanced across and leapt to her feet.

"He's found my ostrich egg!" she shrieked.

Startled, Jonathan dropped the egg.

It did not bounce or roll, but simply thudded on to the polished wooden floor, taking on a curiously flattened appearance; like an apple, he thought, that you take a bite out of to stop it rolling away when you lay it on the table. He was totally confused by the flurry as both his mother and his aunt descended upon him; his mother cuffing him vigorously about the ears, his aunt wringing her hands over the egg.

"My late cousin Charles brought that back from South Africa in nineteen hundred and seven," she moaned. "It's sat there for thirty years, dusted every week. Now look at it!"

When, after much manipulation and discussion, the egg was turned with the intact side facing the room, and another ornament interposed between it and the mirror to stop the broken side being reflected back, he thought it did not look too bad. Clearly though, his aunt was not giving his opinion a great deal of weight. The atmosphere became noticeably chilly, and they were all relieved when it was time to get back to Paddington and the Gloucester train.

This incident appeared to be the final straw, for his mother, when taken together with the events immediately preceding the visit to Wandsworth. In fact she resolved she would never again bring him to London for a day out.

They had started well enough; the train journey, breakfast at Lyon's Corner House on arrival, a ride on a double decker bus, and the rest of the morning in the Imperial War Museum, had all been perfect. But it began to turn sour as soon as they went to Derry and Toms, a sort of middle class Harrods, to do some shopping. He was allowed only five minutes at the toy counter to make an unsuccessful bid for a water pistol – having speculated rather too openly on the effect of using urine instead of tap water – while his mother spent half an hour trying on hats.

"You've had your treat, now it's my turn," she snapped, as he stood by pouting and pulling surly faces at her in the mirror.

It was too cold to eat lunch on the roof garden, so after feeding the ducks with a roll left over from elevenses, they went into the restaurant. He was used to Urches', back at home, where the friendly waitresses knew them, and the other customers, mostly farmer's wives, diluted their middle class pretensions with some rustic homeliness. The clientelle in Derry and Toms had no such saving grace, and his mother, shedding her Norfolk dialect and talking 'posh', constantly bade him 'sit up straight' and 'tuck your elbows in' and 'hold your knife properly', and 'stop wiping your nose on your sleeve'.

Having paid the bill, his mother announced her intention of going to the toilet.

"Can't I come with you?" he asked.

"No," she said. "You're too big to come into the ladies' now; besides, you've been twice in the last fifteen minutes. Also I don't like the way you stare at the ladies coming out of the cubicles."

"It's fun, watching them go all red," he sniggered.

She gathered her handbag and rose from the table.

"Now you're to sit perfectly still until I come back," she said. "I shan't be long."

All through lunch he had caught tantalising glimpses of what he assumed to be the kitchen. Waitresses and waiters were constantly coming through with trays of food for the diners, and each time the swing doors stayed open just long enough for him to observe a huge expanse of white tiling.

Waiting until he was unobserved, he slid through the doors and gazed in awe at the palatial view before him. It was quite unlike the kitchen at home, with its solitary coal range set in the wall. Here, several gas burning cookers paraded down the middle of what seemed like a vast hall, with chefs wearing tall hats working on both sides of them. Nobody seemed to notice him as he embarked upon a tour of inspection.

Coming across a huge tray full of meringues, he took one and ate it as he continued his royal progress up the aisle between the cooking stoves. Chefs and waitresses ignored him completely, until he was accosted by an older chef who had a black moustache and a taller hat than the others.

"Hello little boy, what are you doing here?"

He sounded surprised, but quite genial.

"I'm eating a meringue," Jonathan informed him.

The chef leaned over him.

"Yes I can see that, but who are you with?" he looked around. "Where are your Mummy and Daddy?"

"My Daddy's dead and my Mummy's spending a penny," Jonathan told him frankly.

Having given the chef all the information he thought he needed, Jonathan prepared to move on. But just then a waiter swept along. He did not see Jonathan at first because the chef was standing between them. Putting down the tray he was carrying, he mopped his brow with his sleeve.

"I've come in here to get out of the way," he said. "There's all hell breaking loose out there. Some woman going bloody frantic saying her child's been kidnapped. They're trying to establish whether it's the same kid that was seen leaving with a funny looking bloke – hello." He paused because Jonathan had moved into his line of vision. "You're not him are you? What's your name sonny?"

"Jonathan," he told him.

"That's it," the waiter looked relieved as he held out his hand. "Come on, I'll take you back to your mother."

Jonathan hesitated.

"Is she a bit cross?" he asked.

The waiter grinned at the Chef.

"I think you could just say that," he said.

The scene in the restaurant was reminiscent of a theatrical farce, his mother gesticulating wildly to the head waiter who was begging her to calm down.

"- to allow a perfect stranger to walk out with my child!" she was saying.

The other diners were all frozen in various positions, fascinated, some of them with forks poised halfway to their mouths. His mother, facing in his direction, saw him being led from the kitchen. Sagging with relief momentarily, she immediately tensed up again with anger and bore down on him. He thought quickly and recalled a useful ploy that had diverted her on a previous occasion; balling his fists and plunging them into his eye sockets, he cried loudly and piteously:

"Don't hit me Mummy, please don't hit me again!"

His mother's face flamed with embarrassment as a low murmuring arose from the assembled diners. It was a pity Jonathan could not resist a grin of triumph as she hauled him towards the lift. He held back because he did not want to be alone in the lift with her; a lot could happen while it was slowly descending three floors. He abandoned resistance however when a distinguished looking gentleman in a grey hat, grey tie and grey suit, accompanied by his equally grey wife, preceded them into the lift. He had a kind enough face but he had eyes that looked through people rather than at them. They bored into Jonathan's now for a few moments before he turned and touched his mother re-assuringly on the arm.

"Please do not be distressed by what happened upstairs," he said. "We saw the grin on his face when he had completed that very fine performance."

"You should put him on the stage," said the grey wife. "He's a splendid little actor."

Jonathan's mother gave a sigh of relief.

"Thank you," she said. "You are so kind. You obviously know children."

"My husband is headmaster of a boy's preparatory school at Farnham," said the grey wife. "We know boys."

The headmaster looked them up and down. They were wearing their best clothes for the trip to London, and this obviously misled him into the belief that they were several notches higher up the social scale.

"No doubt you will be thinking of a school for him shortly," he said. "If you are not already committed, could I suggest that you consider St. Giles? Our fees are modest, and we pride ourselves on turning out boys who are polite, well mannered and, – " his eyes bored into Jonathan's again, " – above all well behaved."

"Well how strange that chance should bring us together," said Jonathan's mother, beginning to enjoy herself now that the tables were turned. "I was only thinking the other day that I should be looking for a place for him. There is some financial provision, -" she paused, " – I'm a widow you see – ", she paused again to allow time for the expressions of sympathy to take root, " – I would, of course, be looking for a place with some emphasis on discipline."

Jonathan began to feel uneasy.

She was lying in her teeth of course. She could no more afford to send him to a private school than she could put in a bid for the Crown jewels, but the grey man was not to know that. Neither for that matter was Jonathan; he held the belief that parents actually *received* money for sending children to school; why else was she so rigidly insistent on herding him off there every morning?

The headmaster produced a card from his wallet.

"Do please give me a telephone call when you have had time to think about it," he said.

Jonathan now began to feel distinctly nervous.

"I'll give you a ring tomorrow," said his mother.

"I am quite sure we could help your boy," said the headmaster. "In fact -," his eyes bored into Jonathan's for a third time, "- I would regard it as a challenge!"

As they left Derry and Toms, his mother walked so fast that Jonathan had to trot to keep up with her.

"You wouldn't really send me to that man's school would you Mummy?" he whined.

She pointedly maintained a tight lipped silence.

He did make an effort to conform during the afternoon, even submitting to having his hair cut by a 'posh' barber.

Back in the village his hair was cut by Bob Cheatham, who also thatched hay ricks, dug gardens and hired himself out to do hedging and ditching, and who employed the time honoured method of putting a basin on top of a boy's head and cutting round it.

Then, of course, having been a model child all afternoon, he had to go and break the ostrich egg.

It was as they left Aunt Louise that his mother hissed: "I swear I'll never bring you to London again. And tomorrow," she added, "I'll ring that school."

He eyed her handbag speculatively, and mentally resolved to steal the headmaster's card and burn it.

"And don't think you can steal the card out of my handbag and burn it," she said. "I've had the clasp tightened with pliers since you stole that half crown."

"I didn't steal it," he reminded her. "I took it to give to that poor old tramp."

"Who used it," she reminded him, "to get drunk on cider, and give poor Constable Pogmore a black eye."

As he lay in bed that night, listening to the dialogue filtering up through the floorboards from the room below, he heard his mother haranguing Aunty Barney with an account of the day's events, indignation lending vigour to her delivery.

"I blame myself," she was saying. "I should have sent him to that Masonic school when he was five. Hardly a day goes by but I'm tempted to ring them. He plays with those wretched boys from down Lower End who habitually lie, steal, swear and fight and teach him all their bad habits. You never know what the little swine is going to do next."

Aunty Barney cleared her throat preparatory to making sympathetic response, but his mother was by now in full flow.

"Well, I've had enough," she went on. "He's either going to the Masonic school, or to my parents in Norfolk, because I've made up my mind. I'm going to look for a better job, preferably in London, and somebody else can have a go at straightening him out. I give up."

She paused before resuming with grim satisfaction.

"I'll tell you this much," she said. "My father won't stand any of his nonsense if I have to send him to Norfolk. He'll soon clip his wings and no mistake."

Jonathan did not take all this very seriously.

Hardly a day passed without some menacing reference to the original plan to send him to the Masonic school; a threat which had lost its edge through constant repetition. He became vaguely aware, over the next few weeks, that his mother was spending evenings penning laborious letters, and he heard her confide to Aunty Barney that she still awaited replies from Barts, Guys and St Thomas's, but by the time the weeks had extended into months the incident had faded in his memory.

He was unprepared, therefore, when she greeted his arrival home from school, on the last day of term before the long Summer holidays, with some solemnity.

"Come you here a minute boy Jonathan," she commanded, pulling him up on to her lap.

He was instantly suspicious.

She usually addressed him as 'Johnny' or, wholly reverting to her native Norfolk idiom, 'little ol boy'. When she called him 'boy Jonathan' a serious discussion usually followed.

She took a deep breath.

" How would you like to go and live with Granny and Grandad in Norfolk?" she asked, in the tone and delivery she would have used if asking him if he would like some strawberries and cream as a special treat.

"I wouldn't," he said.

She sighed; confronting him with the awful truth was going to be just as difficult as she had anticipated.

They were going to leave this cottage, which had been home for as long as he could remember; worse, they were going to abandon the network of relationships which they had developed since they came to live in the small Gloucestershire village.

Their lifestyle was reasonably comfortable and secure, despite the professional demands imposed upon his mother by her dual role as District Nurse and Midwife, and Staff Nurse at the Convalescent Home. The cottage, which went with the job, enabled her to have her small son with her until he was old enough to go to the newly built Masonic School for Boys at Rickmansworth. Friends, and members of his father's Lodge, had put Jonathan's name down after the funeral, but when the time arrived her nerve had failed her, and she sent him to the village school instead.

This was only putting off the evil day; she had always acknowledged that she needed to get to London, to one of the big teaching hospitals, where she could obtain the qualifications neccessary to take her to a higher salary level.

Furthermore she was finding it increasingly difficult to reconcile the demands of an emotionally draining job with the equally taxing task of bringing up a seven year old boy; especially as she believed him to be 'running wild' and suffering from a lack of discipline. The disastrous day in London had not helped; perhaps more disturbing was an incident, later in the year, which had led to the older brothers of some of his playmates being hauled before the Juvenile Court.

Seizing an opportunity she had attended an interview in London, where she had been provisionally offered a post.

Jonathan would not be going to the Masonic School.

Correspondence with his grandparents suggested that they may, albeit reluctantly, have him to live with them. His mother now proceeded to devote some time to reminding him of the benefits, to himself, of such an arrangement.

"There will be Sampson, Grandad's big Shire horse," she said. "And Jeb the Labrador retriever, and Snip the terrier, and calves and chickens and cows and pigs and geese – " she paused, while he digested this information, before warming to the task.

"Just think," she breathed. "You will go to the same school that I and your uncles went to. You may even sit at the same desk as I did. There'll be just as nice little boys and girls there as there are here. Nicer," she added, thinking of some of the families with whom he spent a great deal of his time, and who were noted for their general indifference to such trivia as hygiene, social etiquette and the Rule of Law.

She spoke persuasively and with enthusiasm, but this did not really help her case. He found himself reflecting on her use of the same strategy when conditioning him for admission to Gloucester Infirmary to have his tonsils and adenoids out. The nice kind nurses who would make a fuss of him. The other children in the ward who would play with him. The nice doctor who would help him go to sleep and when he woke up he would not have sore throats and blocked noses anymore. The reality, of course, included hard faced nurses too pre-occupied with the next task to worry about their patients feelings, the other children too ill to play, and the doctor, white gowned and masked, who had slapped a sickly smelling pad over his nose and tried to choke him with it.

"For Christ's sake somebody hold the little bugger," the doctor had complained, as Jonathan fought back while watching black and grey concentric rings receding into the distance, heard an increasingly loud ringing in his ears, and eventually awoke to pain in his throat, nose and neck.

When he cried he was ignored. When his mother visited he ignored her, feeling that he had been grossly mislead. When she left, after the visit, he cried because he had ignored her and wished he hadn't. When he began to feel better he decided to explore his environment. This displeased the waspish ward sister, who had him retrieved successively from the kitchen, the boiler room and the operating theatre.

The latter was the last straw.

The surgeon, about to wield scalpel on a recumbent patient, and suddenly becoming aware that a small hospital nightgowned figure was watching his every move with interest, allowed a pained expression to cross his somewhat pompous features.

"Get that damned child out. He's undoubtedly infectious. Everything he's touched will have to be scrubbed again before I can begin."

Jonathan's mother had been instructed to remove him from the Infirmary forthwith.

She had appealed to the Matron.

"Surely you can keep him for two more days?" she had said.

"Not two more hours," the Matron had said firmly.

His mother's next words jerked him back to the present.

"I'm going up to London one day next week to complete arrangements at the hospital," she said. "I shall be away overnight because I shall have to go on down to Norfolk to talk Granny and Grandad into -," she paused and corrected herself. "To talk to them about them having you."

Jonathan maintained a sullen silence.

"It's either that or the Masonic School," she said nastily.

For the next few days he had a little knot of dread in his tummy, not helped by her announcement, during the following week, that she was off to London and Norfolk on Thursday and that he would be staying with Aunty Barney during her absence. She realised that she still had some work to do on him.

"Just think," she said. "If I earn more money I can buy you all the nice things I can't afford now. Nice new clothes for instance."

"Don't want any new clothes," he said ungraciously. "Except -," he suddenly saw an exploitable opportunity, "- a Red Indian head-dress with eagles feathers."

"I'll see what I can do while I'm away," she said.

When she returned, two days later, there was a marvellous head-dress, full of pretend eagle feathers, in a box on the kitchen table.

Also the news that his future was settled.

"Granny and Grandad are really looking forward to having you with them," his mother said. "Isn't that wonderful?"

It may have been wonderful, but it was not strictly true. She had, in fact, had a hard time selling the idea to them.

Well into middle age, and having brought up a family of four boys and a girl, his grandparents had settled down into a steady comfortable routine to take them into the Autumn of their lives. His grandfather still took on a few carting jobs, hiring out himself and the great Shire horse Sampson. He also worked two days a week on the nearby Limmer's farm, supplementing his income from the small milking herd of Friesians and the rearing and sale of livestock on his smallholding. Neither grandparent was enthusiastic about having this comfortable existance disrupted by the introduction of a small boy into the household. They would probably have declined at the outset, but for the fact that Jonathan's grandfather had always found it hard to say 'no' to his youngest child and only daughter; she had learned to get what she wanted at a very early age by gazing soulfully at him with liquid eyes. In fact his attitude towards her contrasted sharply with that towards his sons. With the reputation of being a strict disciplinarian, he had exercised a rigid control over them when they were boys, not hesitating to thrash them with his belt for even the slightest misdemeanor.

He owned his own forty acres of land, described as being 'in the middle of nowhere', behind a wooded rise two miles from the village and eight miles from Norwich. In an age and area where most people were tenants of the Squire, it was unusual to actually own one's land. But Jonathan's great-great grandfather, a horse trader, had enjoyed a boom during the Crimean War by exploiting a sellers market with the Cavalry, and had saved the money to buy the land his forbears had tenanted.

Jonathan's mother had presented her case carefully and persuasively, believing it was her father who had to be convinced.

Obviously he was going to opt out however.

"That's up to your mother," he told her. "I haven't the time to be bothered with a boy. She'll have the job of keeping him from under my feet."

He began to put on his boots in preparation for his return to work.

"Why haven't you brought him with you?" asked her mother. "We'd like to have seen him."

Some of Jonathan's behaviour patterns, which had developed over the past three years, were not exactly calculated to win friends and influence people. His mother had not wished to expose his grandparents to him until they had more or less committed themselves.

"I had nowhere to leave him in London while I went to the hospital," she temporised. "Besides, the double journey would have been too tiring for him."

"One thing I have to say," said her father, lacing up his boots. "Boys can be headstrong, and have to be kept in hand. Now if he misbehave he'll get treated the same as your brothers did, and you'll have to settle for that if you want us to have him."

She supressed her misgivings, recalling her belief that the time had come for Jonathan to be exposed to his grandfather's firmer discipline anyway.

Her father had a final question.

"What happen if we have to say 'no'?" he asked.

She sighed, looked straight at her mother, and played her trump card.

"There's nothing else for it," she said. "He'll have to go to the Masonic School."

"He will not!" her mother spoke with asperity. "No grandson of mine goes into the Workhouse."

A reputable establishment like the Masonic School could hardly be equated with the Workhouse, but Jonathan's mother felt it politic to make no further comment.

For a whole week after her return from Norfolk, Jonathan was able to repress the knowledge that his whole lifestyle was about to suffer a dramatic change. There were still exciting things to do, especially as the harvesting gathered pace, plums and apples ripened and the cider making began. Then one evening he came home to find packing cases and cardboard boxes all over the cottage, and his mother commanding that he sort out his toys and books. The furniture was going into store, but a lot of the bits and pieces were to be given or thrown away.

They were having a taxi to Gloucester train station, and changing trains at Swindon for London. By staying overnight with Aunt Louise in Wandsworth, they would be able to catch an early train out from Liverpool Street to Norwich the next morning.

Despite the early hour, a number of people had turned up at the cottage to indulge in tearful farewells. It was with a heavy heart, therefore, that he waved out of the back window of the taxi and watched the cottage, and the group of well-wishers, disappear round the bend. They sped through familiar countryside until they were out of their territory, and the landscape was recognisable only by virtue of previous trips to Gloucester. All that was consistant and secure was vanishing through the rear window into the past.

That which was unknown, and threatening, lay in the future.

Chapter Two

Sam Sharpe, the driver of the pony and trap hired by Jonathan's grandfather to meet them at Norwich Thorpe Station, was not quite drunk, but was obviously not far short of it.

Not that it mattered; the moth eaten pony, which refused to be coaxed into anything more than a lethargic trot, simply laid back it's ears and – obviously from long habit – took charge and simply ignored the contradictory commands carried on Sam's beery breath.

As they jerked their way around the quieter back streets of the city, to pick up the road out to the village, the buckled wheel uttered a grating screech with every revolution, causing the trap, and the passengers, to judder.

About two miles out Sam suddenly raised his mellow baritone in song. Jonathan's mother, sitting up on the seat beside him, resigned herself to the situation and joined in with her warm contralto. Sitting on his suitcases in the back, and uplifted by the novelty of the occasion despite his gloom at having to abandon home and friends, Jonathan contributed his shrill treble:

"No cares have I to gree-eeve me, No pretty little girls to
decee-eeive me, I'm as happy as a king belieee-eeve me,
As I go ro-o-o-lling home."

Their voices echoed back off the elm and beech trees lining their route.

Fortunately there was no one about, at this point, to see them or hear them, although assorted rooks, pigeons and pheasants, took terrified flight at their noisy approach. Mercifully, after about ten minutes, Sam chose to further remonstrate with the pony, giving Jonathan's mother the opportunity to divert him away from song and into conversation.

The journey seemed endless, but eventually they reached the village. She pointed out various landmarks which were familiar to her but meaningless to Jonathan. The Church, constructed mostly of flint and with a round tower instead of a square one, looked odd to him. She pointed out the Victorian school next to the Church, the King's Head Inn where his grandfather spent some of his time, and the brook running alongside the main street through the village.

"They'll all be in the fields finishing off the harvest," said Sam, in response to Jonathan's comment that there did not seem to be many people about.

Indeed, apart from the odd dog or cat basking in the warm noonday sun, and a few geese on the bank of the brook, the village appeared to be slumbering behind drawn curtains and closed doors.

Jonathan's mother was obviously relieved.

"It's just as well," she told Sam. "I'm calling on my brother Bert, at the Police House, for a few minutes, but I don't want the world and his wife stopping me for a chat. I need time to get out to the farm and get the boy installed before I catch the evening train back to London. I can make time for chinwagging next time."

Sam chuckled.

"There'll be a few as'll be a bit peeved when they know as you a bin down but haven't bothered to look them up."

The turning off the High Street, into the narrow road which ultimately took them towards the farm, brought them to the outskirts of the village. The Police House, which was almost the last dwelling, was virtually identical in construction to that of the village bobby back in Gloucestershire; also common to both were the completely weed free and neatly edged and trimmed paths, borders and lawn.

His mother had arranged to call on her brother, on the way through, so that Jonathan could be introduced to him, and to his Aunty Eliza who ushered them into the parlour.

Sam, slumping sideways on the seat, went to sleep, while the pony reached over the low wall to crop some of the flowers growing near to it.

Jonathan liked Aunty Eliza immediately; she was plump and warm and hugged him as if she'd known him all his life. But his Uncle Bert, who came in ten minutes later, was rather a disappointment. Although he was the village policeman, Jonathan had expected him to be friendly because he was his uncle. But Uncle Bert made it obvious, from his conversation, that he was suspicious of boys and would be keeping an eye on him to make sure he did not get into mischief.

"Although – " with a significant look at Jonathan's mother " – I reckon our father'll take care of that."

As they left, he put on his helmet.

"I'm having a word with that Sam Sharpe," he said. "Unless I'm very much mistaken he's had a drink or two."

"For God's sake don't charge him, or whatever it is you do," pleaded Jonathan's mother. "Father hired him to collect us, and I need him to get me back to Thorpe for the seven o'clock train."

Refreshed by his little nap, and no doubt influenced by the sight of Uncle Bert's uniform, Sam made a passable show of appearing sober.

"Have you been drinking?" Uncle Bert came bluntly to the point.

"Now come on Bert, would I be daft enough to be drunk in charge of a horse right outside the Police House?"

But Uncle Bert had been diverted away from duty to a more personal issue. His eyes bulged, and his face went nearly purple as he observed the massacre of his wallflowers.

"That damned horse of yours have chopped the heads off my best blooms!" he raged.

"Yes, I'm right sorry about that Bert, truly I am," said Sam, trying to sound sincere. "But I can let you have a few from my own garden to plant in."

"At this time of the year? That have to be a laugh!"

But Uncle Bert was not laughing.

Before the situation could deteriorate further, Jonathan's mother climbed up beside Sam and urged him to make good speed. Uncle Bert, morose, lifted Jonathan up into the back of the trap.

"You haven't heard the last of this, Sam Sharpe," he shouted over the noise of the trap wheels, adding in an audible aside to Aunty Eliza: "I'll have him yet, you see if I don't."

Ten minutes later, as they rounded a bend, a jumble of farm buildings came into view among some trees on their right. The bright red of a new Dutch barn looked somehow out of place beside the weather mellowed brick of the other structures.

"Is that Grandad's farm?" Jonathan wanted to know.

"No, that's Mr Limmer's," his mother told him. "Mr and Mrs Limmer are friends of Granny and Grandad, and Grandad works for him occasionally."

For about half a mile now, on their left, a high flint and brick wall had obstructed the view. As they trundled further they observed a magnificent pair of wrought iron gates and, beside them, a small cottage built into the wall. She told Jonathan that Mr Perriman, the Squire's gamekeeper, lived in the cottage with his daughter.

"Enid Perriman and I were friends when we were girls," she added, "and I have found out that she will be your teacher when you start school."

He did not like the sound of this.

His mother had been friendly with his teacher back in Gloucester, with the result that snippets of information about his private affairs were too freely exchanged for his liking.

The gates, and well kept drive beyond, led to the Hall, his mother told him.

"It's where the Squire lives, and you'll discover that Captain Canfield employs a lot of the village men on his estate," she added.

Her words prompted Sam to reminisce.

"You'll remember young Ted Holt?" he said. "Worked for the Squire for ten years, but because he get drunk a few times to drown his sorrows after his little ol' girl died of the Consumption – she couldn't a been more than six years old – the Squire sacked him and threw him out of his tied cottage."

"That's awful," she said. "What happened then?"

"Ted went up to the Hall to beg for his job back," said Sam, "and the Squire got the grooms to throw him out. Foolish like, he went back and threw a brick through the drawing room window. Your brother, Bert, had to lock him up and bring him up at the Petty Sessions, where he got three months. Mind you, the Squire was sitting as a Magistrate, so that didn't come as no surprise to no one – least of all Ted himself."

"What happened to Jean and the other children?" she asked.

"Ended up in the Workhouse," said Sam. "Then Ted got the Consumption himself. He must a had it beforehand without knowing it like. But being in Norwich Jail wouldn't a helped. Only lasted six months after he came out."

"I remember Ted and Jean as a fine young couple", she said sadly. "I think that's a terrible thing to have happened."

This was not an unusual situation in the thirties, Jonathan later learned. Consumption, as it was called, was rife in an area with few T.B. tested cows and the primitive sanitation of the outdoor lavatory, known in Norfolk as the 'petty'.

Worse, people like the Squire held, to some extent, the power of life and death over their employees and tenants. Fortunately most of the big landowners in the county were benevolently despotic, but the local populace had little or no defence against the harsh autocracy of those who were not. The farm labourers had a Union, and it had gathered strength in the twenties, especially after the village of Burston had attracted so much attention from the Labour movement. It had achieved some limited success during the nineteen- twenty-three farmworker's strike, but still lacked the muscle it was to acquire after the Second World War.

Jonathan's unhappiness was submerged by curiosity, and even some excitement, as they turned down opposite the Limmer farm gates. The trap juddered even more as the wheels jolted over the hard baked mud of the winding narrow lane. The green strip running up the middle, where cart wheels did not touch, was lush enough to tempt Sam's pony to pause for a mouthful every so often.

The terrain had changed for the better in the last mile; less flat, though undulating rather than hilly, and the trees, in their red gold and brown Autumn colours, created a warmly welcoming atmosphere.

"There's only about three or four people ever come down here," commented Sam. "Apart, that is, from your father and the Squire's men. There's Jack Smith's milk lorry when he come to collect your father's churns, Ted Limmer to get to the field he bought from your father, and Ted Kemp the Vet. Even the postman leave the letters at Limmer's when he know your father is going to be up there."

"I'm not surprised," said Jonathan's mother. "Talk about living in the back of beyond."

After about half a mile they came to a place where trees closed in on either side of the lane, and his mother and Sam had to duck to avoid low hanging branches. It was cool and restful at this spot, and quiet, apart from the buzzing of insects among the wild flowers and blackberries that proliferated on the sides of the ditch. There seemed to be more of everything here; rabbits, pigeons, rooks, magpies, scores of pheasants, and a couple of weasels hunting the hedgerow.

Then suddenly, as they rounded a bend where the wood gave way to pasture, they arrived at the ivy covered weathered brick walls and red pantiled roof of the farmhouse.

Jonathan's first impression was one of disorder; bits had obviously been added on to the house over the years, and, as he was to learn, you had to go up or down a step when you went from one room to another. The barn and cowshed were definitely leaning, but in that settled way that old buildings have of finding their own comfortable level. The yard, which separated the house and barn, was unevenly cobbled, and seemed, despite its size, to be overcrowded with geese, ducks, chickens, guinea fowls and pigs.

He offered to get down and open the gate, but in the end Sam had to do it because ropes substituted for broken hinges, and it had to be either lifted or dragged along the ground. Also he was diverted by the noisy arrival of the two dogs. Jeb, the grey muzzled soft eyed black Labrador invited hugs, and Snip, the perky Norwich terrier, sought a more boisterous welcome.

Then his grandmother appeared.

As she and his mother embraced, he was struck by their physical similarity; his grandmother seemed just an older version of his mother. He was to discover that they were not quite similar in temperament however; his grandmother was softer, more prone to panic when things went wrong, less able to retain her composure in the face of the unexpected, but more relaxed about general routine matters.

She turned to him now.

"Come and give Granny a hug," she commanded.

He thought she smelled nice; a mixture of lavender and baking bread.

Except for a spotless white apron she was dressed completely in black, wearing a dress that came down to her ankles and which she had to hitch up to avoid the bottom brushing the dung and mud of the yard. Her white hair was drawn back in a bun, with straggly wisps sticking out, and what appeared to be dozens of hairpins jabbed in at odd angles.

He liked her immediately, responding to her warmth.

As they sized each other up, his mother negotiated with Sam Sharpe.

"Be sure to be back here by five o'clock at the latest," she said. "I must catch that seven o'clock train back to London."

Holding his hand, his grandmother gave him a conducted tour of the yard, naming all the pigs as they worked their way slowly towards the dairy.

"I started churning some butter," she explained. "I'll have to finish it or that'll go off. You got here quicker than I expected."

Jonathan was fascinated by the dairy, with its wealth of milky cheesy smells, polished red tiles and large scrubbed earthenware bowls, some of them full of thick cream and covered with white muslin. The wide cold-slab running the entire length of one wall was full of baskets of eggs, plucked and dressed chickens and more butter, ready wrapped in greaseproof paper. Under his grandmother's direction he finished churning the butter, turning the handle to a constant rhythm until the slurping noise from within the churn changed to a wet slapping sound.

She emptied the butter out on to a large wooden board, and began to shape it with a pair of wooden pats.

"Your father is up ploughing Limmer's top field," she told his mother. "He'll be home about half past three, just to see you. But he'll have be off back before you go, because he have to help Ted with something later."

The small outer dairy contained a cream separator, together with gleaming galvanised pails and churns, and had a door leading to the outside. But as he headed towards it his mother warned him not to go near the well.

His grandmother reassured her.

"That's quite safe," she said. "Your father bought a new hasp and padlock."

Jonathan was not unused to wells; most of the houses in the village back in Gloucestershire had no piped water, and were, for the most part, dependant upon them. It was one of his mother's recurring nightmares that he would one day fall down one.

His grandparent's well was different. It had a red tiled roof, looking for all the world like a miniature house with a winding handle sticking out of the end. The door, which took up virtually the whole of one side, allowed a large wooden pail, weighted with a stone to make it sink, to be lowered forty feet to be filled. This door was secured with a shiny new padlock of the same popular make that graced several chicken coops back in Gloucestershire, and which Jonathan's delinquent friends had taught him to open with a bent wire or a hairpin.

He thought he would like to look down the well, and maybe drop a small stone down to see how deep it was.

He went back into the dairy, where his mother had nostalgically taken over shaping the butter with the wooden pats, and tugged his grandmother's apron.

"Could I have one of your hairpins please Granny?" he asked meekly.

"Of course you can my little ol' love," she said, removing one from her white bun.

"Thank you Granny," he said politely.

As he trotted outside again she beamed indulgently at his departing back.

His mother, preoccupied with shaping the butter, had only been half listening, but suddenly she became alert.

"What did he want?" she asked sharply.

"He just asked me for a hairpin," said his grandmother.

"What did he want it for?" asked his mother suspiciously.

"Well I don't know to be sure," said his grandmother, "but I'm not bothered about a little ol' hairpin for Heaven's sakes; I got plenty of them. What are you making such a fuss about?"

"When you get to know him," said his mother grimly, heading towards the door, "you'll learn that when he puts on that innocent face and asks for something, that's as well for you to find out what he wants it for."

"Well bless me," said his grandmother, with a hint of impatience. "He's not going to do any harm with a little ol' hairpin."

A few moments later she stood, visibly shaken, while his mother, holding him firmly by the scruff of the neck, pointed out just what he had been trying to do with it.

"Well! The little devil!" she said. "And me soft enough to give it to him".

"We need a better type of padlock on there," said his mother. "This one's no good."

"That costs money," his grandmother grumbled.

"I'll pay for it," said his mother. "I'd rather be safe than sorry."

"I reckon we'd better go and give him some dinner," said his grandmother. "That'll keep him quiet and out of mischief for a while."

She led the way through another door and into a narrow passage that ran the length of the house down into the kitchen. This was obviously the centre point of the whole house; a typical farmhouse kitchen where everything happened, and around which the life of the farm revolved.

It seemed vast compared with their kitchen back in Gloucestershire; virtually square and almost thirty feet across, with a huge blackleaded kitchen range taking up half of one wall, and shining copper pans on the opposite wall reflecting back the warm glow from the range. Serviceable willow pattern plates and dishes left little room on the big Welsh dresser for anything else, and muslin wrapped hams hung from the oak ceiling beams alongside round tennis ball sized cream cheeses, also muslin wrapped.

His interest was aroused by the double barrelled shot gun, which was strapped to the centre beam that ran the full length of the kitchen.

In deference to the warm Autumn day only a small fire burned in the grate, but the rabbit pie his grandmother produced out of the oven was steaming hot and perfectly cooked; the pastry, supported by an inverted egg cup, was crisp on the outside and moist with gravy on the inside. Served up with runner beans and creamed potatoes, followed by a generous helping of fruit swimming in cream, he satisfied an appetite he thought he had left behind in Gloucestershire.

He was intrigued when his grandmother, in response to his urgent request for the toilet, took his hand and led him across the yard to the 'petty', counselling him to sit on the smaller of the two holes in case he fell through the big one. The tiled floor and white wood seats were scrubbed spotless, but it was nevertheless an attraction for hundreds of flies, who sought to get down the hole while the lid was up while, at the same time, avoiding falling prey to the dozens of spiders laying ambush for them from permanent homes in every corner.

Having completed his toilet, with the aid of squares of newspaper threaded on to a piece of string, he joined his mother and grandmother who were admiring the geese.

"Fattening up nicely for Christmas," his grandmother commented proudly.

His attention was immediately diverted by the lithe hob ferret in the hutch by the harness room wall. Unable to fulfill his desire to own a mongoose, having been inspired by Rudyard Kipling's stories of Ricki Ticki Tavi, a ferret had seemed the next best thing. He had been given one for his sixth birthday, but after many hectic misadventures, including an incident at school where, in his view, the headmistress had over- reacted, his mother had finally put her foot down and found a home for it elsewhere.

"Come on my little beauty," he said, opening the hutch door and lifting the ferret out, after giving it a chance to sniff his knuckles and categorise him as a friend. He enjoyed the warm sensation as it wrapped itself around his neck, nuzzling his ears.

"Oh my God, he a let the ferret out!" yelled his grandmother, turning round at that point. "That'll get at my chickens."

The ferret promptly leapt off Jonathan's shoulder and disappeared into the pile of logs stacked up against the wall.

"Get him back in! Get him back in!" his grandmother flapped her apron. "Close the yard gate.!"

A five barred gate could hardly contain a ferret, but his mother checked that it was closed anyway, while he climbed up the pile of logs and reached down to lift the ferret out. Sensing he meant it no harm, it came quite calmly and he soon had it back in the hutch.

"Don't you ever do that again," said his grandmother crossly. "Your grandfather have your backside skinned if you lose him that ferret; he say that's the best one he ever had. Besides," she went on, "I don't trust the little devil. He soon as anything make off with one of my chickens."

Jonathan realised that his grandmother had the same unreasonable dislike of ferrets that his mother had.

"Let's get him inside and settle him down with his book while we unpack his things," said his mother irritably, and virtually frogmarched him into the house before installing him at the huge kitchen table with his Boy's Own Annual and the command to: "Stay there and don't get up to any more mischief!"

Alone in the kitchen he had the leisure to look around and examine things. A large cupboard by the scullery door contained very little of interest apart from jars of fruit, home made jams and pickles and blue packets of sugar. The drawers of the Welsh dresser were stuffed full of promising odds and ends however, including some ancient packs of cigarette cards which might come in useful for swops later. A smaller cupboard by the kitchen range contained an enormous pair of black shiny boots and a black Homburg hat; obviously his grandfather's Sunday wear.

Snip and Jeb followed him with their eyes, thumping their tails on the stone flagged floor as he continued his exploration.

"He's very quiet down there," he heard his grandmother say, from upstairs. "What are you doing boy Jonathan?" she called in a louder voice.

"Just reading my book," he shouted back, opening the remaining cupboard by the door to the passage that led to the parlour and the dairy. This yielded finds of passing interest; roughly kept account ledgers on one shelf, vet's medicines on another, and farming periodicals on another. The latter, when he opened them, contained pictures of Friesian cows and bulls, with scrawled handwriting in the margins. On the very top shelf sat three boxes of cartridges, too high up for him to reach.

Observing them, he was reminded of the shotgun.

He could only reach it by climbing up on to the kitchen table, so he kicked off his shoes in case they made a noise.

The two leather straps unfastened fairly easily, but the gun was so heavy that he could not support it once he had undone the second one. His knees buckled and he sat down with a resounding thump, the gun across his chest pinning him to the table. His screech of pain, as his buttocks hit the table, coincided with the rattle of crockery as the force of his fall vibrated the cups and saucers set for tea.

There was a brief breath-holding silence from upstairs followed by his grandmother's cry of: "My God! What's he done now?" and then a tremendous clatter as both she and his mother vied for first place down the narrow stairway.

"I was just sitting here reading my book and it fell on me," he claimed indignantly, but with no real expectation that he would be believed.

His mother replaced the gun in the beam straps, maintaining a thin lipped silence which he recognised as the prelude to a storm, so he dived under the kitchen table.

"Come out you little varmint," his grandmother hauled him out with thumb and forefinger expertly grasping an ear. "Edith, this'll not do. He'll have me in the Asylum in a week if he carry on like this.!"

Controlling her temper with a visible effort, his mother piloted him towards the scullery and the back door.

"I'll take him for a walk up the lane, and have a serious talk with him," she promised his grandmother. "Just give him a chance to settle down. He'll soon learn what he can and cannot touch."

As they crossed the yard, stepping around the pigs who were basking on their sides in the sunshine, he warily acknowledged the geese, who seemed to be the most belligerent of the inhabitants of the yard.

Out of earshot of the house, his mother pulled him up short.

"Now look," she said. "If you think that by behaving badly you can make your grandmother change her mind about keeping you here, you can think again. I cannot have you with me in London, so you have to stay here whether you like it or not."

"Yes," he said. "Can we go and see where Sampson lives?"

She jerked his arm angrily.

"Are you listening to me?" she said. "Because I'll tell you this. You may have got the idea you can twist Granny round your little finger, but you'll run into trouble if you try it with your grandfather. I've already told you how he used to deal with your uncles when they were boys. You can take it from me that he'll take his belt to your backside if you so much as say anything out of place, let alone do anything wrong."

"Yes," he said. "Come on, show me where Sampson lives."

She gave a sigh of exasperation and let go of his arm.

Sampson was not in his stall; the only occupant of the barn was a small Friesian calf which took Jonathan's hand into it's mouth and sucked vigorously.

"Grandad will have Sampson with him if he's ploughing," his mother said. "For goodness sake wipe that slime off your hand," she added, the calf having salivated freely in an effort to extract nourishment.

He knew enough about animal husbandry, from his village life in Gloucestershire, to know why the calf was alone in the barn.

"Grandad must be weaning her from the mother cow," he said. "She'll be feeling a bit sad," he added, a lump rising in his throat.

His mother hurriedly changed the subject.

"Come on," she said, with forced cheerfulness. "I'll show you the woods."

He forgot his gloom for a while as he found trees to climb, and rabbit holes to investigate with Snip. The wood, which belonged to his grandfather, was coppiced to provide fencing posts, a seemingly never ending supply of firewood, and as many rabbits and pigeons as could be snared or shot.

His mother, complaining bitterly at the grubby knees and filthy hands resulting from his activities, had left him there while she went back to spend a penny.

He became so engrossed in helping Snip in a vain attempt to dig out a rabbit, that he did not hear his grandfather come down the lane. Abandoning the rabbit, he had wandered back towards the barn when Snip suddenly took off to chase, and welcome, the tall figure, viewed briefly from the rear, who turned into the yard.

He ran after Snip, and reached the gate just in time to hear his mother exclaim "Father!" and throw her arms around his grandfather to hug him.

Jonathan felt a twinge of jealousy; he had never observed his mother embrace anyone, and found it difficult to cope with the realisation that a big man, who he could not even remember meeting before, had a claim on her love.

His grandfather lifted her easily off her feet and returned her hug. By so doing he enabled her to see over his shoulder, where she observed Jonathan hanging shyly back.

"That's something to write home about," his grandfather's deep voice rumbled. "Seeing my daughter twice in one month, after not setting eyes on her for five years."

"And there's your grandson right behind you," she said.

He gently let her down on her feet again.

Following her eyes over his shoulder, he swung round to face Jonathan.

Chapter Three

They surveyed each other for a good ten seconds without moving or speaking; curiously enough both adopting the same stance – legs apart, hands on hips. Jonathan was all of three and a half feet high; his grandfather nearly twice that. Jonathan, born in nineteen thirty, carried almost seven years; his grandfather, born in eighteen seventy, nearly ten times that.

Jonathan's mother watched nervously from the side, later confessing to his grandmother that she had kept her fingers crossed behind her back.

As a result of his activities in the wood, Jonathan presented the appearance of a thoroughly disreputable urchin, but his grandfather's face, completely expressionless apart from a hint of shrewd appraisal, gave no indication of what he was thinking or feeling.

Jonathan saw a big man, six feet tall and as muscular and straight backed as a man half his age. The bulging waistline, accentuated rather than contained by the three inch wide brass buckled black leather belt, appeared to be the only concession he made to advancing years. His heavy hobnailed boots made his feet look enormous. Patched and worn grey serge trousers, supported by braces, were topped by a faded blue and white striped collarless shirt. Instead of a jacket he affected a moleskin waistcoat, unbuttoned and not quite hiding the braces, and a red neckerchief knotted around his throat. A battered felt hat, greasy from contact with the flanks of generations of cows milked over the years, completed his workday attire.

His square weatherbeaten face, adorned with a bushy grey moustache and flint grey eyes, now turned to Jonathan's mother.

"He carry his head well," he said.

He beckoned brusquely.

"Come you here boy," he commanded, and putting his enormous ham like hands under Jonathan's armpits, he lifted him, as though he weighed no more than a straw doll, to stand on top of the ferret hutch. He grasped Jonathan's ankles, and, quite impersonally, ran exploratory hands up his calves, thighs, hips, chest, upper and forearms and shoulders. His hands were surprisingly gentle for so large a man; Jonathan felt curiously restful, and could later understand why fractious animals stood quietly, even if in pain, while being examined.

"Open your mouth boy," his grandfather said. "Wider now," and peered at Jonathan's teeth, putting an enormous finger inside to pull his cheek open. Jonathan could not resist biting it, hard, partly for fun, but also to see how his grandfather would react.

It was like biting solid rubber.

His mother tensed up, and gave a sharp hissing intake of breath.

His grandfather gave no indication of having felt it, but clearly recognised the implicit challenge as their eyes locked briefly. Without any rancour, almost indifferently, he raised his other hand as though to cuff Jonathan to make him let go.

"Now," he said, lifting him down, "you see that gate over there? I want you to run to it as fast as ever you can and then turn and run back. As fast as ever you can mind."

Jonathan complied, and threw himself at his mother on his return, nearly knocking her off her feet.

His grandfather delivered judgement.

"He turn his right leg under him a bit, but he have good bone and his wind's sound," he said.

She looked pleased.

"He's a bit skinny though," his grandfather went on. "He need feeding up a bit."

She bristled slightly.

"I always give him plenty," she said indignantly. "But he's so finnicky over his food."

"He'll eat what's put in front on him here," said his grandfather, "or your mother will know the reason why."

Months later Jonathan watched him go through almost the same motions, using the same words, while examining a foal at Norwich Market. To his grandfather, it seemed, he was simply an addition to the livestock on the farm.

He followed them into the house and watched his grandfather, sitting on a low chair just inside the scullery, unlace and take off the mud caked boots before walking through to the kitchen in his stockinged feet. Sinking into the big chair by the kitchen range, with an enormous tin mug of tea in his hand, he began questioning Jonathan's mother about her new job. Normally Jonathan was bored by adult conversation, but this was one of those few occasions when he sat quietly and listened, while his grandparents brought his mother up to date on local gossip before drifting into more general matters.

"What about all these posh friends of yours in London, Edith?" asked his grandfather. "Do they reckon there's going to be a war?"

"I haven't been in London for the past eight years," she said. "But a lot of people feel it to be inevitable; why else would they turn a complete factory in Blackburn over to making gas masks?"

"Your brother Bert saw that in the paper," said Jonathan's grandmother. "He say the police have already been told what to do if ever there's an air raid."

"A doctor I know has just spent some time out in Spain with a medical team," said his mother, "and he tells some horrible stories of German aeroplanes being used to bomb villages, and the awful injuries they inflict on women and children."

Too young to understand the issues, or identify the protaganists in the current struggle in Europe, Jonathan could see nothing significant in this. Thrilled by stories of Sir Francis Drake and the Spanish Armada, which he was not yet able to give their perspective in time, he felt the Spaniards deserved all they got.

"One thing I'm sure of," said his grandfather with some feeling, "the likes of you and me'll have no say in it. That's these damn politicians that'll muck it up again, like they did in nineteen fourteen. I don't trust them no farther than I could throw them. Look what they a done to farming in this country."

To Jonathan, sizing him up while the conversation continued, his grandfather seemed, somehow, a little threatening; he had virtually ignored his grandson from the moment they had entered the house, but there was something about his 'presence' that discouraged any demand for attention. Although Jonathan did not dislike him, he did not like him either at this stage. This was unusual for him because he tended to divide adults, at first sight, into the black or white categories of hostile or friendly. He was reserving judgement; instinctively recognising his grandfather's invisible mantle of authority, but feeling impelled to test it out and challenge it.

He did not have to wait long for the opportunity.

Absently glancing upwards while he talked, his grandfather suddenly froze in his chair.

"Who a been fiddling with my gun?" he asked. "That strap were tighter fastened than that."

"I could not have pulled it tight enough," said Jonathan's mother.

She hesitated, and then went on: "I'm afraid Jonathan got it down to look at, but – " she held up a placatory hand as he rose out of his chair " – he knows now he must not touch it. He won't do it again."

"That's a fact he won't," said his grandfather frostily, taking the gun down and checking it thoroughly, opening it and squinting up the barrels as he pointed them at the window. "I'll tell him now, him and me'll fall out good and proper if ever he touch that again."

Jonathan stared at him insolently.

A flicker of anger crossed his grandfather's face, but he was interrupted before he could say more.

"He gave us a fright I can tell you," said Jonathan's grandmother. "In fact he give us a few frights this afternoon. He let the ferret out before he'd been here an hour."

His grandfather opened his mouth, but again Jonathan's mother held up her hand.

"It's alright," she said. "It was only out for a few minutes; he soon managed to get it back in again."

"If he ever – " began his grandfather, but was interrupted again.

"And while I think of it, you'll have to get a new padlock for that well door." said Jonathan's grandmother. "He can open that one with a hairpin."

Jonathan's grandfather sat, cold and distant, his anger silently building, as he was given an account of the events of the afternoon. In an attempt to divert him, and defuse the situation, Jonathan's mother suddenly bustled to clear the pots off the table, she and his grandmother both disappearing into the scullery.

Alone together, his grandfather gave him a hard stare.

"You chalked up a good score," he said, looking at the clock. "You been here no more than three hours and – " he ticked off his fingers one by one – "you picked the well padlock, you let the ferret out, and you take down my gun."

He paused.

"And you bit my finger." he added.

In the cool silence that followed, he stared hard again.

Jonathan used to play a challenging game with his playmates back in Gloucester. Known as 'staring out' it consisted simply of locking eyes with your chosen adversary and attempting – by sheer will power – to get him to blink or look away first.

He tried to stare out his grandfather.

To help, he counted the tick-tocking of the big long-case clock which stood against the wall by the door leading to the stairs.

One, two, three, four, five – he was determined not to look away. Nine, ten, eleven, twelve – his mother and grandmother chattered away in the scullery, unaware of what was happening, their voices muted by the closed door. Sixteen, seventeen, eighteen – he was still determined not to look away. Twenty one, twenty two – he looked away.

He pretended he had dropped something down his shirt front, and made a great thing about scraping it off.

His grandfather suddenly grunted, and unfastened the wide black leather belt. He drew it from round his waist and folded it in half before leaning across the table to hold it up in front of Jonathan's face.

"Now look at that," he said. "Because I have to tell you this – " he paused to make sure Jonathan was concentrating on his words. "If ever I have to fetch this across your backside, you'll know to it. And you a come pretty close to it already. Now, do you have anything to say?"

Jonathan knew what he was going to say, and he did not really want to say it. But he could no more have not said it than he could have stopped breathing.

"You hit me with that and I'll kick you in the bollocks," he told his grandfather flatly.

Like most of his more dramatic pronouncements there was nothing original about it; it was a straight quote from someone else – in this case an older boy back in Gloucestershire during an altercation with another youth in the school playground. As he finished saying it his mouth became dry, his tummy churned, he began to feel curiously lightheaded and he had an overwhelming urge to urinate.

To give his grandfather his due, he allowed not one flicker of emotion to show on his features, but his face, indeed his whole body, became absolutely still. For what seemed like several minutes, but were probably only seconds, neither of them moved. Even the ticking of the clock seemed subdued. Only the distant voices of Jonathan's mother and grandmother invaded the silence as they carried on their conversation in the scullery, both of them quite oblivious to the drama that was being enacted in the kitchen.

His grandfather, diverted by the sound of a moist drip, looked down and noted the small pool that had collected under Jonathan's chair. For an instant his eyes showed a change of expresssion; a brief awareness. He looked thoughtfully out of the window before rising slowly to his feet. Jonathan prepared for flight, but – still thoughtfully – his grandfather rebuckled the belt round his middle before moving over to stand with his back to the kitchen range.

"Edith! Eliza!"

His voice was pitched no louder than was neccessary to penetrate the scullery door.

The expressions on their faces must have been revealing because neither Jonathan's mother nor his grandmother said anything, but simply stood apprehensively looking from one to the other of them.

"He've wet himself, needs mopping up," his grandfather waved a hand in Jonathan's direction. "No, not you Edith," as she started forward, "I want a word with you."

Although his grandmother made tut-tutting noises as she cleaned him up in the scullery, they were both straining their ears to listen to the conversation through the closed door, most of which had little meaning for him at the time.

"I have this to say," his grandfather began crisply. "For years now you been telling me what a bad job I made of bringing up your brothers; how you could see, since you got an education and went up a couple of notches, and got on to that new fangled cycle-ology or whatever you call it, how you could see that bringing boys up to fear the belt across their backside was all wrong. Well – now I see what a shape you made of bringing up that youngster, there's nothing you can say on that score that I want to listen to – "

"If you knew the problems – " she began, but he would not let her interrupt.

"You needn't come across with that business about being left on your own," he said sharply. "You knew when you married a fellow as had been gassed in the war that it could happen; me and your mother warned you often enough but you had no mind to listen. And you saw enough of it around here when you was a girl; men back from the trenches coughing their lungs up and lucky to last five years, some of them, before ending up in the Churchyard."

"What happened while you had him in here?" she asked with some apprehension, "did he -"

"Never mind that," he waved his hand dismissively. "I'll tell you something – you remember when you was about ten years old – I was daft enough to buy in a young colt that had been badly broken in. That Suffolk Punch – Toby. That horse gave me more trouble than enough. Well, I'm too old to start that game all over again."

"Are you saying that you don't want me to leave Jonathan here?" she was close to tears.

"You'll have to leave him here for the moment I know," he said. "But that might be kinder in the long run to put him in that Masonic place, which is maybe what you should a done two years since."

He went into the scullery to prepare for his return to work.

"Go you back to your mother in the kitchen, boy Jonathan," his grandmother sounded determined. "I'll walk across the yard with your grandfather; there's something I have to say about all this."

Jonathan's mother looked defeated, and sat gazing into the fire for several minutes before drawing him close to her.

"I'm going to see if there is any way I can have you near me in London," she said dispiritedly. "If not, I'll have to see if I can get a job somewhere else."

He made no response, but played with the tassels on the cushion of her chair.

"In the meantime you have to stay here and behave yourself," she went on. She suddenly grasped hold of his shoulders and held his eyes intently. "Now you do understand what I'm saying, don't you? I'll do my best to have you back with me if only you will be a good boy, and hold on here for a few weeks until I come to fetch you."

"When you come," he said, "I'd like you to bring me some of those big marbles with the blue and green colours in them like you got me before."

His mother stood up abruptly and joined his grandmother who had just returned to the scullery.

"I swear I'll half kill the little sod one of these days!" she said savagely.

"Edith! You don't use that word in this house," his grandmother snapped.

He experienced, briefly, the usual little twinge of triumph at having worked his mother up to the edge of her temper. Suddenly remembering they were soon to be parted however, he felt enough remorse to follow her through and give her a hug. She sighed, briefly hugged him back, and then did something she rarely did, and then only in the evenings. Going back through to the kitchen she groped in her handbag, produced a packet of Craven 'A's, lit one and inhaled thankfully.

His grandmother was aghast.

"How long you been smoking them things,?" she demanded to know.

"A lot of women smoke these days," said his mother defensively.

"Well you'd better not let your father see you," said his grandmother, "or he'll soon have something to say."

"Give me a puff Mummy?" Jonathan begged.

His grandmother looked horrified.

"My God! You never teaching him to smoke them things are you?"

But his mother was beyond caring.

"I've had a word with your father just now and softened him down a bit," his grandmother said. "You'd better look up that Mason's place just in case that don't work out, but we'll see how that go over the next week or two."

"What did you say to him?"

"That's not often I argue with him," his grandmother's tone was overlaid with some satisfaction, "but when I do he listen more often than not. I told him I have some say in this, and I want to give the boy the chance to settle before we make up our minds whether he stay."

They carried on a low murmured conversation while Jonathan explored the shelf between the range and the window. Their discussion was mostly about him, but he was used to adults talking about him as if he were not there, and had learned to tune his senses to filter in only that information which was vital to his continued well being.

Pushing aside a pile of papers he disclosed an old wireless set, but an experimental turning of each knob failed to produce any sound.

"That haven't worked for a few weeks," said his grandmother. "Your grandfather just haven't got round to fetching that old accumulator from the village."

Having developed a passionate interest in the Nordic Sagas of L. Du Garde Peach, as well as enjoying 'Uncle Mac' as Derek McCullough was known to thousands of children nationwide, he was relieved to know that the wireless was usable. Reference to the accumulator drew his attention to the fact that his grandparents had no electricity; there were no lights suspended from the ceiling, and no switches to give instant and reassuring relief from darkness.

"There's always a storm lantern left alight outside the back door, and a small lamp turned low on the wall at the top of the stairs," said his grandmother. "Although you use the pot under the bed if you want to go to the lavatory during the night."

"How about school, dark evenings and mornings?" his mother wanted to know.

"We got plenty of them little storm lanterns," said his grandmother. "He have to get himself up the lane and down the road to the Perrimans, and Enid'll take him from there on the back of her bike."

Jonathan clambered up on to his mother's lap, knowing that the time was fast approaching when Sam Sharpe's trap would be arriving to take her to Norwich Thorpe and the London train. He felt his throat tighten as she began to collect her bits and pieces together, and hand over some money to his grandmother.

"He'll need new boots within a month," she said. "And new shorts."

Then came the sound he had been dreading all afternoon; the grating sound of Sam Sharpe's trap wheel, and his whistle as he drew up at the barnyard gate. His grandmother held his hand as they walked with his mother across the yard.

"Now be a good boy and help Granny, and I'll be down again in two or three weeks," his mother said briskly and matter of factly. But neither the briskness, nor the matter of factness, could stem the flood of tears or the howl of anguish he let out as Sam helped her up on to the trap.

"Get going quickly," she muttered to Sam, but Jonathan broke away from his grandmother and ran after the trap, still howling. Afraid he would fall under the wheels, Sam stopped.

She got down again.

"Now you have to be sensible," she said firmly, holding him tightly for a moment. "I have to leave you here, and that's that. You know perfectly well I cannot have you with me in my new job."

His grandmother caught up and held him again, while his mother mounted the trap and set off a second time. His howls rising to a crescendo, he tore himself away from his grandmother and ran after the trap again. Sam had to stop once more. Looking desperate his mother got down, and Jonathan clung to her like a leech.

Suddenly she pushed him roughly back to his grandmother.

"For God's sake," she said. "Don't you understand? I don't want you with me. I want a rest from your constant demands. You get on my nerves. I *want* to leave you here. I dont *want* you round my neck all the time!"

"Edith, really – " his grandmother began nervously.

Jonathan stood, still howling, and watched the trap disappear round the bend in the lane, knowing nothing of the cost, to his mother, of the scene they had just enacted; how she broke down and sobbed on Sam's shoulder once the trap was out of sight; how close she came to giving in, and sending Sam off to Norwich without her.

Jonathan refused to be comforted by his grandmother.

He howled as she led him, unresisting, back to the house, and was still howling an hour later.

"I tell you," she told his grandfather later that night, "I thought he was going to cry himself into a fit."

As it grew dark, she sat him up on the draining board in the scullery to wash him ready for bed. Pulling his nightshirt over his unresisting head, she put him down on the rug, in front of the kitchen range, with a plate of bread and cheese which he ignored. By this time his howling had changed to a repetetive moan, snivel and hiccough.

"Now eat your supper," she said. "I'll not be long. I have to go out and shut up the chickens and geese before that nasty old fox come and get them."

He was left alone, a forlorn and desolate little creature, sitting in his nightshirt on the hearthrug in the rapidly darkening kitchen. As he looked around, his misery was overlaid with another sensation – fear.

A fear which began to escalate into terror.

The furniture, the grandfather clock, the oak beams, all so warm and friendly this afternoon, now took on a threatening aspect as the shadows deepened and the darker corners of the room turned black. The restful ticking of the clock was no longer restful, but sinister in its measured beat. His terror increased as he sat, shrinking and immobilised, on the hearthrug. The beating of his heart became the predominant sound in the room. Then, just when it seemed that his fear and anguish would evolve into screaming hysteria, his grandfather came in.

Without a word to Jonathan, who continued his snivelling hiccough at five second intervals, he kicked off his boots in the scullery, before padding in to poke the fire into a blaze, and sit down in his chair.

He stirred after a few moments.

"You can stop that noise," he said. "Your mother have been gone two hours now. Well on the way to London. You a had plenty of time to get over it."

Jonathan continued to snivel and hiccough.

His grandfather stirred again.

"I'm telling you to pack it up," he said. "Or I'll take my belt and give you something to cry about."

In the light of his uncompromising attitude, Jonathan could not have explained why he did what he then did. Neither, probably, could his grandfather have explained his own reaction.

Rising to his feet, Jonathan clambered up on to his grandfather's knee and, sucking his thumb, buried his face into the moleskin waistcoat and closed his eyes.

His grandfather, almost in a reflex action, crooked a supportive arm under Jonathan's bottom.

Bustling in a few moments later, Jonathan's grandmother stood open mouthed in amazement.

"Well! I never thought to see you cuddling a little ol' boy," she said. "Here, give him to me and I'll pop him up into bed."

He clung to his grandfather's waistcoat as she tried to lift him off.

"Let him be for now," said his grandfather.

"I'll see to the lamps first then," she said, and busied herself lighting and trimming the big brass oil lamp which was placed in the middle of the kitchen table once dusk fell. She repeated the performance with smaller lamps kept in the scullery and at the top of the stairs, and with the lantern hung outside the back door.

"I'll take him up now," she said, holding out her hands for Jonathan.

Once more he clung to the moleskin waistcoat.

"Let him be," his grandfather said again.

"I'll get the supper then," she decided, and went through the process of setting out plates, slicing bread, and uncovering a dish of pickled herring. His grandfather ate his supper one handed, while an hour passed in low murmured conversation between them.

She suddenly looked at the clock.

"I thought you were supposed to be meeting Bob Harrold down at the King's Head at nine o'clock?".

"That'll do another night," his grandfather said.

A few minutes later, as she darned socks, holding them close to the paraffin lamp, his grandfather began to doze. His head drooped until his chin was resting on the top of Jonathan's head. Clasping the waistcoat with both hands, Jonathan buried his face even further into his grandfather's chest.

They both slept.

Chapter Four

He awoke in the morning while it was still dark, uncertain where he was but reassured by the flickering candlelight through the open doorway which connected the two bedrooms. Listening to the rustle of his grandfather pulling on shirt and trousers, he decided to investigate.

"Hello! What are you doing up and about?" his grandfather looked startled to see him standing in the doorway sucking his thumb, a habit his mother believed she had cured by coating it with alum.

"I'm coming down to help you with milking," he announced, knowing this was his grandfather's first job in the mornings.

His grandfather considered this for a few moments.

"You'll have to put your clothes on first," he said.

"They're downstairs," Jonathan told him, and followed the flickering candle down to the kitchen, moving quietly to avoid disturbing his grandmother who was still snoring.

He dressed while his grandfather poked the range into life, adding more kindling wood and coal from the big brass and oak scuttle. The huge black kettle, kept permanently on the banked up fire, was almost boiling by the time they had washed themselves in cold water in the scullery. As his grandfather made, and then sipped, an enormous can of black tea, Jonathan suddenly found his tongue and began to chatter about a neighbouring farmer's cows back at home, and how he would sometimes help to fetch them in for evening milking on his way home from school.

"You can make yourself useful then," his grandfather told him, and later watched him run around the field shouting at the slow movers. He even let him milk for a while, sitting on the three legged milking stool while Jonathan squatted between his knees.

Prior to this, while tethering the cows to the mangers, Jonathan had his first meeting with Sampson.

Well known – at nineteen hands and turning the scales at twenty four hundredweight – to be the biggest Shire horse in Norfolk, his kind patient eyes and searching nostrils inspected Jonathan. Lifted over the side of the stall by his grandfather, he walked underneath Sampson's belly and ran a hand along his flanks. The big gelding lowered a head almost as big as Jonathan's entire body, and sniffed and snorted all over him, before standing restfully in that position while his nose and white blazed forehead were stroked.

Jonathans's grandfather reached down and lifted him back again.

"That's you and him settled then," he said, as he resumed milking. "I know I don't have to worry now that he knows you. You'll come to no harm with him so long as you're sensible."

"I want to help," Jonathan told him.

His grandfather thought for a moment.

"You can use the yard broom to fetch up that muck," he said. "But don't use too much water. That rainwater barrel's nearly empty."

Feeling grown up, and important, Jonathan worked with a will, and caught his grandfather looking at him speculativly from time to time.

"You can't lift that heavy barrow," his grandfather said, at one point, as Jonathan tried to wheel the muck across to the midden.

"Yes I can," Jonathan insisted, struggling to move it, and of course tipping it and losing half the contents.

"Sod it," he said peevishly.

"That's not a word I want to hear you using again," his grandfather stared at him coldly. "You hear me?"

Jonathan stared back at him, and for a moment their wills clashed as they had done on the previous day.

"I said do you hear me?" his grandfather repeated.

Jonathan wasn't about to fight a battle he knew he could not win.

"Yes Grandad" he said sulkily, shovelling up the muck.

Later, having returned the Friesians to pasture, and helped to feed the pigs, he realised he was hungry. Not having eaten for several hours, he tucked in, with some enthusiasm, to a huge plateful of bacon rashers, fried bread, tomatoes and eggs, while his grandmother looked on approvingly. He chattered all the way through breakfast, and caught both of them grinning once or twice at his responses to their questions about his mother's methods of dealing with his shortcomings.

"The way you put it," said his grandfather, "that's always somebody else's fault when you get into trouble!"

He felt himself go red, but wisely decided to say nothing.

After they had finished eating, his grandfather scraped his chair round to face the fire, gazing thoughtfully into the coals for several minutes.

"You'll be late up at Limmer's," said Jonathan's grandmother, surprised to see him still sitting there after she had cleared the breakfast table.

"I'm thinking," was all he said.

As she disappeared out to collect the eggs from the chicken pen just off the yard, he looked across at Jonathan, who had been romping on the hearthrug with Snip.

"Come you here a minute," he said.

He seemed surprised, momentarily, when instead of standing in front of him as he had expected, Jonathan climbed up on to his knee. They were both silent for several minutes, Jonathan also gazing into the coals, until his grandfather suddenly cleared his throat.

"Now your mother will be coming to fetch you back in a couple of weeks," he said.

Jonathan shook his head.

"She won't," he said.

"What do you mean 'she won't'?" his grandfather asked.

"She just won't".

"How come you say that?"

"She means promises when she makes them," Jonathan told him, "but things always happen. Like when she said she would take me to see Snow White and the Seven Dwarfs in Gloucester, and then a baby got born and she couldn't, and she said she'd take me the next week but she got called into the hospital, and in the end Aunty Barney took me."

Another several minutes passed in silence until his grandmother came in; she looked quite startled to see them still sitting there.

"Ted Limmer will wonder where you a got to," she said.

His grandfather put him down and rose to his feet.

"I'm off now," he said. "But I'm sending young Eric down on his bike to get Bert to telephone Edie, and let her know the boy's staying."

Jonathan's grandmother beamed and gave him a hug as his grandfather left. His own reaction was matter of fact; he had known all along he would be staying because that was what his mother wanted.

He wanted to spend the rest of that first day with his grandfather, but that was vetoed by both of them; his grandfather was at Limmer's all day, and his grandmother particularly wanted him with her to meet Miss Perriman. They would be calling to see her on their way up to the Hall to deliver the butter that had been made yesterday.

Before they could embark upon this adventure however, the front parlour had to be dusted and polished, even though it had not been used during the week. Indeed the only time it was used, apart from family gatherings at weddings, funerals, Christenings and Christmas time, was when people of 'quality' like the Squires wife, Lady Mary, or the Vicar came to visit. Despite this his grandmother insisted on a weekly clean. When she began operations later, Jonathan gazed in awe at the showroom of the house as he stood in his stockinged feet in the middle of the flower patterned Belgian carpet. It was a strange experience to walk into this room; almost as though he had left the house behind and walked up the road to a totally diferent abode, so much in contrast was the parlour with the comfortable – albeit strictly functional – atmosphere of the kitchen and scullery.

Not that the parlour was lacking in comfort; rather it provided a warm restful sleepy kind of comfort as opposed to the bustling active warmth of the rest of the house. Facing into the afternoon sun, which was almost reflected off the heavy starched chintz curtains and chair covers, it seemed to soak up the sun's heat, into the plain yellow plastered walls, and redistribute it into the evening. Bric-a-brac of all kinds, including the biggest collection of Toby jugs Jonathan had ever seen, adorned the surfaces of the smaller tables and dresser, while the large round table in the centre of the room was covered with a beautiful chenille cloth which draped down to the floor.

The only slight flaws in the decor were the vertical and horizontal dust lines on the end wall where his mother's piano, now in store in Gloucester, had once stood.

The oak pannelled chimney-breast and red brick open fireplace, with winking brass tongs and poker and shiny copper kettle on a chain, conjured up visions of crackling logs on winter evenings. In fact, the fire was seldom lit more than once a year, when the family, or at least those who could manage to get home for Christmas, arrived in force.

Jonathan's eyes were immediately drawn to the family photographs, including some of his mother, and one of himself taken when he was tiny, which shared space on the two occasional tables. Pride of place however was given to two large framed potographs which were hung on the wall immediately behind them. These were of his grandfather when he was a much younger man and standing, in each case, at the head of a much decorated Shire horse. The captions, in copperplate writing, indicated second and first respectively, at the Royal Shows in nineteen twelve and nineteen twenty one.

"Now that mare there," his grandmother told him, pointing to the latter, "was grandmother to old Sampson. Your grandfather say she was the best horse he ever had."

He scrutinised, with interest, the prominently displayed photographs of his uncles, all in the uniform of the Norfolk Regiment. Uncle Bert he recognised of course, but he had never met Uncle Jack, who was a gamekeeper over at Thetford, or Uncle Jim, who had abandoned agriculture in nineteen-twenty-seven to 'emigrate' to Wallsend-on-Tyne to work in Swan and Hunter's shipyards.

He was puzzled though, because he had a more than vague idea that his mother had four brothers.

"I thought I'd got four uncles -," he began, but his grandmother cut him short.

"Three," she said. "As far as you're concerned you have three uncles."

"But I'm sure Mummy said there was four," he pursued, and was rewarded with a crisp cuff on the back of his head.

"I've now told you, you have three uncles," she said, some irritation evident in her tone, "and that's the end of the matter. Now come on and get ready to go and see Enid Perriman."

His curiosity was aroused by her reaction, but he was also a little wary of it. He decided to shelve it for the time being; he could always ask his mother when she came on her first visit.

Because the stubble field was not yet under plough, they were able to cut across it to the Perriman's cottage, the chimney pots of which were just visible from the front gate. Coming out on to the road just short of their destination, they found the lodge gates open. This was a sure sign that the Squire was at home, rather than in London where the family owned another house in South Audley Street.

"Round the back," commanded his grandmother as they turned in at the gates. "They don't use the front door."

Full of curiosity he scampered on ahead, and almost ran full tilt into the tall figure poised in the act of throwing a handfull of corn to a dozen clamouring chickens of all shapes and sizes. His first impression, as he stood and gazed up at her, was of a person of immense calm. A rather grave face, with level grey eyes and brown hair falling in curls around her ears, created an impression of quiet beauty.

"You have to be boy Jonathan."

Her voice was warm and clear, and so quiet that he had to listen to hear what she said. She seemed too mild and gentle to be a teacher; not a bit as Jonathan had imagined her. He had pictured someone like his mother, because they were friends. She addressed his grandmother as 'Granny Cooper', and he later learned that everybody did this to avoid confusion with Uncle Bert's wife. His grandfather was referred to simply as 'The

Master', or Master Cooper; a hangover from the days before he had inherited the farm, when he travelled the County as a Gangmaster in the harvest fields.

Taking Jonathan's hand, she gave them a conducted tour of the back premises, discussing late flowers with his grandmother. For his benefit they ended up at the kennels, where he made friends with two labradors and some Norfolk terriers who looked a bit like Snip except that their ears did not stand up. Half a dozen ferrets were curled up asleep in a hutch, and he warmed to Miss Perriman when, without hesitation, she lifted an old jill ferret out for him to hold.

"That's the old mother of your grandad's ferret," she told him.

Back in the house, she produced a bottle of Stones ginger beer, and then joined him at the kitchen table while he drank it.

She asked him several questions in her calm gentle way. At first he answered 'yes' or 'no' but he then began to chatter away about school in Gloucester and how he would miss all his friends. She seemed to sense his anxiety about going to a new school, and encouraged him to talk about that. She gave him a great deal of reassurance, which comforted him, because he trusted her without question.

She puzzled him on one point though.

"You have lots of little cousins who'll look after you," she said.

"Ive only got one," he said, thinking of Uncle Bert's daughter Daphne, "and she goes to the girl's High School in Norwich."

It was her turn to look puzzled as she raised a questioning eye at his grandmother.

"Second and third cousins," his grandmother told him. "He don't seem to know about them," she said in an aside to Miss Perriman; and to Jonathan again: "Haven't your mother told you about Colin and David and Cecily and Joan and all the others?"

He looked blank.

"I'll tell him about them later," his grandmother told Miss Perriman, who held his hand as they walked towards the gate.

As they left, he responded to an impulse to hug her.

"I'm sorry I wasn't here yesterday," she told his grandmother. "I would have loved to have seen Edith again. But now she is in London I can arrange to meet her; as you know I go up occasionally."

He had gathered, from his grandmother, that Miss Perriman was courting a young man who was a soldier in London.

"He's a Corporal in the Grenadier Guards," she told him. "And he's your Great Uncle Silas' boy. Now Great Uncle Silas is your grandfather's cousin. He's called Silas Bews and he always thought a lot of your mother. You'll be meeting him tomorrow, and all your cousins."

Jonathan began to feel confused as they walked up the drive to the Hall to deliver the butter, eggs and two plucked and dressed chickens, all wrapped in cloth in the large wicker basket she carried on her arm.

"What's this about cousins?" he asked.

"I can't understand why your mother haven't told you all this," she sounded irritated. "Haven't she mentioned your Uncle Percy and Aunty Doris and all that side of the family?"

He had a vague memory of his mother's description of people in the village, but he had not realised they were relatives. He also remembered her talking about people who were identified as relatives, but he had not realised they lived near his grandparents.

His grandmother gave a sigh and stood the basket down. Using a beech twig she drew a diagram in the soft earth at the side of the drive.

"Now here's me and here's your grandfather," she said, drawing dots with lines connecting them to more dots. "And here's your Uncle Bert, your Uncle Jack, your Uncle Jim up North, and here's your mother."

"What about the other uncle?" he asked. "The one you wouldn't tell me about while we were in the parlour?"

"Never mind that," she said sharply.

"But why's there only three photo's – " he began, and had to dodge the clip she aimed at his ear.

"I said never mind that," she began to sound angry. "Now will you be told boy?"

Breathing heavily she waited until she had gone off the boil before resuming.

"Now here's you," she connected a dot under his mother. "Here's Daphne," another dot under Uncle Bert. "Anne and Linda", dots under Uncle Jack, "and Betty and Marion," dots under Uncle Jim.

She paused to collect her thoughts.

"Now Daphne's the only cousin you got around here, because Jack live over at Thetford and Jim up near Newcastle."

"Now – "she paused again while she drew some lines horizontally away from herself and his grandfather. "Here's my sister Bertha – she's your mother's aunty and her son Bob is your mother's cousin and his children, David, Cecily and Joan, are your second cousins, as are Terry and Colin because their mother, Doris, is your grandfather's brother's daughter."

She drew similar lines and dots depicting his grandfather's other brothers and sisters, all of whom had children ,who in turn had children, who were all related to Jonathan by blood.

He began to feel thoroughly confused, but his grandmother reassured him.

"Most of them live miles away," she explained. "My side of the family are mostly over at Wymondham, and your grandfather's side have some in Yarmouth, some down in Suffolk, and some in East Dereham."

Even so, he began to believe that half the children he would meet in school would be related to him in some way.

As they continued up the drive, he shed his interest in various relatives on rounding a curve and taking in his first view of the Hall. Having heard so much about the Squire from his mother, and having a fantasy of someone like the wicked giant in Jack and the Beanstalk, he felt a little apprehensive in case they should meet him.

Not that there would be much likelihood of that; their passage took them very firmly round the back of the house to the tradesmen's entrance. He caught only a glimpse of the imposing facade, and the neatly trimmed lawns and flower beds, before he found himself being led down some stone steps to basement level. His grandmother, being a regular visitor, opened the door and walked straight in. She paused briefly to exchange greetings with a pleasant looking young man polishing silver at a table off to the left.

"That's the butler's pantry," she whispered, "and that's John, the footman."

Turning off down a stone floored passage, they turned into a huge kitchen where the cook, Mrs Musgrove, presided. She was a jolly looking woman, of ample proportions, who immediately made quite a big fuss of Jonathan.

"Bless his little heart," she indulged. "Let me find him something special."

The 'something special' turned out to be a generous helping of delicious chocolate mousse, something he could not remember ever having before.

The kitchen maid, Ellen, took charge of him while his grandmother and Mrs Musgrove discussed business, and showed him the 'dumb waiter', a sort of miniature lift worked by ropes. This carried the hot dishes straight upstairs from the kitchen to the dining room. Of more interest to Jonathan was the voice pipe, which enabled staff upstairs serving at table to talk to those down in the kitchen.

He blew down the whistle of the voice pipe, much to Ellen's anxiety.

"That Mr Fulton will be down to see who's playing about," she giggled, and ran with Jonathan down to the pantry, where she began flirting with the footman.

Mr Fulton was the butler, and from the awed tones in which Ellen spoke of him he sounded a formidable person.

Jonathan was fascinated by the soda water cylinder outside the pantry. He had only seen soda water in siphons, but at the Hall they made their own by filling a specially strengthened bottle with ordinary water, and injecting gas into it under pressure. The huge cast iron cylinder, which held the gas, stood taller than a man, and was as thick as a tree trunk. It stood against a wall in the passage, and John, the footman, showed him how it worked, lifting him up to operate the valve lever.

Taking advantage of John's pre-occupation with Ellen a few moments later, Jonathan stood on a chair to discover what would happen if he pulled the lever without a bottle in place. He found that it had a simple, but ingenious safety device. The thick metal shield, protecting the user should the glass shatter under the pressure, could not be pulled right down unless a bottle was in place displacing a ratchet. If the shield was not right down, the top of it restricted the movement of the valve lever.

He worked out however, that by putting his elbow where the bottle should be – thus depressing the ratchet – and lowering the shield into the crook of his elbow, he could just turn the valve lever enough to send a blast of gas hissing through the air.

It was unfortunate that Mr Fulton should choose that moment to come down to investigate the blowing of his whistle.

Mr Fulton, who Jonathan's grandfather later described as 'like a strutting peacock,' epitomised the small minded person who acquires power. He had pop eyes and a receding chin, and was dressed in the standard English butler's daytime uniform of pin striped trousers, black jacket and tie. He walked, and talked, with his head held back in an attempt to compensate for his inadequate jaw, and this created the impression, reinforced by a slight nasal drawl, that he was always talking down his nose.

The noise of the escaping gas masked his approach, so Jonathan's first intimation of his presence was the firm grasp of one hand on his collar and the other on the seat of his trousers. It was not surprising that he should, in fright, lash out with his feet.

Hopping about on one leg while clasping the other and uttering most unbutler like oaths, completely destroyed Mr Fulton's dignity. Unfortunately poor Ellen and John got it in the neck for being 'too busy spooning' to keep an eye on Jonathan.

His grandmother grumbled all the way home, but his grandfather, to whom she told her tale of woe, surprised him by rumbling his deep belly laugh.

"That butler Fulton have it coming to him," he chuckled. "Every time I go up to the Hall he look at me as if I have manure on my boots."

"You nearly always have," she retorted tartly. "And I expect you to tell the boy off, not laugh at him."

But his grandfather only chuckled the more.

That evening, as Jonathan sat on the rug in front of the kitchen range, clad in his nightshirt, he was still simmering from the dispute with his grandmother over what constituted bed time. He had stuck out, not too hopefully, for ten o'clock; telling her – untruthfully – that this was his mother's stipulated time. His grandmother had expressed disbelief, and opened the bidding at seven o'clock. The subsequent heated negotiation had finally been resolved by his grandfather, who came in at that point and grunted "Half past eight," in a tone, and with an expression, that discouraged further argument. In any event Jonathan soon found ways of extending it to nine o'clock and beyond.

His grandmother was now out shutting up the chickens, and he needed comfort, the excitements of the day having become submerged in the realisation that his mother was over a hundred miles away and he might not see her again for several weeks.

"Can I sit on your knee Grandad?" he asked, and clambered up without waiting for an answer.

"I want a story," he added, settling against his grandfather's chest.

His grandfather paused for thought.

"I can't be bothered with them old fairy stories," he said. "But I'll tell you about the time I went to see the old lady there."

He nodded towards the sepia reproduction of Queen Victoria on the wall over the dresser.

"But Mummy told me you'd never been to London in your whole life," said Jonathan.

"And she's quite right," his grandfather chuckled, "but the ol' gal came down to Norfolk once on a visit. That were nigh on fifty years ago, when I was a young man."

He then proceeded to enthrall Jonathan with his account of what had been, for him, a momentous occasion. Although it was supposed to be a closely guarded secret, word had got out, probably through the house servants, that the Queen was to be the guest of an aristocratic family in the West of the County. Due largely to his Liberal politics, he was not an ardent

Royalist. He had, nevertheless, walked thirty miles through the day and, with others, had waited several hours by the lodge gates for the briefest glimpse of the old lady. He had then walked the thirty miles home again.

"You know," he looked pensive, and even a little moist eyed, "you never see pictures of the old Queen with a smile. And that's a pity, because she had a lovely smile. She smiled at us that day, and that made the thirty mile walk each way worth every step. She were dressed all in black, and of course were a lot younger than she's shown in that picture. But she were a beautiful lady."

He approved less of the old Queen's successors.

"I never had a lot of time for the old King, Edward, as a young man," he said frankly. "George were alright; your Uncle Bert say the troops in the trenches in nineteen fourteen thought a lot of him. Then we have this Abdication business, and then we get the Duke of York. He seem alright, although he have a bit of a stutter, but we'll have to wait and see how he shape up if this war come that they're all talking about."

Jonathan had found a way of delaying bedtime; not only this, he had unwittingly created a happy precedent. From then on it became an established routine, almost a ritual, that he would sit on his grandfather's knee, once he was ready for bed, and listen to his marvellous stories; all of them factual and reflecting an era long since vanished. An era when rural folk lived their lives within the constraints, but also within the security, of custom and tradition. His grandfather, as their relationship developed, was to fascinate him, especially during the long Winter evenings, with tales of his own childhood. How, having left school at the age of eleven, he had worked as a horse boy for a farmer some miles away, having to sleep in the loft above the stables in order to rise at four thirty in the morning to prepare the great Shires and Suffolks for work. How he would accept, without resentment, a beating from the farmer if he was late or made a mistake.

Jonathan learned something of his grandfather's attitude to religion.

"If you wanted to keep your job you had to be sure to be in Church at least once every Sunday. Every farmer in the parish was judged on how many of his men he could get into Church, and the Vicar would do a head count. That went on until people started going to Chapel because Methodism had more to offer the ordinary working man."

He had considered Methodism, but in the end had decided that as his father and grandfather were buried in the village Churchyard he would, in effect, be deserting them.

Although not fanatically devout, he seldom missed attending at least one of the Services on Sunday, usually Communion at eight o'clock. If there were not too many tasks to be done back at the farm, he would sometimes wait in the village and join Jonathan's grandmother for Matins as well.

Jonathan not only discovered a great deal about his grandfather during those evening story telling sessions, but the very closeness engendered by sitting on his knee, forever asking questions, and responding to his occasional gentle teasing, enabled the development of a close emotional bond between them.

A great deal happened to both of them in the weeks that followed that first night, when the old man had responded spontaneously, as he would have done to any small animal in distress, when Jonathan had clambered up upon his knee to seek salve for his emotional bruising. As time went on, the hitherto inflexible attitude to discipline was carried less easily, and became less evident. This despite the fact that he had been conditioned, by his Victorian upbringing, into the belief that the male head of the household should establish a rigid and unsentimental authority over any young human male for whom he had a responsibility. This was backed up by tradition, and supported by custom and practice in a heirarchical rural community, and was also reinforced by the teaching of the Church. In consequence he had imposed a regime upon his sons, when they were boys, which had demanded the enforcement of obedience to a degree which was harsh to the point of being oppressive.

He now found himself questioning these old values, and having to come to terms with the consequent discomfort.

For his part, Jonathan brought almost the exact opposite experience into their relationship, having lacked any male authority figure in his environment. His early male chauvinism had asserted itself to a point where his mother's attempts to enforce discipline, hindered rather than helped by Dr Elizabeth Sloan Chesser's 1925 edition of "Health and Psychology of the Child", had resulted in pitched battles which neither of them had won. He had never experienced domination to any degree, and only reluctantly would he relinquish any of his freedom.

Ultimately, both he and his grandfather were able to compromise.

Jonathan discovered the feeling of security that benevolent control engenders.

His grandfather discovered, and accepted, that the excersise of skill and patience neccessary for good animal husbandry – he had never been known to physically punish a horse or a dog – could be equally effective when applied to a young human.

Together, over those first few weeks, they both discovered that love enables the sacrifice required by compromise to be made with only a little pain. The foundations of that love were probably laid on that first evening, at the end of which the old man had himself carried Jonathan's sleeping form upstairs, lowering him gently on to the huge feather mattress.

Jonathan's relationship with his grandmother had also developed in those first weeks. It was similar to that which he had with his mother, although his grandmother was softer, more gullible, and therefore more easily exploited. His grandfather's looming presence in the background prevented him from going too far in that respect however.

She had not got over that first day when she had naively given him the hairpin with which to pick the well lock, and he exploited that too.

"Pass me the salt Granny," he would ask at the meal table, having first twisted his face into an expression of low cunning.

"What do you want it for?" she would ask suspiciously, her hand pausing over the salt pot.

"To sprinkle on my dinner of course," he would claim indignantly.

As soon as he had carefully, and with much slow deliberation, sprinkled the salt on his plate, she would snatch the pot back and place it as far away from him as possible, continuing to glare at him as though still not convinced of the innocence of his request.

There were problems of communication similar to those he had with his mother; like his mother she tended to skip certain essentials of dialogue. Quite often she would cuff him before he had completed his explanation of why he was doing what he was doing, and then give him an apologetic hug when she finally got at the truth. Not that her cuffs were hard; even when they were he pretended they did not hurt, and this frustrated her as much as it did his mother.

She used similar descriptive language.

"All over the place like the Devil found Sixpence!" she would grumble, when he constantly ran everywhere or he was getting in her way. He later learned that this expression was vaguely East Anglian in origin, and that both his mother and grandmother were misquoting; it should have been: "All over the place like the Devil *lost* Sixpence."

Sometimes a word or phrase of his grandmother's would have a different meaning for him.

"Don't let that dratted dog lick your face," she snapped, on observing Snip demonstrating his affection one morning. "He sit in that scullery licking his private parts, and then go straight and lick you."

He assumed, vaguely, that by 'private parts' she meant the various doggy toys and bedding, in the wooden box under the disused oven that Snip had staked out as his own territory. Why it should matter if Snip should want to lick his toys or bedding, or why this should adversely affect Jonathan, was not clear to him.

Later, on his way out to that corner of the barn that he had established as his play area, and where he kept some of his own toys, Jonathan interrupted a conversation between his grandmother and Mrs Limmer, who was visiting.

"I'm going out to play with my private parts," he announced, causing Mrs Limmer to look startled, and his grandmother to flush a bright red before handing him a hefty clout on the ear.

Sometimes he would contribute to misunderstanding by his over eagerness to help.

"That dratted boy," she said angrily as she held up a bandaged finger on one hand, and the evil looking gin trap, with its vicious serrated jaws in the other. "That's a miracle that did no more than graze my knuckle. And you," she rounded on Jonathan's grandfather "and you soft enough to set it for him!"

"That were meant for that ledge in the barn where the cats can't get," said his grandfather, trying to keep a straight face. "I didn't reckon on him fetching it in and hiding it behind the cheese dish in the pantry."

"I was doing you a favour," Jonathan protested. "You been trying to get that ol' mouse for weeks. I just thought a bigger trap would stand more chance."

Despite these and other set backs, he gradually became aware, during those first weeks, of a feeling of well being. He was too young to think introspectively. Only in retrospect was he able to identify this as the beginning of the happiest period of his childhood. He had fitted in to his new environment as though he had always been a natural part of it; as though he were where he belonged.

He loved both of his grandparents, and he knew that they loved him.

His grandmother's love was demonstrative; she enjoyed giving and receiving hugs.

His grandfather's love was not so overtly expressed, but it did not need to be. When Jonathan scurried up the lane, to meet him coming home from Limmer's in the evening, the two dogs would run ahead to demonstrate their own affection, tails thrashing in ecstasy.

Jonathan had not got a tail to wag, but he knew exactly how they felt.

Chapter Five

Jonathan's early initiation into Sunday School provided him with the oppportunity to meet most of the relatives who lived in the village.

Curiosity about their hitherto unknown cousin brought them all flocking around, when Jonathan and his grandmother arrived at the home of Aunty Mavis, David's mother, just before Sunday School. Terry and Colin arrived a few minutes later, with Uncle Bert's daughter Daphne, and Jonathan found himself being inspected.

Colin and David, his second cousins, he took to straight away – finding similarities between them and his companions back in Gloucestershire. They were from different families, were both almost a year older than himself, and were to become his constant companions. Colin had an older brother, Terry, who had a multiplicity of roles, being not only 'cock of the school' and gang leader, but school prefect, head choirboy and Scout patrol leader. This resulted in his having to cope with the conflict of having two life styles, one respectable and the other disreputable. The three of them, together with David's older twin sisters, Cecily and Joan, were Jonathan's closest relatives in the village and immediate area, apart from Daphne. Many of the children he subsequently met in Sunday School and school were either third or fourth cousins. He gave up trying to work out exact relationships; it was only important insofar as it gave him immediate entry into what could be loosely defined as a clan or sect, membership of which carried obligations as well as privileges. For example, if a fight broke out in the school playground, he was expected to immediately close ranks if one protaganist was connected by blood - even only loosely - and the other not.

It was a fact though that their corporate mischief was of a fairly benign nature; possibly Uncle Bert's oversight ensured this. As the village bobby he felt that his own relatives, however distant, must be seen to be law abiding.

Jonathan was immediately made to feel part of the family group, despite some problems of communication arising from his West Country dialect, which they seemed to find fascinating. He discovered that blood kinship gave all the adults a controlling interest in the distribution of both reward and punishment; Colin, David or himself were either clouted, or hugged, by whoever happened to be around whenever either was required.

Mrs Morven, who was also Sunday School Superintendant as well as day school Headmistress, Wolf Cub Akela, Choir boy marshaller, Sanctuary Guild organiser, Deputy Organist and anything else that the Vicar wanted to thrust upon her, greeted Jonathan kindly but firmly.

"David and Colin will look after you; do as you are told and we'll get along fine."

Sunday School over, he was collected by his grandmother.

"We're now a going to see your Great Uncle Silas," she said. "Now he'll be right pleased to see you, 'cos he used to think a lot of your mother when she was a girl."

The rather bulky old man sitting in the wheelchair, and looking for all the world like Lionel Barrymore in some of the films Jonathan was to see years later, beckoned him to sit on a cushion he threw down on to the floor by his side.

"My Lord, he do favour Edie," he said, looking Jonathan over intently. "He look just like my little ol' maid what used to come a tripping in with her little basket all the way from the farm."

Jonathan knew quite a lot about Great Uncle Silas of course. His mother, who loved the old man, regarded him as her favourite uncle, and had often shown the photographs of him which she kept in her family album. She had been a regular visitor to him, when she was a child, right from the time of the unfortunate shooting accident which had left him crippled for the rest of his life. Carrying a covered basket with gifts of eggs, butter, and the odd chicken, she would set it down and tidy up his house, organise any neccessary help from neighbours, and then sit for an hour or more listening to his reminiscences. He had developed a special affection for 'my little maid' and had been delighted to learn that her boy was to come to live at the farm. Jonathan wandered around the cottage, fascinated by the relics of service in the Norfolk Regiment in South Africa. He was particularly interested in the weapons; a Zulu assegai, a funny shaped bayonet which, the old man told him, came from a German rifle, and one that he did not like at all; a hefty axe that was used for dispatching horses that had been wounded in battle.

"Have the boy pop in to see me from time to time," Uncle Silas told Jonathan's grandmother, as they were leaving. "That'll be like having Edie back again."

She was anxious to get home to cook the Sunday dinner, but they stopped briefly to call on Colin and Terry's parents, who he was to know as Aunty Doris and Uncle Percy.

Aunty Doris asked him how he had enjoyed meeting all his little cousins.

"I like them all, but they live too far away for me to come and play with them," he said, having identified the major drawback to living with his grandparents.

There were no children at all within two miles of the farm, and this was a bit of a blow to someone as gregarious as himself. He would be deprived, for whole chunks of time, of companions of his own age.

It was Aunty Doris who partly solved this problem.

"He can stay on in the village for an hour or two after school sometimes; play with boy Colin and boy David, and then I'll give him his tea and set him off home before that get too dark."

This arrangement ensured that he had some opportunity to spend time with his playmates, although it led, fairly quickly, to his first confrontation with Uncle Bert.

"Why is Uncle Bert so *awkward* Grandad?" he asked, using a favourite word of his mother's, as he sat on his grandfather's knee, ready for bed, while his grandmother ironed a sheet.

"He take after his father," she cut in tartly, some coolness having developed between them because she wanted him to chase Jonathan off to bed instead of telling him stories.

"Have he been awkward with you?" his grandfather wanted to know.

"He chased me and Colin today and caught me and hit me with his glove," Jonathan told him.

"You must a been up to some mischief for him to want to do that," his grandmother interrupted again.

Jonathan hurriedly rearranged his facial expression into one of injured innocence, and tried to move the discussion on.

In fact he felt Colin had rather let him down.

They had been using an ornamental iron vase, on a grave in the Churchyard, for catapult target practice; enjoying the satisfying 'ping' when a pebble scored a direct hit. Colin had seen Uncle Bert appear, and had taken off without saying a word. Jonathan had made a belated dash for safety, but Uncle Bert could move like a greyhound despite his size. He carried his spotless white gloves tucked into the front of his uniform tunic, and when he had taken them out and whipped him across the back of the head with them, Jonathan had expected no more than a mild stinging sensation; that was when he discovered that Uncle Bert kept a twelve sided brass threepenny bit tucked into each finger end of one of the gloves.

Uncle Bert had also confiscated the catapult.

"You might a told me he was coming," Jonathan remonstrated with Colin later, rubbing his painful ear.

"He's usually satisfied with catching just one of us," Colin told him frankly. "If I hadn't a let him catch you he might a chased and caught me."

Jonathan decided not to burden his grandparents with this information.

"What you have to remember," said his grandfather, "is your Uncle Bert have a job to do, and if you get up to mischief he'll tell me about it, and then I'll have something to say."

"He had a bad time in the German war," his grandmother said. "He see a lot of good men die in the trenches in France, and that make him feel sort of bitter and that make him act strict towards everybody."

Only a very few people understood Uncle Bert's philosophy.

As he saw it many men, some of them his closest friends, had sacrificed their lives in 1915 to preserve the Englishman's right to continue to enjoy his liberties and to practice his traditional customs and beliefs. From his vantage point as a policeman he saw these rights being abused, and made a mockery of, by scroungers, thieves and workshy ne'er-do-wells. The fact that some of these thieves and scroungers were ex-servicemen made their behaviour less excusable in Uncle Bert's view; they, having survived the trenches, had watched their comrades die, and should have been more rather than less rigorous in honouring their sacrifice.

Uncle Bert's attitude towards his job was strongly conditioned by this philosophy, and found expression in the vigorous policing of his parish which was particularly irksome to small boys.

Jonathan's grandmother, feeling unable to even attempt to explain all this, changed the subject.

"There's a long letter from your mother today," she told him. "She might be coming down the week after next."

His mother had experienced a rather depressing journey back to London, and quite failed to appreciate the Autumn beauty of the countyside flashing past the train windows. The scene they had enacted, as Sam Sharpe drove her away, had taken a toll and left her emotionally drained. Also she was grappling with uncertainty; her parents had made it clear that Jonathan's continued stay with them must be subject to review. The fact that there was a doubt, neccessitated re-opening negotiations with the Masonic School.

She began to feel the fates were conspiring against her.

Tomorrow she would be struggling with a new job, and feeling her way into a whole network of new relationships; the last thing she needed was an ongoing unresolved problem with her small son. Nevertheless she created time during her lunch hour, on that first day, to telephone the Masonic School.

The Headmaster was sympathetic but not encouraging.

"I shall have to put it before the Board again," he told her. "In fact it will have to be treated as a new application. The original sponsers will have to be approached and invited to support it."

He was even less encouraging when he 'phoned her back later that day.

"You appear to have incurred the displeasure of the sponsers by declining to take up the original offer," he told her.

This was an understatement; she had, in fact, had a boiling row with them when – their attempts to persuade her having failed – they tried emotional blackmail by suggesting that her late husband would rest uneasily in his grave if she did not send Jonathan to the school. Because Jonathan's father had never confided in her with regard to his Masonic activities, she knew nothing about the organisation and suspected, quite wrongly, that they were trying to spirit her only child away, removing her parental rights completely.

"This does mean," the Headmaster went on, "that the Chairman will have to decide, on his next visit, whether the matter can be placed before the full Board in November."

"November!" she almost choked, "I was hoping to have him admitted in three weeks!"

She was not helped by the message she received from her brother Bert when she reached the Nurses Home late that night. Unable to talk to her directly, he had left a message with the switchboard operator who had, somehow, got an 'r' into the word 'staying'. The boy is *straying* she read in panic, thinking Jonathan had run away from her parents and was wandering around the countryside in the middle of the night. It took a midnight telephone call back to Bert, getting him out of bed, to straighten that one out; the gaps being filled in by her mother's poorly punctuated letter to her a week later.

'Your father have changed his mind' she wrote.

> 'he seem to have taken to the boy for some reason. Enid Perriman have taken to him as well as have your Uncle Silas. Your brother Bert and the butler Fulton up at the Hall are the only ones that say we did the wrong thing in having him and Bert say we should keep him away from the village apart from school in case he get in with the wrong crowd.'

On the matter of her own feelings she was somewhat reserved.

'He play me up a bit and he tell fibs but your father put a stop to that but I never knew such a boy for being able to be in three different places at the same time he want to be in everywhere and all over the place like the Devil found Sixpence and he argue blacks white and I box his ears but that make no difference he just laugh at me he let me down when we went up to the Hall he kick that butler Fulton on the ankle just because he tell him off for playing with the soda machine and the pantry staff thought that was funny but Mr Fulton say I must not take him up to the Hall again I tell you Edith I did not know where to put my face.'

She finished her letter on a cautiously optimistic note however.

'He get on well with boy Colin and boy David them being the same age and play with them but Bert say that dont have to be a good thing seeing as how there both a couple of right little varmints but I dont see it myself I think they can be fairly good boys some of the time but Bert dont see no good in no one since the War and since he been a Policeman.'

With some relief therefore, Jonathan's mother had been able to thank the Head of the Masonic School and firmly close that particular door. Later letters from her mother had confirmed that Jonathan had settled, and seemed to have adapted quite well to school and particularly to the regime of the farm.

He particularly loved the evening routine, especially the hour before bedtime when all the livestock would be shut up, the wind would be rattling the loose window frames, and the chill outside seemed to emphasise the cosy warmth of the big kitchen.

His grandmother, pushing her specs up on her nose, would complain about the poor light from the oil lamp, while she wrote laborious letters to relatives, or sewed or darned socks. He would sit at the other side of the table drawing, or making plasticine models, or fighting innumerable battles with his toy soldiers. If his grandfather was in, they would sit gazing into the fire while listening to the wireless, or repairing boots or rabbit snares and nets. The bedtime battle between Jonathan and his grandmother over, he would climb on to his grandfather's knee and settle down to listen to a story.

His mother had warned him that his lifestyle would be subject to some changes. Apart from having no other children in the immediate vicinity, there was a feeling of isolation engendered by the very remoteness of the farm, and the absence of any form of public transport on the road which passed the end of the lane.

One respect in which his lifestyle was not allowed to change was in the matter of personal hygeine. At the age of seven he would probably never have washed at all if left to his own devices, but his grandmother, like his mother, was almost obsessional about it.

"Cleanliness is next to Godliness," she would say, slapping a cold wet flannel around his neck and knees as she was getting him ready for school in the morning.

"How can I be dirty?" he would yell. "I been lying in bed all night!"

It was a matter of pride for her that he should at least start the school day clean and tidy, even if he arrived home looking: "Like you been drawn through a hedge backwards."

She carried this obsession over into the management of the house, despite the fact that the place was a dust trap, the range and oil lamps belched out smuts and soot like an LNER locomotive, and every drop of water used for cleaning had to be laboriously manhandled from the well in buckets and churns.

Because of the isolation he was sometimes driven back on to his own resources for play, and had to invent his own games.

The morning after Uncle Percy had taken him, together with Terry, Colin and David, to Carrow Road football ground to watch the Canaries beaten three two by Aston Villa, he chalked out a table sized football pitch on one of the larger flagstones in the barn. He then assembled twenty two of his toy soldiers, and a marble, with which to play his own version of 'Newfooty' – a game which was subsequently acknowledged to be the forerunner of modern Subbuteo. After a few minutes of play he realised he needed some means of separating the two teams, his soldiers all being Guardsmen. The winning team had to be the Canaries of course, so he resolved to give them all yellow shoulder bands, like they used for school sports.

"Please may I have some yellow cotton from your workbox Granny?" he asked politely

"What do you want it for?" she asked suspiciously

The only yellow thread she had was silk, neatly wrapped around a card.

"You're not having that to play with," she told him. "That's far too expensive."

He waited until she was out of the way before whipping it out of her workbox, and escaping to the barn with it, but then found that manufacturing eleven shoulder bands would be far too time consuming, so settled in the end for winding the silk round the Guardsmen's waists.

The trouble was that his hands were grubby, and by the time he had finished, the silk remaining on the card had turned from bright yellow to drab grey.

Appreciating the folly of returning it to the workbox as it was, he gave it a bit of thought before plunging it into the rainwater butt and swishing it around a bit. The card promptly pulped and disintegrated, leaving a mess of ravelled silk floating on the surface of the water.

He hoped that sufficient time would pass, before she missed it, for his grandmother's memory to become dulled, but it was just his foul luck for her to decide, the very next evening, to finish some embroidery. His heated denials fell flat when she scurried out to the barn, returning a few moments later with his Guardsmen – each with the incriminating yellow waistband. He was cuffed and sent to bed with the advice that his grandfather would be invited to deal with him as soon as he arrived home.

Subsequently there followed a dialogue which, through frequent repetition, was to become almost a ritual.

"Where's the little ol' boy then?" his grandfather would ask, unlacing his boots, surprised that Jonathan had not met him at the top of the lane to enjoy the customary ride home on his shoulders, holding on to his ears like horse's reigns.

"Well might you ask!" Jonathan's grandmother would start slamming pans and crockery around in her indignation. "He been sent to bed without any supper. And what you have to do as soon as you get your boots off, you go you upstairs and you take your belt and you give him a good thrashing, 'cause that's what he have to have. He a been a little heathen all day today. He play me up something savage and that's a fact!"

By this time Jonathan would be out of bed, sitting on the top step of the stairs in his nightshirt, elbows on knees and chin cupped in hands. As the predictable dialogue progressed, so would Jonathan; shuffling his bottom down one step at a time until, at the conclusion of the debate, he would be sitting on the bottom step.

The next line would be his grandfather's.

"He play you up, you give him a hiding."

"Oh no," his grandmother was firm about role definition in matters of discipline, "that's not a woman's job not when that's a boy. Any more than that's a man's job when that's a girl."

After a pause she would then produce the line Jonathan was waiting for, and which would send his hand reaching out for the door knob in anticipation.

"But you won't do it I know 'cause you're too soft with him. That's beyond me how you're as soft with him when you was so hard with your own when they were boys, but you'll regret it I know. He'll come to a bad end you mark my words, and that'll be all your fault 'cause you a been so soft with him."

"That can't be right to send him off with no supper," his grandfather would grumble. "He's such a skinny little beggar, there's nothing on him as it is. He want feeding up not starving."

"That's up to you," she would wash her hands of the affair. "You want to give in to him, you fetch him down. I'm not giving in to him."

"Boy Jonathan! – " his grandfather would bawl, but he would be through the door, grinning at his grandmother, before the first syllable was out.

"The little devil been sitting there listening to every word," she would say angrily.

But she had always set three places at the table, with three rounds of bread and three portions of pickled herring on the side.

Ted Perriman would often accept her invitation to have a bite of supper with them, and would always have great difficulty in suppressing his mirth whenever he was witness to this little ritual. Apart from Ted Limmer he was the most frequent visitor, often handing over a pheasant or a brace of partridges 'for the oven'. As he was especially fond of Jonathan's grandparents, the birds he brought were always young tender and succulant. His affection stemmed from the days when his wife was dying from a very long drawn out illness, and they had supported him through this very difficult time, virtually taking over the care of his little daughter Enid.

There were very few other visitors to the farm, especially in winter when the lane, a quagmire in wet weather and like furrowed concrete after a frost, discouraged all but the most enthusiastic. Even tramps, or 'roadsters' as they were called, gave them a miss unless they knew Jonathan's grandparents and enjoyed being treated like human beings instead of scroungers. The oil man, delivering paraffin for the lamps, would leave it at Limmers', as would the postman with the letters. Very rarely a pedlar would come and grind scissors and knives, while Jonathan's grandmother drew out distant as well as local gossip from him. The rabbit skin man used the lane as a short cut between the main roads, and always called in to collect any skins left for him at a penny a time.

He was a cheery soul with a red beery face and a great sense of humour. He carried his skins impaled on two long sticks which he carried one over each shoulder.

"Well now Mrs Cooper," he would say, grabbing hold of Jonathan's collar. "Here's a one the Master forget to skin. And he's still alive. I'll have to skin him for you."

He would then tickle Jonathan until his giggling became uncontrollable and then sit and drink home brewed beer while she pumped him for all of his gossip.

She believed in keeping herself well informed, and as both the pedlar and the rabbit skin man were veritable mines of information in this respect, she was able to startle her friends, on her next visit to the village, with her knowledge of all notable events within a twenty mile radius.

Occasionally the Squire would ride through on his way from one part of his vast estate to the other, but would only call in if he had business to discuss.

Jonathan's grandmother baked all her own bread, so the only tradesman who called on a regular basis was the fishman, Mr. Bellini, and even he left his wares at Limmer's if he had been told in advance what was wanted. He was an Italian who had settled in England after the war, and had recently exchanged his pony and trap for a green 'Bullnose' Morris van. Bumping this down the lane with a casual disregard for the springs, he would reverse up to the yard gate, and open the van doors with a flourish, to reveal bloaters, hake, mackerel, shrimps, herring, cod and plaice.

"You're having me on," she would say when he tried to convince her: "All caught this morning Mrs Cooper," when he was at the gate by ten o'clock, having completed his village rounds, and Yarmouth thirty miles away.

Mr Kemp the Vet also visited quite often. Usually he had some task to perform, but sometimes he would just pop in for a chat. He had great respect for the skill, with sick animals, which Jonathan's grandfather had developed, and would sometimes take him with him on his rounds, either for advice or practical help.

"I have a fractious beast to work with, there's no one can hold them like Will Cooper," he would say.

Jonathan liked Mr Kemp, who would haul him up on to his knee, and tell him stories arising from his experiences, before giving him a ride to the top of the lane in his car.

"I'm going to be a Vet when I grow up," Jonathan told everybody after one such visit, but as he had, within a week, announced his intention of being a soldier, a pilot, a footballer and a poacher, nobody took him seriously.

Sometimes his grandmother would take him with her on her monthly shopping trip into Norwich, but finding him 'an infernal nuisance' to drag around shops, she would arrange to leave him at the Market to be brought home by his grandfather. One Saturday, after making their way to Castle Meadow, they met at the pig pens. His grandfather took possession of him, and headed straight towards the spot where he had left his bicycle, a sly grin reaching his face when they suddenly met Uncle Bert.

"How come they let you over the border line then?" Jonathan's grandfather teased, referring to the rivalry, not always good natured, which existed between the Norwich City force and their country cousins in the

Norfolk County Constabulary, of whom they tended to be somewhat contemptuous. This antipathy found bureaucratic expression in the rule that a county officer could not enter the city, in uniform, unless he had a specific duty to perform or was 'in hot pursuit' of a malefactor.

"I had to check some pigs as had been moved without a certificate," grunted Uncle Bert sourly.

Ensuring that sheep had been dipped, and that the movement of livestock was properly controlled, was a regular feature of a rural policeman's job.

"I can't stop," he said after a few minutes conversation, "I have to get these papers to the Auctioneer."

This was the first time Jonathan had seen his grandfather and Uncle Bert together. He studied them with interest, noting the physical similarity, but noting also that – because they were together – the authority vested in Uncle Bert by his uniform was somehow diminished. It was evident in the way they stood; the old man dominating the exchange by his legs apart hands on hips stance, while Uncle Bert stood virtually at attention.

From the security of his grandfather's side, Jonathan gave Uncle Bert an arrogant stare, remembering the clout he had been given, and the confiscation of his catapult. If Uncle Bert noticed, he did not acknowledge it.

As they parted company, Jonathan had a sudden idea. He ran back and booted a tin can, which his grandfather had stopped him from kicking along the gutter, so that it rose in the air and landed right behind Uncle Bert. His grandfather had stopped to wait for him with an expression on his face that was not pleasant.

"Do you want to come to market with me again," he asked.

Jonathan dropped his eyes and said nothing.

"Go and pick it up."

He watched as Jonathan sulkily retrieved the can.

"Now you can carry that around in your hand until we get home," his grandfather said. "That'll be about an hour and a half from now. Maybe by that time you'll a learned something."

This incident epitomised many of a similar nature during those first weeks, and could perhaps be described as the growing pains in their relationship.

This was something which they both had to work through; the process probably helped by the onset of winter, and the reduced daylight hours which curtailed Jonathan's after school activities away from the farm.

He was allowed to stay in the village after school if someone, usually Uncle Percy, was willing to run him home, later, on the crossbar of his bike.

"You're not walking all that way in the dark on your own," his grandmother was adamant.

To Jonathan's amazement Uncle Bert occasionally volunteered to run him home on the crossbar of the big Police bike, usually when he wanted to call at the farm anyway. The bigger surprise was that Uncle Bert was sometimes quite relaxed and affable when they were alone together, a kind of cosy intimacy possible as they sped along through the pitch blackness, cocooned in the pool of light from the headlamp.

He was seldom able, however, to part company from Jonathan on these occasions without reverting back to his official self.

"Now see you keep you out of mischief, boy Jonathan," he would caution. "I have my eye on you mind."

Playing around in the village became a less atractive pastime as the weather worsened, and Jonathan found himself eager to get home to the warmth of the farm kitchen.

The cows were kept in because the fields were covered in frost, and the weather was bitterly cold. He went to school clad like an Arctic explorer, with two pullovers under his overcoat, two pairs of socks, and one of his grandmother's enormous scarves wrapped around his head under his cap.

The rabbit skin man had produced a pair of rabbit fur mitts on his last visit.

"The Missus made them up specially for the little ol' boy," he said. "I told her all about him and the chilblains on his fingers, and she run these up out of a few skins and a bit of shammy."

Jonathan began to spend more time indoors, hugging the kitchen range.

Sometimes, if his grandfather was out, his grandmother would tell him stories at bedtime. Provided he egged her on enough, she could be relied upon to forget the time, and he would watch the hands of the clock move way past nine o'clock before she would suddenly exclaim and rush him upstairs.

She loved telling him about his mother's activities as a little girl, and would gaze into the middle distance in pensive mood as their conversation evoked pleasant memories of years past. Noting her relaxed manner on one such evening, Jonathan wondered if he might have better luck in persuading her to talk about his mysterious uncle.

"You know that day at Miss Perriman's, when you was telling me all about my cousins," he said. "Well, why did you get all cross when I asked about my other uncle?"

"That's not something we talk about," her voice suddenly hard, "haven't your mother told you that?"

"She told me his name once," he said, "but I've forgotten it. What is it?"

"That name's not to be mentioned in this house, especially to your grandfather," she snapped. "Now I want to hear no more about it, otherwise I'll box your ears."

Perceptive of the real tension his apparently innocent question had created, he wisely dropped the subject. His curiosity was like an itch that needed to be scratched though.

He was suddenly struck with an idea; he would ask his cousin Terry about it when he next saw him at school.

Chapter Six

His grandfather had given up breeding and showing Shire horses in the early nineteen thirties.

"That's for a young man with time to spare to go traipsing all over the County," he said. "But there's times, when I look at Sampson, when I have my regrets; I'm sure he'd a won me some prizes."

His stories of the horses he had owned and loved down through the years were fascinating and highly entertaining, especially when related while in a group of farm workers, all of whom would try to cap them with stories of their own.

"I tried Suffolk Punches once," he reminisced. "But they didn't suit me. They was faster for straight pulling with carts, but they didn't have the strength for heavy loads or ploughing on heavy soil, unless you ran them as a pair."

They would take Sampson to be roughshod by the village blacksmith, who was quite happy to turn his forge over to Jonathan's grandfather and sit smoking his pipe.

"That Will Cooper do as good a job as I've seen," he would say. "And he's trusted by his own horse."

A Shire horse's collar must be an exact fit to avoid chafing and soreness, and as there was no saddler in the village, the collar had to be made in Norwich. Jonathan went with his grandfather when Sampson's old collar wore out, and watched a craftsman at work.

Sampson was strong, even by Shire horse standards, but amazingly gentle. He would stand quite still, showing no sign of discomfort, even when Jonathan literally climbed him as though he were tree; shinning up a foreleg and grasping handfulls of mane to pull himself up. He would help his grandfather to harness up, walking with impunity under the big horse's belly and through his legs to fasten the straps. Sampson was a gelding, but people who were thinking of putting their mare to his sire would come considerable distances to look him over.

Sometimes Jonathan's grandfather would harness him in tandem with one of Limmer's horses for ploughing, but on the lighter soil of the top fields he preferred to work him alone. Men spoke admiringly of his ability to work an acre and a half in a day.

His grandfather was very particular about grooming, especially the long hair around the legs which almost hid the hooves. This well known Shire characteristic had the disadvantage of soaking up damp and mud, causing 'Greasy Leg' a kind of infection which could result in lameness if neglected.

When Sampson was not working, he either shared the pasture with the Friesians or stood dozing on three legs in the yard. His stall was built into the end of the barn, and when he came home warm from work, on a chilly day, he would be immediately visited by the feral cats who made the barn their home. Sometimes three of them would find a space on his back to curl up in, and even when they stretched their claws he did not seem to mind.

The cats were never allowed in the house.

The word 'allergy' was in very few vocabularies in the thirties; certainly Jonathan's grandmother was not diagnosed as allergic or treated for the quite distressing symptoms she would evidence on being brought into contact with a cat. She would sneeze non-stop; her eyes and nose discharging copiously.

Successive generations, culled from time to time to prevent a population explosion, had grown progressively wilder over the years. Despite her antipathy she put food out for them every day, but for the most part they lived off what they hunted. As this included Ted Perriman's partridge chicks out of the hedgerows, he contributed to the culling exersise whenever he caught them at it. The barn owls did their share by grabbing the tiny kittens should the mother cat relax her vigilance as it was getting dusk. The cats in their turn tried to get at the baby owls, but the nest was usually far out of their reach. They were totaly anti-social and rejected any friendly overture. Jonathan did eventually persuade some of the kittens to come to be fussed over, but this made Snip jealous; he simply barked his head off until the kittens took fright and left. The whole tribe was led by a battle scarred and patriarchal old Tom, who was as vicious as he was ugly.

Cornering him once, Jonathan told him he only wanted to be friends, and to prove it he would stroke him gently. As his grandmother later dried his tears and iodined and bandaged his lacerated arm, Jonathan resolved to reserve his affection for Snip and Jeb.

He was able to develop a fondness for the school cat though; it really belonged to Mrs Morven, but had the run of the school and would visit each classroom in turn. At first they thought it was generously sharing itself between the children, but it was simply following the sun around the building, finding successive warm patches to snooze away the entire day. Terry, as school monitor, had the job of ensuring that it was not shut in the building all night.

During school playtime one day, Jonathan remembered his resolve to ask Terry about his missing uncle, but Terry was not able to be very helpful.

"I remember something about it," he said, wrinkling his brow in concentration. "He was the one as went off to Canada to be a lumberjack, then he came back and had a fight with Uncle Bert, then he went off again and haven't been seen since."

This sounded exciting, but Terry knew no more than that. He did promise to ask his parents however.

"I got a right telling off through you," he twisted Jonathan's arm up behind his back, next day, as a punishment. "Mum get right huffy and tell me to mind my own business and not bring up things that happen before I was even born."

"Did she say what his name was?" Jonathan asked trying to ignore the pain in his arm.

"No," said Terry. "And Dad didn't either, and he get huffy and all, and say he'll clout me if I keep on asking questions."

Jonathan's curiosity was thoroughly aroused now, but he could see no way of satisfying it; questions about his fourth uncle seemed to arouse hostility in everybody. He toyed with the idea of asking his grandfather, but his grandmother had left him with the impression that the old man should be the very last person to raise the subject with.

Then a sudden thought struck him: Uncle Silas enjoyed talking about the past, wistfully remembering the good old days before the German war. Perhaps he would throw light on the situation.

With the year drawing to a close, Jonathan began to anticipate Christmas; an exciting time for him but a rather disappointing one for his grandparents. They had hoped to reinstate the 'family get-together' – an event which had become traditional up to the time of his mother's marriage – by getting all three uncles and their families to come.

"Your mother was the one who badgered the others into coming," his grandmother told him "Even Uncle Jim from up North. But since your mother left home that fell off."

Their efforts met with failure.

Jim could not afford the train fare for his family, due to short time in the shipyards. Uncle Jack, being a gamekeeper, had a Boxing Day shoot to organise, and with no public transport would not have been able to get back to Thetord in time. Indeed he would be spending most of Christmas Day putting up markers and beating round the outskirts of the estate to drive the pheasants into the woods he intended to draw first. Uncle Bert was already committed to spending the day with Aunty Eliza's mother in Kings Lynn.

In the end only his grandparents, his mother, Uncle Silas and himself would be sitting down to Christmas Dinner together; he and his mother having pushed Uncle Silas' wheel chair all the way from the village after Matins. She had arrived three days beforehand, and Miss Perriman had collected Jonathan to take him to meet her at Norwich Thorpe.

"I want to see your mother," she had told him, "and as I shall be away over Christmas this is the only chance I shall have."

He was impressed by the warmth of their greeting and their obvious affection for each other. Sending him on ahead, as they walked from the village, they chattered and giggled like two schoolgirls. They talked a lot about Uncle Silas, his mother having a continuing concern for the old man's welfare.

Jonathan had been told of the sad background to his invalidity.

"After the Regiment came home from South Africa he married his Sergeant Major's daughter," his mother had said. "But Mary had seen enough of the Army and wanted him to buy himself out."

Uncle Silas had done so, reluctantly, and had taken a job as a farm labourer on the Squire's estate. As was the custom, the farm labourers were pressed into service as beaters during the shooting season, driving the pheasants, partridges and hares towards the waiting guns. One of the shoot guests had accidently discharged his gun into Silas' lower back, damaging several vertebrae and leaving him permanently disabled. This was a tragedy for an able bodied man with a wife and small son to support, but as such accidents were not uncommon there was a recognised procedure. The onus was on the guest to arrange adequate financial compensation and, as etiquette demanded, he discussed it with the Squire.

"I think two hundred pounds and a hundred pounds a year thereafter," he said.

This was considered to be reasonably generous; the average weekly wage at that time was twenty two shillings a week.

But the Squire would not hear of it.

"You're creating an unacceptable precedent," he had told his guest. "You'll have every damned labourer, who gets a pellet in his backside, trying to exploit the situation. In any case it is highly immoral for a man to sit around with no incentive to do anything for himself. He can take up basket making or something to supplement what you give him."

"What would you suggest?" asked the guest.

"Fifty pounds and fifty a year, " said the Squire.

So Uncle Silas had to struggle to make ends meet.

Mary cleaned at the Hall two days a week for five shillings, while Silas, helped by his small son, had cut blackthorn from the hedgerows to make into walking sticks, all with intricately carved heads, which he could sell for a few coppers. He would carve while sitting outside his front door on warm days, pausing for conversations with passers by.

Then Mary had died of Consumption.

With the help of willing neighbours and relatives, including Jonathan's grandparents, he had stuggled on until his son, Jim, was old enough, at thirteen, to enlist as a boy entrant in the Army.

Despite his infirmity Uncle Silas was, Jonathan found, fun to be with over Christmas. He drank far more home brewed beer than he should have done, but apart from having to be repeatedly helped out to the petty he appeared to suffer no ill effects.

He was able to bring them good news about his son.

"Jim's been promoted to Sergeant," he told them proudly. "That mean he can get his Commanding Officer's permission to get wed."

"I'm delighted," said Jonathan's mother, "but Enid didn't say anything when she met me at Thorpe."

"Not a word to her," cautioned Uncle Silas. "Jim right particular that he tell her himself when he see her in London next week."

Jonathan's grandmother had begun her preparations early; the geese had fattened well and two had been earmarked for the family table. His grandfather had butchered a pig in the Autumn and passed some of the meat to the Limmers. In return they had butchered one at Christmas.

Jonathan had his first pair of roller skates as his main present, and was very full and contented at the end of the day.

Christmas week concluded with the traditional Epiphany bonfire and carol singing at the Hall.

They processed up the drive from the Church, the choir in their thick robes, swinging lanterns, until they came to that edge of the wood which was closest to the house. The foresters had built the huge bonfire, while the cook had provided enough jacket potatoes and soup to feed an army. The Choir had disappeared through the front door to sing their usual carols, and on their return found that the crowd had been swelled by almost the entire population of the village. They were followed out by the Squire and Lady Mary, with their various guests, including the Vicar and the Doctor. The Squire made a speech in a clipped staccato voice, sounding as though he were telling everybody off, concluding with the comment that the estate must pay if full employment were to continue through the New Year, and that every one of his workers must pull his weight with no slacking.

As an afterthought he hoped everybody had had a happy Christmas.

In order to cook the enormous geese, and the huge leg of pork, Jonathan's grandmother had decided that the disused oven, which was set into the back wall of the scullery, should be brought into use. This had involved disposing of a lot of paraphanalia that had accumulated in it over the years. Before coaxing the fire into a blaze, a way had to be found of securing the oven door with a wedge, the latch having long since broken off.

After Christmas, the oven no longer in use, Jonathan discovered that it was roomy enough to acommodate him if he sat in a hunched up posture. Trying it out one morning he observed, through the hole where the latch had been, his grandmother enter and begin to prepare vgetables at the sink. He sat perfectly still until she had finished before letting himself out and standing behind her.

She nearly leapt out of her skin.

"How the devil did you get in here?" she demanded. "You didn't come in through the back door or through the kitchen."

"I've been in here all the time," he told her. "It's just that I can make myself invisible, so you couldn't see me."

For a brief second she looked – almost – as if she believed him; her eyes, darting all over the scullery, telling her there was no place he could have hidden. For some reason the oven as a hiding place never occurred to her.

He decided to repeat the experiment an hour later, and again watched through the hole, as she decided he must be outside and went to the back door to call him in to dinner.

"Boy Jonathan," she yelled.

He slid out and stood behind her.

The effect was quite gratifying, especially as she happened to be holding the knob of the closed kitchen door, which was next to the back door in which she was standing, so he could not have entered through either.

"I want to know how you do that," she yelled, getting exasperated and nearly wrenching his ear off.

"I keep telling you I can make myself invisible," he insisted. "I've been standing behind you all the time."

The third time was even more rewarding.

"That's easy," his grandfather had told her when she complained to him. "Don't you remember when Edie was little? How she used to hide from the boys by climbing into the copper?"

"Of course! The little varmint! Why did I not think of that.!"

The next day, before calling him in for dinner, she looked all around the scullery before, eyes gleaming, she advanced upon the huge copper, as the washboiler in the corner was known. With a dramatic gesture she swept off the lid, and then looked baffled at not finding him in there.

"He have to be outside then," she muttered, but gave a final check around all the corners which might have secreted him, before going to the back door and calling him.

"I'm here," said Jonathan, the wind, howling around the eaves, drowning any noise he might have made sliding out of the oven.

She flew across the scullery and began cuffing him around the ears.

"I have to know how you do that," she yelled. "Now you tell me this instant. I shan't rest till I know."

"I keep telling you. I can be invisible," he said. "Why don't you believe me?"

She threw logic out of the window.

"Alright, do it now then," she demanded. "While I'm watching you."

"I can only do it while no one's watching," he explained. "That won't work if I try to do it in front of someone."

She poked and prodded around the scullery for the next half hour before finally giving up, and glaring at him suspiciously for the rest of the day.

He tried it out on his grandfather, who was shaving prior to an evening visit to the Kings Head and scraping away at his chin with his cut throat razor.

"I'd come out of that oven now if I was you," his grandfather suddenly said, conversationally, as he paused to apply more lather to his whiskers.

"How did you know?" Jonathan demanded, pummelling his grandfather's buttocks with his fists.

"That's easy," his grandfather said. "I'm looking in the mirror, and behind me I see that Snip, looking up at the oven and wagging his tail."

"Don't tell Granny," Jonathan begged.

The old man rumbled his deep belly laugh.

"Alright," he said. "We'll keep her in the dark a little while longer."

Like many elderly people who spend a lot of time alone, Jonathan's grandmother had developed the habit of talking to herself; in fact she would frequently stand at the sink preparing vegetables, or washing up, while conducting an imaginary conversation. Sometimes this would be a replay of a dialogue she had already had, but with the addition of witty repartee that she wished she had thought of at the time; another dialogue would be a rehearsal for a forthcoming debate. On more than one occasion Jonathan had run into the scullery thinking they had a visitor. She was obviously self-conscious about it, and only did it when she believed herself to be alone.

His grandfather knew she did it, and pulled her leg.

"You know what they say about people as talk to themselves," he would joke. "They reckon that's the first sign of madness."

"Only if you answer yourself back," she would also joke; but she would redden nevertheless.

Unaware that Jonathan was hidden in the old oven one morning, she tried out several lines of approach to Mr Bellini, the fishman, who had sold her a piece of cod the previous week which was off when she came to cook it.

"Now Mr Balony," fiercely, "That cod you sold me last week was off; now I reckon you have to give me my money back, or you can stop coming and I'll buy elsewhere. I'm not buying off people what sell me bad goods."

A pause while she considered the effect of this; then a milder alternative:

"That cod you sold me last week was a bit off Mr Balony. I reckon you owe me another piece seeing as how we couldn't eat it."

Another pause, then a much more aggressive approach.

"You can stop coming after today Mr Balony. I'm not buying off people what twist me by selling me bad goods. That cod you sold me last week was near to rotten; walking off the dish it was. I'll have my money back and I don't want to see you down here again."

By this time, hunched up in the oven, Jonathan was stuffing his pullover sleeve into his mouth to prevent her hearing his giggles; the more so when Mr Bellini arrived and she went across the yard to meet him at the gate.

Jonathan scrambled out of the oven to listen.

"Now Mr Balony," she greeted him. "That's a nice morning to be sure."

"It's a Bellini, Bellini," said Mr Bellini automatically, although he had long ago given up any hope of her ever getting his name right.

"I'll have a few shrimps, and a piece of halibut if you have it, and just a few more herring for pickling."

Only after the transaction was completed did she lower her voice confidentially.

"Fact is Mr Balony, and I don't want you to worry about it, I'm only telling you so as you'll know. Likely that was passed on to you so you wouldn't know when you give it to me. So no ill feeling. Like I say, I'm only telling you so as you'll know. I'm not asking for my money back. That's the first time that's ever happened, and knowing you that'll never happen again."

She beamed at him kindly.

Mr Bellini gaped in bewilderment.

"What is you are telling me?" he groped.

"That's nothing really," she said. "I'm not a going to have you worrying about it. In fact I won't mention it again."

"But what is you won't mention again?"

Mr Bellini's frustration, at not knowing what she was talking about, was evident.

"In fact that weren't wasted," she went on. "The cats had it."

"The cats have what?"

Mr Bellini was almost desperate.

"Why the cod of course."

"You give best cod to the cats?"

"Why yes, well we couldn't eat it."

"Why not? Is nice cod."

"That's what I'm telling you," she still beamed at him, "It was off."

"Off?"

"Bad."

"My God! – you telling me I sell you bad fish? – why you not say? – here, I give you another piece."

Jonathan's grandfather enjoyed the piece of cod on his plate that evening.

"You get that sorted out with that Eyetalian fellow?" he asked.

"I gave him a piece of my mind I can tell you," she bustled aggressively round the kitchen table. "Sent him off with his tail between his legs and that's a fact."

"What are you snickering at?" the old man asked Jonathan.

But from the twinkle in his eye it was obvious that he knew.

Mr Bellini also sold poultry from his fish van, and would sometimes order a batch of oven ready birds from Jonathan's grandmother. Provided she had enough left over after meeting her own orders, particularly from the

Hall because they were her best customers, she would always let him have some.

In order to ensure white succulant meat, the method employed to dispatch them was the time honoured one of slitting the carotid artery with a sharp penknife after first hanging the unfortunate bird up by the feet on a fence post. Strangely enough they seemed to feel no pain but simply looked peeved, as though they minded the loss of dignity more than the loss of their life blood. Only towards the end, when life had virtually drained away, did some belated survival instinct send them flapping frantically in a futile effort to escape.

The fence by the yard gate was her killing ground, and groundsell and other weeds proliferated in the soil underneath it, fertilised by the blood of countless generations of chickens over the years.

Forty years earlier she had worked as a kitchen maid at the Hall, and when she left to marry, she brought with her, as a wedding present, the contract to supply the Hall with chickens, butter and eggs at current market prices. She was still smug about having cornered that particular market, and used to earmark special birds for the Hall.

Jonathan would spend some time looking after the chickens, and had formed a close relationship with a young cockerel called, unoriginally, Chanticleer, after a story his mother used to tell him. His grandmother did not have an incubator, so the young chicks would spend their first days in a box by the side of the kitchen range, and for some reason Chanticleer seemed tamer than the others as a result. Jonathan even managed to persuade the bird, fully grown by this time, to sit on the back of his hand while being fed titbits. Having recently read something about falconry, in the Eastern Evening News, he made a little hood out of an old glove, but Chanticleer had such a hostile attitude to wearing it that the exercise had to be abandoned. For the same reason he also abandoned tethering Chanticleer's feet to his wrist with a bootlace.

He also had to live with his grandfather's ire because he had taken the bootlace out of one of the old man's best boots; the discovery made on the following Sunday morning when they were already running late for Church.

Notwithstanding these setbacks, Jonathan still nurtured the hope that Chanticleer might one day be persuaded to hunt game. Obviously the bird could not fly, but could, maybe, run along the ground after rabbits. Anyway, he felt, having read about the old fashioned sport of fighting cocks, he could always arrange a change of career for Chanticleer if resistance to becoming a bird of prey continued.

Then, one day when he came home from school, the cockerel was nowhere to be found.

"I think Chanticleer has got lost," he told his grandmother.

"That's not lost that can be found," she replied briskly. "He's hanging up in the pantry, plucked and ready to be taken up to the Hall."

He rushed, unbelieving, along to the pantry.

He could not quite equate the naked limp corpse, recognisable only by the handsome head and comb, with the warm, albeit somehat eccentric and unpredictable creature that he had come to regard as special.

"I hate you!" he screamed at his grandmother, in a temper tantrum, and ended up in bed with his backside smarting.

They made it up later with a conciliatory cuddle on the settee, while she explained that she would have stayed the knife had she realised how much Chanticleer meant to him.

"I was going to train him to catch rabbits, like a falcon," he said, staring suspiciously at his grandfather, who seemed to be having difficulty controlling the corners of his mouth.

"I don't reckon you could get a cockerel to catch rabbits," said his grandfather gravely, looking up at the ceiling, into the corners of the room, out of the window – in fact anywhere rather than directly at Jonathan. "That not being in his nature like."

"That boy have some queer ideas and that's a fact," his grandmother told his mother in her next letter. "He only try to turn one of my chickens into a hawk!"

He had a brief flirtation with the idea of capturing and training one of the barn owls, but abandoned that after he fell while trying to climb up to where they roosted.

The next day his grandfather was teasing him for making a fuss over the grazed knee acquired during the attempt, so Jonathan told him how brave he had been when having his tonsils out in Gloucester Infirmary, and gave him a dramatised account of the event.

"And how long was you in the Infirmary, and how long off school afterwards?" his grandfather's eye held a mischievous twinkle.

"Five days, and I was off school just over a week afterwards." Jonathan told him..

"I had mine out when I were ten years old," his grandfather said. "Know where?"

"Norwich hospital?"

His grandfather shook his head.

"Right there on that kitchen table. Old Doc Shelly was the sawbones then. And there was no chloroform. He reckoned that weren't needed. He just told me to lie flat on the table, propped my mouth open with a wooden ring that nearly made my jaw lock, and my father held my head while he dug in with a pair of long handled scissors and snipped them out. Then he cauterised them and told me to go to bed. He weren't in the house above fifteen minutes."

Jonathan listened in awe.

"Didn't it hurt?" he asked.

"That hurt a bit, but next morning my father say that work make you forget pain, so he put me out in the field scaring crows off the barley."

Jonathan's grandmother, who had been listening to the conversation while she sewed, bit off a length of cotton.

"There's half the things they now push you off to that old hospital for that used to get done at home," she said. "Your uncles were always getting knocked and banged when they were boys. More than once we had broken bones when they fell off a haystack, or even the barn roof your Uncle Jim fell off."

"That Dr. Dunbar came out in his pony and trap," said his grandfather. "He take one look at Jim and he say he have to have him in the surgery because his wrist was clean broken. He take him to his house in the trap, fix the break and plaster it in his kitchen, and then send our Jim to walk the two miles home."

"And when he sent us the bill, that included three shillings for the pony and trap," added his grandmother disgustedly.

This talk of his uncles as boys reminded Jonathan that his curiosity, about his fourth uncle, had been submerged in the exitement of Christmas; he had even forgotten to mention it to his mother before she had returned to London.

He remembered his resolve to talk to Uncle Silas about it, and decided to call round one evening.

He liked to gaze at the painting, on the parlour wall, of the soldier in the dress uniform of the Norfolk Regiment. With navy blue trousers, scarlet jacket, white pipeclayed belt and small cap with the Britannia badge prominent, it seemed to epitomise military perfection.

"I would like to grow up to be a soldier and wear a smart uniform like that," he told Uncle Silas.

"I found this for you," the old man rummaged in a drawer and producing a shiny Britannia cap badge.

"Thanks, Uncle Silas," he said. "I'll shine it up with Granny's brasso every day."

Just as he was about to leave, he recalled his main reason for being there. He decided against the direct approach; the subject seemed to evoke too many negative reactions from adults.

"Granny says my uncles joined the Norfolk Regiment because of the stories you told them," he said, cunningly. "Did they all join?"

"That was funny how that work out," said Uncle Silas pensively. "There was your Uncle Bert who was the eldest and boss your Uncle Jim around, and Jim being the second eldest boss your Uncle Jack around. Then when they get in the Regiment they end up with your Uncle Bert a sergeant, Jim a corporal and Jack a lance-corporal. So they was still bossing each other around in the same order."

He chuckled as he gazed into the middle distance.

"What about my other uncle?" Jonathan asked. "What was he, an ordinary private?"

Uncle Silas suddenly went very quiet, still gazing into the middle distance. Jonathan waited with bated breath for his next pronouncement, but it was disappointing.

"No," said the old man, "but that's not something we talk about."

"Why not?" Jonathan asked, emboldened by the lack of hostility.

There was a long silence while Uncle Silas puffed thoughtfully at his pipe.

"Fact is my little ol' boy," he said with an air of finality, "that's not my place to tell you, seing as how that's more closer family business. You have to ask your mother or your granny or grandad if you want to know anything about Arthur."

Arthur! That was it! At least Jonathan had the name now, and indeed he had only needed the jog to his memory to recall his mother's words.

"After your Uncle Jim left to get work in the shipyards up North, that only left Granny and Grandad at home, because no one knows where Arthur went to."

Obviously Uncle Silas was not prepared to divulge more; Jonathan realised that he would just have to be patient, and await his mother's next visit, and hope that she would be more forthcoming than the rest of the family.

Chapter Seven

Jonathan's grandfather very rarely missed Norwich Market, even if he had nothing to sell or buy, and he always had his lunch in the Woolpack, where he could usually count on seeing most of his old cronies, including Mr Kemp. The landlord normally objected to children, but Jonathan was granted special dispensation because of his grandfather's standing. He would sit in the stone hearth, cuddling Mr Kemp's Old English Sheepdog, while his grandfather ordered cheese and pickles for both of them.

The clientelle included both gamekeepers and poachers, who appeared able to suspend animosity for the duration of the drinking hours, and to indulge in ribald boasting about how they had outwitted each other. Because his head was filled with tales of their exploits, and was consequently fertile ground for ideas, Jonathan pricked up his ears one day when he heard the familiar thread of conversation running through the chatter, as he sat tailor fashion in the hearth.

"That seem like a waste of good whisky to me," commented George Fuller, who had previously been pointed out to him as a poacher of some repute and a thorn in the flesh of gamekeepers, including that of his Uncle Jack at Thetford.

Another of the regulars, whose job frequently took him up into the north of the County, had just completed a lengthy tale about feeding alchohol soaked raisins to pheasants.

"Not when you can pick up a half dozen or more pheasants in one go," said the regular. "All you have to do, so this fellow tell me, is soak them ol' raisins or currents in spirits, scatter them around where the pheasants feed, and they go for 'em like a thirsty man in the desert."

"And what happen then?" asked George Fuller, a note of scepticism evident in his tone.

"Why they get as drunk as lords," said the regular. "They can't fly, run, flap about or shift for themselves at all. They just keel over as quiet as mice; all you have to do is walk on and pick 'em up. No squawking or noise to let the keeper know you're around. Just shove 'em in the sack and be off."

"I'd have to see it to believe it," said George Fuller. "What do you say Master?".

"That seem to me that you have to ask the pheasants what brand of whisky they take," Jonathan's grandfather chuckled, making a joke of it. "No use to give 'em Haigh if they're only partial to Johnny Walker."

"Do you think that might work Grandad?" Jonathan asked later, as they were wending their way homeward. Sampson's roughshod hooves, clacking steadily on the tarmac road, made him feel drowsy.

His grandfather chuckled, and still made a joke of it.

"We'll try it on your granny's chickens," he said. "If that make them drunk, that'd work on pheasants". He rumbled his belly laugh and slapped his ribs. "We could all get high on the eggs then!" he chortled at his own wit.

Jonathan felt a rising excitement as the idea that had been unwittingly sown took shape in his mind, but he felt it would be wise to keep his own counsel for the moment.

The next day he approached his grandmother as she rolled pastry on the kitchen table in readiness for the evening meal.

"Can I have some raisins or currents please Granny?" he asked politely.

"Course you can," she answered absently, reaching up to the top shelf for the jar, and emptying a handful on to a saucer.

"I need more than that," he said.

"More!" she looked indignant. "You'll not want any dinner if you stuff yourself with them."

"I don't want to eat them, I want to play with them," he said, perhaps rather unwisely.

"I should say not!" she snapped angrily, emptying the saucer back into the jar. "Using good raisins at threepence a pack to play with. I never heard the like of it!"

But she left the jar on the table.

Jonathan knew it would not be long before she paid a visit to the petty, so he hung around.

When she suddenly stared into the middle distance introspectively for a moment, before hurrying out of the back door, wiping her hands on her apron, he moved swiftly. It was but the work of a moment to grab three handfuls of raisins out of the jar and shove them into the pocket of his shorts. Still moving at high speed he nipped into the parlour and dragged a chair over to the corner cupboard. The bottle of brandy was kept on the top shelf 'for medicinal purposes,' and he grunted with exertion as he lifted the heavy coal scuttle up on to the chair and climbed on top of it. He still needed a few inches, so he dismounted and lifted the heavy family bible off the side table, placing it on top of the coal scuttle.

He did not pause to return the various items of furniture to their proper places; he could always sneak in and do it later. It not being her day to 'do' the parlour, it was unlikely his grandmother would go in there before he had completed his project, and the first priority was obviously to get clear of the house, with his illicitly acquired equipment, before she returned.

Kicking off his boots, he crept barefoot past the petty and then raced across the yard and thankfully let himself into the chicken run.

"Come on then my little ol' pretty ones," he mimicked his grandmother, as he emptied the water out of the hollowed out flat stone that served as a drinking bowl for those hens that chose to remain in the pen during the day.

Emptying his pockets into the hollow, he liberally doused the raisins with brandy, stirred them around with his finger, and stood back to await results, coughing slightly as the fumes rose up and enveloped him. The chickens looked at him suspiciously, but made no move to sample the delectable offering. Becoming impatient he threw a handful in front of them, noticing as he did so that the raisins hardly seemed to have soaked up the brandy at all. He tried to mash them with a small pebble before scattering them further round the dirt floor of the pen.

One hen advanced cautiously and, in the gormless way that chickens have, inspected the raisins with first one eye and then the other before moving on and scratching industriously a few feet away.

"You stupid bird," he said angrily. "Why don't you try it to see if you like it?"

He tried to herd some of the others in the general direction of the raisins, but apart from the odd one or two who went through the same motions of inspection before moving on, they ignored the offering.

He was disappointed, but the thought occurred to him that regularly fed chickens might not find the bait as tempting as would pheasants, who would have to depend solely on their own foraging for sustenance.

Morosely he sat cross legged on the floor of the run and began picking up the raisins, one by one, to taste them for himself.

His grandmother had enjoyed her session in the petty. That, together with the fact that it was a nice sunny day, and her first batch of pastry had emerged from the oven in perfect shape, had given her a feeling of well being; the psychological uplift that accompanies the knowledge that the day had started off well. She decided to enhance her feeling of contentment by walking round to the pen to feast her eyes on the fat pullets she was bringing on for market. She hummed her favourite happy little hymn tune as she rounded the corner.

Her feeling of well being evaporated rapidly as she beheld the diminutive figure of her grandson engaged, to all intents and purposes, in picking up pieces of chicken excreta and putting them in his mouth.

"Stop that you **dirty** little devil," she yelled angrily. "What in Hades do you think you're a doing of?"

Startled at this unexpected attack from the rear, Jonathan leapt to his feet, knocking over the unstoppered brandy bottle in the process, and heard the contents glug-glugging out on to the chicken run floor.

His grandmother's eyes swivelled to the source of the noise, and then bulged.

"Great God Almighty in Heaven!" she screeched. "He a got my brandy!"

Casting around for a weapon, she lit on a cane supporting a late chrysanthemum by the outside wall. The chrysanthemum executed the dying swan scene from Swan Lake as its life support system was wrenched away.

As she began to manipulate the catch on the wire mesh door, Jonathan realised he had a problem.

The only other means of exit was through the door into the chicken house itself, and then on through to a door right at the other end. Unfortunately the first door was at right angles – and immediately adjacent – to the one she was coming in by. The double width mesh fence around the chicken pen was twelve feet high, so there was no way over that. The only other outlet was a rectangular timber framed hole, cut into the wire mesh at ground level, to allow the chickens to forage in the wood next to the run. To discourage foxes this was only about ten inches square however, and any mathematician could have calculated the size of Jonathan's head, shoulders and hips, and concluded that there was no hope of his squeezing through there.

In fact the mathematician, who would have excluded the x factor of sheer fright, would have been wrong. By virtue of rolling over and over while remaining in the same place, Jonathan virtually corkscrewed his way through, the chrysanthemum cane thudding to the earth a fraction of an inch behind his departing bare feet.

From the comparative safety of the other side of the wire he prepared to negotiate, but negotiation requires a minimum of two people and his grandmother was clearly not prepared to be one of them. First trying to rip the stout wire mesh apart with her bare hands to get at him, she then resorted to ineffectually poking at him through the wire mesh with the chrysanthemum cane. Spots of spittle, gathering on her lips, created the impression that she was foaming at the mouth.

Jonathan was considerably slowed up by having to traverse the brush in the wood, and the hard stubble of the field, in his bare feet. Fortunately for him, his grandmother was more concerned with crooning a requiem over the dead brandy bottle than with immediate pursuit. He was therefore able to make it to one of his secret hiding places with time to spare. Such was her strength of feeling, she actually conducted a search; a pastime she normally abandoned as fruitless, because Jonathan had developed the technique, of hiding, to an art form. Muttering imprecations, she poked around the neighbourhood of the barn for ten minutes before stumping off into the house.

Descending from his hide, he flopped down on to a pile of hay and contemplated his immediate future. He could not expect leniency from his grandfather this time; with good brandy twenty two shillings a bottle, at a time when the average man's weekly wage was little more than twice that, his grandfather would not find it easy to forgive him. It began to look as though the unthinkable would happen, and that he was doomed, after many stays of execution, to feel the wide black leather belt across his rear end. There was no point in meeting his grandfather up the lane to put his side of the story first; he had not got a feasable one to put. Neither was there any point in hanging around the barn in the vain hope that his grandmother would cool off.

"I've come to give myself up," he announced dramatically, marching boldly up to the kitchen table where she stood polishing the lamps.

This was a direct quote from a James Cagney and George Raft film he had once seen, but with the difference that James Cagney was not soundly cuffed by his grandmother and sent upstairs to await later retribution at the hands of his grandfather.

With as much dignity as he could muster he mounted the stairs, put on his nightshirt, and climbed into bed.

She started on his grandfather as soon as he came in the door.

Jonathan could not hear what was being said, and felt this was one occasion when it would not be at all politic to creep out and sit on the stairs to listen. He could however detect a note of indignation in his grandfather's response which boded ill for the immediate future.

His heart sank as he heard him begin to climb the stairs.

When he came into the bedroom Jonathan saw that he had taken off his belt, and was holding it coiled for action in his right hand. Resigned to his fate, Jonathan threw back the bedclothes, knelt with his bottom sticking up in the air, and hoped it would all be over quickly. He remembered that cowboys in Western films used to bite on something while Red Indian arrows were being extracted from their shoulder – always their shoulder – by a colleague. He wondered if biting on the corner of the pillow would help.

"Just a minute," said his grandfather, "I want to know a bit more about this first."

"It was your idea," Jonathan told him, opening one eye. "When we was coming home from Market yesterday, you said we should try it on Granny's chickens and get high on the eggs."

His grandfather looked stunned.

"Don't you remember?" Jonathan went on, returning to a sitting position. "That man as was telling George Fuller about making pheasants drunk and easier to catch?"

There ensued a long silence during which neither of them moved or spoke. Then, to Jonathan's relief, his grandfather returned his belt to its normal position around his middle.

"Stay there a minute," he muttered. "I have to have another word with your Granny."

As Jonathan lacked the nerve, for the first five minutes, to move to his usual position sitting on the stairs with his chin cupped in his hands, he missed the beginning of the discussion. By the time he got within earshot it was almost concluded.

"What that mean, at the end of the day, is that he a got away with it again!"

His grandmother spoke in the frustrated tones of one whose lust for blood remains unsatiated.

As he sat – still in his nightshirt because permission to get dressed again had been witheld – he felt the need to break the stony silence that followed his grandmother exhausting her repertoire of invective.

"I'll give up half my pocket money for a few weeks to pay for the brandy," he said.

99

His grandmother had done her arithmetic.

"You'll give up all your pocket money for forty four weeks," she said.

She also went on at length about the coal scuttle on the chair in the parlour and, almost the greatest sin, using the Family Bible to stand on. She only let Jonathan off the hook when his mother's weekly letter promised a replacement bottle of best brandy on her next visit.

As the evenings began to draw out, and the weather turned milder, his grandfather had varied his routine to include ten minutes or so, as it grew dusk, leaning on the five barred yard gate gazing pensively over the pasture at his herd of grazing Friesians.

With his grandfather's hands clasped around his middle, Jonathan would sit on the top bar, leaning back against the old man's chest. More often than not they would simply enjoy a companiable silence as they watched the hares disporting themselves in the field or, more rarely, a particularly bold fox trotting along the hedgerow.

Sometimes, with a little encouragement, his grandfather would reminisce.

"I remember my grandfather doing this," he said one evening. "That were when it were a proper farm, not just a smallholding, and he have more land to plan what to do with, even though it weren't his own."

"Why is it smaller now?" Jonathan wanted to know.

"That's 'cause we been hard up from time to time," he said, "and have to sell off bits to keep our head above water."

He paused a moment to collect his thoughts before he continued.

"My great great grandfather, began as a tenant farmer of the Squire's family," he said. "But my grandfather wanted to be his own man so he bought the farm, about ninety acres there were, with the money he made from dealing in horses. He got it at a knock down price because the Squire's family were hard up then, and were glad to let it go. But when the old Squire inherited, and married into a wealthy family, they were pleased to buy bits of it back off him."

Originally the farmhouse was little bigger than a cottage, consisting of what was now the parlour and the dairy. It was not big enough for a growing family, so a whole field had been sold to raise the money for improvements, which included the addition of the huge kitchen and the rooms above it, making the cottage L-shaped. The new kitchen had linked the house with two outhouses which had now become the scullery and the harness room. The stairs, which had risen from just inside the front door, had been ripped out and reversed so they now rose straight out of the new kitchen. The seventeenth century barn had been added to, and part of it converted into horse and cattle stalls.

"He bit off more than he could chew, my grandfather did, and that's a fact," Jonathan's grandfather went on. "He did a good job of draining and ditching some of the poorer land, but, years later, my father made the mistake of thinking he could gain some land, to replace the field as had been sold, by cutting down half of the wood. He did it alright – that's how he made the small field just as you turn into our lane – but he spent so much on draining it that he'd no money left against poor harvests and dropping markets."

When he had inherited the farm, Jonathan's grandfather had sold off more land to finance his ambition to breed Shire horses, and to build up a reputable herd of Friesians. For five years he had struggled, but had flourished for the next fifteen, especially after he had backed his judgement and set aside a promising young foal to be stallion founder of his line.

"That was Hercules," he said. "Won Second Prize for stallions at the Hunstanton Show. I had people from as far as Yorkshire wanting to put their mares to him."

The formation of Kitchener's Army, following the outbreak of the Great War in nineteen fourteen, had robbed the land of men to work the horses, and breeding had declined.

"I'd put my eggs into the wrong basket," he said ruefully. "I was left with a horse that cost me more money than he made, and by the time the war was over, and the horse trade had picked up again, Hercules was past his prime."

The Depressions of the nineteen twenties and thirties had worsened the situation, and he had to sell off even more land in order to survive.

As he gazed out over his pasture, quite clearly transported back in time, Jonathan wondered if he could take advantage of the easy mood of gentle nostalgia.

"Tell me about Uncle Arthur," he said. "The one that went to Canada and got to be a lumberjack?"

It was too dark to see the expression on his grandfather's face, so he felt – rather than saw – the relaxed manner replaced by a stiffness, a sudden tension.

The silence which followed was uncomfortable; Jonathan wished he had kept his mouth shut.

His grandfather suddenly moved away from the gate, taking out his pocket watch and glancing at it before heading towards the back door.

"I don't know how much your mother told you," he said, his voice not exactly cold but certainly distant. "And I don't want to know. All *you* have to know is that that is a matter which is never talked about in this house. Ever."

His mood abruptly changed again as he swung Jonathan up on to his shoulders.

"Come on," he said. "Let's get your granny to get you ready for bed, then I'll tell you a story."

Jonathan felt a sense of frustration; his curiosity about Uncle Arthur seemed doomed never to be satisfied, but even as he ducked under the top of the back door, and his grandfather lowered him to the floor, he recalled the letter from his mother which had arrived that morning. It confirmed that she was coming on a visit the following week-end, so he would contain his impatience, and fall back on his idea of asking her.

His grandmother toyed with the idea of clearing a space in the lumber room for her, and re-assembling the spare bed. In the end she decided not to; Jonathan's, bed, which many years earlier had been his mother's, was big enough for two, so she would sleep with him as she had done over Christmas.

In the process of exploring the lumber room however, he had come across a pile of ancient family photographs, mostly of relatives long dead.

One of them, faded and brown, and bearing the legend 'Jerome Lowestoft', depicted the standard family group, in postcard size, which had probably been taken on an impulsive visit to a studio while on a day out at the seaside. His mother could have been no more than ten, his Uncle Jack about seventeen. Neither his Uncle Bert nor Uncle Jim were in the photo, but the rather sullen looking boy of about thirteen could only be Arthur.

On impulse, he thrust it into the pocket of his shorts, with the idea of smuggling it up to his secret hiding place, and studying it at leisure.

His mother arrived too late on the Saturday for him to find time to be alone with her; a neccessary pre-requisite he felt, in view of his grandparents' hostile attitude to any raising of the subject in their presence. His opportunity came next morning.

He had climbed over her sleeping form to go to help his grandfather with the milking, and as she was 'having a lie in' he crept upstairs while his grandmother was cooking breakfast. He turned somersaults on the bed and bounced up and down until she got annoyed and threatened to cuff him, then settled down under the eiderdown beside her.

"I'll lie still and not disturb you if you tell me something I want to know," he said.

"What?" she asked sleepily.

"Tell me about Uncle Arthur?" he said.

"What about him?" she asked cautiously.

He gabbled out all his questions in one breath

"Why do Granny and Grandad get cross when I ask about him and where is he and did he go to Canada and why did Uncle Bert have a fight with him and was he a lumberjack and I bet it was fun being a lumberjack and I'm going to be a lumberjack when I grow up unless I get to be a poacher and why do Uncle Silas say he can't talk about him?.."

"Does say, not do say," she corrected, but she was playing for time.

She was silent for so long that he thought she had gone back to sleep, and opened her eye with his thumb and forefinger.

"Stop that," she said crossly, and sat up.

"I found this," he said, producing the studio photo he had retrieved from the lumber room.

She studied it for a few moments, and then gave a sigh which was partly resignation and partly irritation.

"Now listen," she said. "Have you been pestering Granny and Grandad and Uncle Silas about – about – this?"

"I only want to know," he said. "Why is it all a secret?"

"It's something we don't talk about," she said.

"Why?"

"We don't talk about it because it upsets your grandfather," she said.

"Why?"

She gave a sigh of exasperation.

"I suppose if I don't tell you, you'll go on and on and on like you usually do, and end up by upsetting someone," she said irritably.

He said nothing, but waited expectantly while she gathered her thoughts.

"Arthur was the youngest of my four brothers," she said. "He was three years older than me. He wasn't a bit like Bert or Jim or Jack. He was sly and spiteful and rude and told fibs."

She paused, and added what Jonathan felt to be an unnecessary aside.

"In fact, a bit like you when the mood takes you."

"I'm not like that now," he told her, "because I don't want to make Grandad cross."

She looked at him searchingly.

"Because he would take his belt to you?" the question was rhetorical.

"Oh no," he said confidently. "Grandad would never hit me."

She gaped at him in surprise, in fact remained silent for so long that he became impatient.

"Go on about Uncle Arthur," he said.

She settled back on the pillow, and again marshalled her thoughts.

"I want you to promise that you won't talk to anyone about this," she said.

"I promise," he said.

"Particularly Granny or Grandad."

"I promise."

There was another long silence.

She lowered her voice to ensure that his grandmother, in the scullery below, should not hear.

"When my brother Arthur was about twelve, he did something very bad," she began.

From time to time Jonathan's grandfather grazed and cared for other people's horses, particularly hunters, to bring them up to condition for the season. On this particular occasion he was convalescing a horse for Dr Dunbar which, having responded to treatment for a lung infection, was almost back to normal. To show off to some of his friends Arthur had ridden it at a gallop around the field, retarding its progress by weeks, and putting it at risk of a relapse.

Arthur had been taken by his father into the barn and, to quote Jonathan's mother, thrashed to within an inch of his life. This had caused the relationship between father and son, never very good, to deteriorate even further. When Arthur was sixteen he ran away from home and began working for a farmer halfway across the county. He was found and brought home, but at eighteen he ran away again and was missing for a whole year before returning, destitute. The final severance had happened in nineteen sixteen, when conscription into the Army had been introduced.

His parents had been embarrassed by his refusal to follow his three brothers into the Norfolk Regiment; he avowed he 'had no time for this King and Country nonsense' and had been, apparently, quite indifferent to the white feathers publicly handed to him. It was customary, during the First World War, for men who appeared reluctant to join Kitchener's Army to receive white feathers – the symbol of cowardice – usually from women who had seen a husband, sweetheart or brother off to the Trenches.

To avoid conscription Arthur had simply vanished; it subsequently transpired that he had travelled all over the country, working on railways and canals – even in a munitions factory at one point – always staying far enough ahead of the authorities to avoid being conscripted. Three years after the end of the war he had suddenly reappeared at the farm, at a time when his father was absent, and persuaded his mother to give him some of her hard earned egg and chicken money. He needed the cash, it seemed, to take him Canada where he had been offered the opportunity of working as a lumberjack.

At this point Jonathan's mother became reticent.

"It's true he and your Uncle Bert had a fight," she said, "but I'm saying nothing about that."

To her surprise Arthur had visited her, at the hospital she was working at in London, to ask if she would write to him in Canada, as he felt the need to maintain some link with the family and he appeared to have alienated everybody else. She had agreed, and they corresponded intermittently for just over four years, at which point he wrote that he was hoping to return to England early in nineteen twenty six.

She then heard nothing for nearly three years.

In the middle of nineteen twenty eight, by which time she was working in Scotland, she had been startled to receive a letter, in unfamiliar handwriting, from Bury St Edmunds, and addressed to her at a hospital she had left two years earlier.

"Dear Edith," the letter had said. "I am writing to tell you that your brother Arthur and I are to be married at a Civil Ceremony next Saturday. We would like you to come as Arthur does not want any other member of his family to be invited, and there will be no one from my side there."

The letter, which had been re-directed several times, went on to say that they would both be going to Canada soon after their marriage, and was signed : 'Your Sister-in-Law to be, Polly Lathgreen.'

"By the time I got the letter they must have been married and settled in Canada, with no way of my finding out where they were," Jonathan's mother told him. "My guess is, that when they heard nothing from me, they must have thought I was just not interested. Anyway," she went on, "your father and I were planning to get married at the time I got the letter, so, to be quite frank, I had other things on my mind. Although," – she paused and looked a little embarrassed, "I must confess I've often felt a little guilty about not following it up."

There was a long silence, while Jonathan digested the information she had given him, and she gazed at the ceiling, deep in thought.

Suddenly she roused herself up in the bed and spoke with heat.

"Although why the hell I should feel guilty I don't know! He made my life a misery, when I was a little girl, if your Uncle Jack wasn't around to stop him bullying me. And he caused no end of grief for all of us in the end."

"So where is he now?" Jonathan wanted to know.

"That was ten years ago," said his mother, "and none of us have seen hide nor hair of him since."

Jonathan felt partly satisfied by his mother's disclosure, although he would have liked to have been told why his two uncles had fought. Caught up in the jingoism of his generation, he hated the idea of a close relative avoiding military service, and could understand some of the reasoning behind his grandparents' hostility.

Walking across the yard with his mother later that day, he became aware of her pensive manner.

"You've made me think," she said, looking at him thoughtfully. "I've still got a bit of a conscience about the whole thing. I think it's about time I tried to find out where Arthur is, and maybe get in contact again."

She waited until Jonathan was in bed and asleep that night before telling her parents that she proposed to try to trace her brother.

Her father had sat stony faced and silent, but her mother had hit the ceiling.

"Why you have to turn up stones after all these years I don't know," she said angrily. "But that's typical of you Edith, to want to stir things up. I'm of the opinion that's better to let sleeping hornets lie," she added, mixing her metaphors. "What do you think Will?"

He stirred briefly in his chair.

"I said all I had to say ten years ago" he said. "And that's the end of it."

Having advised them of her intention, even though she did not have their approval, she gave thought to how she could set about it, and cycled into the village to invite her brother Bert to place the resources of the Norfolk Constabulary at her disposal.

"Have you gone mad Edith?" Bert's voice cracked with emotion. "Have you any idea what they'd do to me if they found I'd been using police time to find my own brother? Besides, I wouldn't even if I could 'cos I don't hold with it. As far as I'm concerned he can rot in Canada or wherever he is."

"I don't see how I can take it any further," she told Jonathan as she packed ready for her return to London.

He remembered his favourite comic strip.

"I bet Sexton Blake could find him," he said.

She laughed, and then suddenly paused and looked thoughtful.

"Out of the mouths –" she left the quotation unfinished.

By persisting in his attempts to satisfy his curiosity, Jonathan had awakened feelings in his mother which had lain dormant for ten years. In so doing, he had unwittingly precipitated events that were to have far reaching consequences for the whole family.

Chapter Eight

"You got a good little voice," Jonathan's grandmother said one day, having arrived silently at the door of the harness room where he was singing a duet with Master Ernest Lough, courtesy of his mother's old wind up gramaphone. "I'll talk to Mrs Morven about getting you in the Church Choir."

"I'd like that."

He knew that the choirboys had the benefit of outings, and seaside trips to places like Yarmouth and Lowestoft, far more often than other children. Some of the older boys at school were in the choir, and gave glowing accounts of the additional privileges they enjoyed. Not only that, but being in the village Church choir was a far better proposition than one of his mother's earlier plans for him.

"I like to hear him sing," Aunty Barney had said one evening, while at the cottage back in Gloucestershire. "Just think, if he were good enough to get into the Cathedral Choir, you could get him a first class education and it would cost you virtually nothing."

His mother played the piano fairly well, and in return for her playing 'The Maiden's Prayer', which was one of his favourites, he would sing the easier nursery rhymes to her accompaniment while Aunty Barney sat and listened.

The comment had provoked, in his mother, a line of thought which – like so many of her flashes of inspiration – seemed a good idea at the time. It coincided with one of her periods of doubt as to the wisdom of having withdrawn Jonathan as a candidate for the Masonic school; if, however, his singing voice could get him into King's, in Gloucester, he would be close at hand and would be educated like a young gentleman.

As a first step she had forged ahead with her cultivation of the Ffoulkes-Weedons, a couple with whom she had a professional contact and whose son, Benedict, was in the Cathedral Choir. Being a member of the Board, Dr Ffoulkes-Weedon had a peripheral involvement with the selection of boys for the choir.

"I want you to be on your best behaviour," his mother had told Jonathan firmly, having angled for – and got – an invitation to take tea with the Ffoulkes-Weedons one Sunday afternoon.

Benedict and Euphemia, both rather older than Jonathan, so over-awed him that he sat as quiet as a mouse throughout tea, which was taken on delicate china plates, and seemed largely to consist of postage stamp sized cucumber sandwiches. They were incredibly well mannered and polite, moving around with the food like diminutive waiters, and calling their parents 'Mama' and 'Papa' with the emphasis on the last syllable.

"You realise that I do not actually audition," Dr Ffoulkes – Weedon had told Jonathan's mother as he led them, through a drawing room almost the size of a tennis court, to where a Baby Grand piano stood by the French windows. "But my position on the Board enables me to make suggestions, and I can tell you whether Jonathan can sing well enough to make it worth while taking it further."

He beamed approvingly as Jonathan correctly sang the notes he picked out on the piano, especially when he was able to sing the middle note out of three played simultaneously.

Benedict and Euphemia were encouraged to let him play with their toys, and Benedict's polite smile remained in place, albeit freezing a little, when Jonathan accidently wrenched the smoke stack off one of his model trains. The rot set in when they were sent out to play in the conservatory, and Jonathan attempted to compensate for his feelings of inferiority by boasting about his exploits with the local gang. He rather overdid it as his imagination took flight, and ended up making himself out to be some sort of miniature Al Capone. Then, making a little model man out of a lump of plasticine, he stuck a penis on to it as an afterthought. Euphemia looked puzzled, and Benedict haughtily disapproving.

"We don't do things like that at my school or in front of girls," he said. "Euphemia would not know what it is."

"The girls in my school would know what it is," Jonathan told him.

As they made their way home, his mother had seemed quite pleased.

"Dr Ffoulkes-Weedon seemed quite impressed," she said, "and will arrange an audition at the school when you are a little older."

She was disappointed when the Ffoulkes-Weedons politely declined the invitation to tea the following week. When three invitations in a row were equally politely declined, she began to suspect something had gone wrong. It fell to Aunty Barney, who was close enough to her to be able to speak frankly, to tell her what she had learned from the Vicar's wife, Mrs Edwards, who had seen Mrs Ffoulkes-Weedon at the Cathedral.

"She seemed a pleasant enough person," Mrs Ffoulkes- Weedon had told Mrs Edwards. "But that awful child quite upset Benedict, and my little Euphemia, with his shocking stories about his friends in the village. And after they had left, Benedict showed me a quite disgusting effigy the boy had made out of modelling clay."

Because she loved Jonathan, Aunty Barney had only given his mother an edited version, but it was enough to decide her that he should be confronted.

"What did you say to those Ffoulkes-Weedon children," she had demanded, grasping him by the throat.

"Nothing ," he whined. "I just told them about the games I play with the village boys."

She groaned as she held her head in her hands.

"How can I possibly develop any kind of social life?" she complained bitterly to Aunty Barney. "And as for getting him into King's school, I can imagine Dr Ffoulkes-Weedon going to considerable lengths to keep him out!"

The concept of Jonathan becoming a boy chorister had sunk without trace thereafter, but now his grandmother was resurrecting it in a far more acceptable form.

"That would fit in nicely," said Mrs Morven, when the subject was broached. "We need three boys, and I'd already decided to enlist Colin and David. In fact Jonathan could come into Wolf Cubs at the same time."

While singing the morning hymn at school assembly next morning, he became aware that Mrs Morven had moved round to stand behind him. She was obviously satisfied because she told him, together with Colin and David, to turn up at the next choir practice and Cubs.

He knew enough about both organisations to have no qualms about belonging to either, although it meant a longer day because he stayed in the village, and did not go home until after the Cub meeting on Tuesdays and choir practice on Fridays.

He wore handed down green pullover, cap and garters for cubs; this was organised by his grandmother after negotiations with the parents of various second and third cousins who had graduated to Scouts. His mother, in her letter, wanted his grandmother to take him into Norwich and buy new, but she changed her mind when she learned how much it would cost.

Mrs Morven was Akela, and the Vicar was the Scoutmaster. His was a nominal role because he never turned up, but left everything to Uncle Percy.

For a relatively small Parish Church, the choir was unusual in that it enjoyed both affluence, and a standard and quality of singing, which could almost match a Cathedral choir. This had been entirely due to the generosity of the Squire's late mother, who had a passionate love of Church music.

"She were from a family that had money you see," Jonathan's grandmother explained. "And the Old Squire had lost all his. They do say as that's why he married her, to get her money into the estate. And then this Squire did the same, married for money because the estate haven't paid, and swallow it all up."

By setting aside a considerable sum of money each year for treats and outings, there had been no problem with recruiting boys; in any event it was a day and age when village boys did not consider it 'sissy' to sing in the Church choir, in fact it was a coveted honour.

After the First World War the money had dried up, but the chorister's robes, purchased with the original grant, were of such outstanding quality that they remained servicable, even if slightly threadbare. The cassock with which Jonathan was issued was in even better condition than the others, even though it was thirty years old.

"It's hardly ever been worn," said Mrs Morven, as she tried it on him, "with there not being many boys as young as you in the choir before.".

The administration of choir and Cubs overlapped to such an extent, probably because of Mrs Morven's dual role, that it became confusing at times. They had to wear Cub uniforms to choir practice in case Mr Price, the Welsh choirmaster, did not turn up, while on other occasions Cub night would be cancelled and an extra practice substituted. This caused problems for the parents of the few boys who were in one or the other but not both. Dismissed to go home one evening, because most of the others were in choir practice, some Cubs had gone marauding instead. Their parents, secure in the belief that they were at Cubs, were horrified to find them on the doorstep with an enraged Uncle Bert holding them by the collar.

Notwithstanding isolated incidents of this nature, the boys' collective response to the regimented discipline of Cubs and Scouts was amazing when one considered their aptitude for non-conformity during their normal day to day activities. They lapped it up, and evidenced a dedicated fanaticism to the pursuit of prompt obedience, and loyalty to King and Country and to each other.

On the 24th May they had to wear their Cub uniforms to school in acknowledgement of Empire Day, which was to end with a party in the village hall, the Mother's Union providing the refreshments.

It was also Jonathan's first meeting with Sergeant Bews, who was going to spend the whole day at school helping Miss Perriman tell them all about the British Empire, and the various battles the Grenadier Guards had fought. He had called round at the farm during the previous evening, and Jonathan noticed the affection with which he greeted 'Uncle Will and Aunty Eliza'. He was also very fond of Jonathan's mother, who had looked after him a lot when he was very small and she was in her early teens. He and Jonathan took to each other immediately, despite Jonathan's slight feeling of resentment because Sergeant Bews was going to 'take away' his beloved teacher. It was a foregone conclusion that they would be getting married now that he had been promoted from Corporal. There was something about his conspiratorial wink, when regaled with an account of Jonathan's misdeeds, that told Jonathan he had found an ally.

He was in khaki, with puttees that came nearly up to his knees, and boots with toecaps that reflected like a mirror. Jonathan was fascinated by his uniform cap, which had the peak slanted down so that his eyes were virtually hidden; in fact he couldn't see ahead of himself unless he threw his head right back. He told Jonathan that was why; the Guards were expected to stand ramrod straight with head thrown right back; the low peak forced them into that posture.

He was staying the night at the Perriman's instead of going home to Uncle Silas.

"Her father's away overnight in Saxmundham," he said, "and I don't like to think of her being on her own in that cottage."

Jonathan's grandmother disapproved, and spoke her mind.

"Thats not right for you and Enid to be alone together all night in that cottage, and you not yet married," she said.

Sergeant Bews hurriedly changed the subject.

When, clad in his Cub uniform, Jonathan went to collect Miss Perriman for school next morning, Sergeant Bews was there and, to the envy of Jonathan's friends, carried him in on his shoulders.

After the village hall tea they all went back to Uncle Silas' house where they played games with him, and Sergeant Bews showed him how to play cards for money, letting him win tuppence. Jonathan saw quite a lot of him during his weeks leave, and was rather disappointed when the time came for him to return to barracks. He and Miss Perriman had been childhood sweethearts, and Jonathan's grandmother still dabbed her eyes with emotion as she described their parting when he went off into the Army Boy's Service.

"There were the two of them, this little boy of thirteen in a soldier's uniform, and this little maid of twelve, kissing and clinging to each other, and her crying her eyes out on Thorpe Station platform," she would say, with a catch in her voice.

The Coldstream Guards were due to parade in Norwich in June as part of a recruiting campaign, and Sergeant Bews was to be one of a Colour Party of four Grenadiers accompanying them. He made Miss Perriman promise to take Jonathan.

"Does that mean you'll be wearing your bearskin?" Jonathan asked eagerly.

"And his scarlet tunic and white belt," Miss Perriman smiled.

"How will we pick you out from all the others?" Jonathan wanted to know. "All Guards look alike."

"Easy," he said. "Me and the other Grenadiers will have white flashes on the side of our bearskins; the Coldstreams have red."

A week after his departure Jonathan enjoyed another significant experience.

He had noticed his grandfather becoming increasingly restless; he seemed to spend a lot of time walking about peering up at the sky and sniffing the breeze. The explanation was provided one morning, when he surprised and delighted Jonathan by telling him he could have the day off school to help him.

"Haysel time," he said. "We start the mowing tomorrow and I need you to keep a sharp look out for any stones or tangles that could jam up the knives."

Jonathan's grandfather was envied locally for his expertise – some sourly claimed it was luck – in choosing just the right time to begin his haymaking. Invariably his mowing would be followed by just the right number of sunny but breezy days for the lush green grass to be transformed into yellow gold hay of just the right texture. Of all the farming events, Jonathan enjoyed the haysel the best; it was probably because the hayfield was just small enough for the work to be done by one man – or in their case one elderly man and an enthusiastic small boy.

Given an early start, they could complete the mowing before evening milking, his grandfather sitting on the machine while Jonathan sat on Sampson's shoulders, peering down to give early warning of any obstructions or tangles likely to foul the cutting blades.

After a day or two, Ted Limmer's swath turner would be borrowed to aereate the hay, but Jonathan's grandfather had his own horse rake to draw it into windrows later. When it was ready, Jonathan would stand in the Suffolk cart and distribute the hay evenly, as his grandfather pitchforked it up to him. Sampson, responding to litle more than grunts, would haul the cart slowly along the rows. The height of the load being restricted, because of the low branches of the trees in the lane, they had to make several trips with smaller loads, but this gave them more opportunity for much needed rests.

All the hay was stored in the far end of the big barn; any that could not be crammed in was sold to Ted Limmer.

"I never make a hayrick now," Jonathan's grandfather told him. "I make a rick I have to go to the trouble of thatching it. That barn hold all I need, and always some left over."

Given the job of evenly distributing the hay, as the stack rose gradually towards the roof, Jonathan had to work almost bent double towards the end. Then, all finished, his grandfather would make a big soft pile of hay on the barn floor for Jonathan's moment. Spurning a ladder he would half jump, half slide, landing with enough force to take his breath away.

The sweet smell of the new cut grass, the slightly musky smell of the finished hay, the bright breezy June days, the companionship of his grandfather and Sampson, all left an indelible mark of contentment and satisfaction on Jonathan, with which few other activities, then or in later life, were able to compete.

Strangely, neither Miss Perriman nor Mrs Morvern objected to his being kept away from school to help.

"Up to only a few years ago it used to be regular practice, during harvest especially," Miss Perriman told him. "In fact all the village schools would be emptied of boys until it was all gathered in, and then emptied of girls the next week because they were all gleaning."

She gave him another surprise a few days later; outside her gate, on the way home from school, she suddenly, and for no apparent reason, bent down and hugged him.

"If I have a little boy I hope he's like you," she whispered, and then looked embarrassed as though she felt she had said too much.

Jonathan expected his grandmother to be pleased when he told her this, but she looked annoyed instead.

"Fancy her saying that to the little ol' boy," she complained to Mrs Limmer. "I never reckoned her as brazen, having brought her up as my own for the most part. I would have expected her to keep it to herself, at least until after the wedding."

Later he heard her talking to his grandfather.

"I said at the time that that was wrong, him staying overnight at the cottage," she said in the self satisfied tones of one who has been proved right.

Miss Perriman came to see them the next day.

Jonathan and his grandmother were engaged in the messy task of blackleading the kitchen range when the flurry of barking dogs, and a soft footfall in the yard, signalled her arrival. His grandmother, having wrestled him for possession of the blacklead brush and won, had compensated him by setting him the task of relaying the fire with Uncle Percy's recently delivered coal.

"Some as big as walnuts to start it off," she said, installng him in front of the big brass and oak coal scuttle, "and some as big as apples to keep it going."

Miss Perriman settled into the high backed chair as his grandmother put the kettle on the paraffin stove.

"As you know, we have settled on the date for the wedding," Miss Perriman said.

His grandmother allowed her eyes to hover briefly on Miss Perriman's waistline.

"I was right glad to hear it," she said, perhaps rather tactlessly.

"I've come to talk about having boy Jonathan for a page boy," said Miss Perriman.

His grandmother looked across to where he sat, tailor fashion, in front of the coal scuttle. His bare legs and feet were encrusted with grime from playing in the barn, his hands were covered in blacklead and his face was streaked with coal dust and mucus from wiping his runny nose with the back of his hand.

His grandmother, who already knew of the proposal, decided to play a little game at his expense.

"Are you sure you want him?" she allowed her voice to rise on a note of incredulity.

"Quite sure," said Miss Perriman, trying to look solemn.

His grandmother pretended to be still uncertain.

"Are you sure you're not mixing him up with some other little boy in your class?" she said.

"Quite sure," said Miss Perriman again

"Well there's no accounting for taste," his grandmother said. "If that's what you want. Mind you," she went on as though trying to justify the sale of a suspect car to an over eager purchaser, "he look alright when he's cleaned up and wearing his Sunday best clothes. Now there's a thing. What do you want him to wear?"

She paused and looked Miss Perriman straight in the eye.

"That depend what you and the bridesmaids wear," she said. "Are you getting married in white?"

Miss Perriman avoided both the question and the implication.

"Actually we would like to dress him," she said. "A friend of Jim's was married in uniform, and their pageboy, who is about the same size as boy Jonathan, wore a small Grenadier's uniform. They will be happy to let us borrow it."

"Has it got a real bearskin?" Jonathan asked excitedly

"No, they only wear those on parades and sentry duty," she smiled. "They wear dress caps at other times."

Little Melanie Wright and Susan Oldfield were to be the bridesmaids. It would be Jonathan's job to appear to be looking after them, and help them hold the bride's train.

The uniform arrived in a huge cardboard box a week later, and he had to try it on to be sure it fitted. His mother was coming down for the wedding of course, and had written to his grandmother with rather complicated plans for arriving on time.

In the same letter she informed his grandmother of the progress she had made in her efforts to trace her brother.

The man in the Colonial Office, who had given her an appointment a week after her return to London, had smiled indulgently.

"I could give you the address of a Private Enquiry Agent in Canada," he said. "But do you have any idea how much it would cost to make enquiries on that scale?"

As she was leaving, feeling rather deflated, he called her back.

"Have you thought of trying the Salvation Army Missing Person's Bureau?" he asked. "They do seem to have a phenomenal amount of success."

She did not take him seriously at first; she was under the misconception that Arthur would have to be a regular attender at Salvationist meetings for them to have any contact with him, and, from her knowledge of her brother's attitude to religion, she felt that to be very unlikely. But the Hospital Almoner, with whom she had become friendly, encouraged her to pursue that avenue.

"I had a dying patient from Stepney who had heard nothing of his daughter for twenty years," she said. "They found her in a remote fishing village on the West coast of Ireland, and she was a devout Catholic with no Salvationist connections whatsoever."

A week later, on her next half day off, she climbed the narrow dusty stairs of the Salvation Army Missing Person's Bureau.

"You do realise," the kindly Captain told her, "that if we do find your brother we cannot tell you where he is. Not without his consent. The most we can do is tell him that you want to get in touch. The rest would be up to him, although we would of course let you know that we had spoken to him."

After asking more questions the Officer looked puzzled.

"We are really looking for two people are we not?" he said. "Presumably his wife will be with him in Canada. Will her relatives not know of their whereabouts?"

"There were going to be none of her relatives at the marriage ceremony," said Jonathan's mother. "So I assume she does not have any."

"Leave it with us," said the Officer. "We'll contact you as soon as we have some news."

The day of the wedding dawned clear and bright, with enough of a breeze to keep Jonathan cool in the heavy serge Guardsman's uniform. He had spent an hour pipeclaying the belt and polishing the brass buckles, and, with some help from Uncle Silas, the toecaps of his boots looked like black mirrors. His mother, taxied from the delayed London train, had brought a jar of Brilliantine to plaster his hair down with, but, to his immense relief, she had arrived too late to apply it. They arrived at the Church, in Mrs Limmer's car, to find Melanie and Susan already at the West door, looking very demure and pretty in their white dresses and pink sashes. Bolstered by the splendour of his Guardsman's uniform, he decided to assert his authority.

"The bridesmaids have to do what the pageboy tells them," he announced pompously. "So don't let's have any messing about."

Melanie lowered her eyes in acquiescence, but Susan developed an ugly glint in hers.

"You're only seven," she said. "I'm a year older than you, so don't try bossing me around."

"But you're only a girl," he pointed out quite reasonably.

"How would you like me to punch you in the mouth you little sod?" she bared her teeth nastily.

Jonathan suddenly remembered that his cousin Colin, who was bigger than him, had emerged second best from a confrontation with Susan. He therefore cast around for a way of backing down without losing face.

"You hit me and I'll hit you back," was all he could rather weakly come up with, but fortunately a rather breathless Mrs Morven arrived, and began to fuss around straightening the bridesmaids sashes and doing up his buttons.

As they waited for the bride and her father, Mrs Morven realised that the organist had not turned up, and that she would have to deputise.

"I'll have to go in and start up," she looked annoyed. "Now you all know what to do. Melanie first, then Susan and Jonathan. Now are you alright?"

Jonathan hesitated.

"I want to spend a penny," he said.

"There isn't time," she raised her eyes heavenwards. "Why didn't you go earlier?"

"I didn't want to go earlier," he said.

"I can't do anything about it now," she glared up at the Church clock. "You'll just have to wait until after the service."

Miss Perriman looked breathtakingly beautiful as her father, who Jonathan had never before seen without his gamekeeper's plus fours, led her up the aisle with the three children in solemn procession. Jonathan did not take a great deal of notice of the actual service, being pre-occupied with an almost overwhelming urge to pee. He knew there was no lavatory in the Church, but perhaps there was a bucket or something in the vestry. He began to sidle that way, stopping every time the Vicar glanced in his direction.

The Vicar liked to give the impression of concentrating emotional effort by talking with his eyes closed most of the time; this meant that every time he opened them, Jonathan was standing in a different place. His voice faltered as he tried to make some sense of this, but he quickly resumed, this time keeping his eyes open and staring fixedly at Jonathan. When at last, his voice throbbing, he closed his eyes once more, Jonathan scuttled as quickly as he could into the vestry and began to cast around desperately for anything that could be pressed into service as a toilet. His heart leapt thankfully when he beheld a large brown decorated earthenware jug standing in a corner behind a curtain. On closer examination it turned out to be half full of a brackish looking liquid which he assumed to be the product of the Vicar's own bladder, so with a groan of relief he urinated copiously and noisily into it. As the sound of tinkling water escaped through the vestry door, he heard the Vicar's voice falter again before resuming with over compensatory vigour.

Jonathan's back had been turned to the body of the Church as he hed entered the vestry, but of course he had to face the congregation as he made his way back to his place behind the bride and groom. He felt himself go red as everybody looked at him. With three exceptions all faces were split with a broad grin; even Sergeant Bews glanced sideways showing all his teeth, while Miss Perriman's lips curled in frank merriment. The three exceptions were the Vicar, who looked bemused, and his mother and grandmother who looked as though they would like to kill him.

He carefully avoided meeting his mother's eye as they processed down the aisle, and even contrived to keep out of arms length while they were posing for the photographs. To delay retribution he dodged into the Church porch, and found himself in the company of Mr and Mrs Margoles, a young couple with a baby awaiting Christening. Curious about a noise just inside the door, he pushed it open. He beheld the Vicar lifting the lid off the font, which stood just inside, before striding briskly off into the vestry, from which he emerged a few moments later carrying the large brown decorated earthenware jug. Jonathan watched, fascinated, as the Vicar carefully balanced the jug on the edge of the font before tipping half the contents in. Stooping to stand the jug on the floor, some sixth sense must have told him he was under observation.

Raising his head, his eyes met Jonathan's.

Suddenly he froze into immobility while his thought processes took him through the sequence of events leading up to the present moment. His eyes, gleaming with dawning insight, flew from Jonathan to the jug, the jug to the font, the font back to the jug and the jug back to Jonathan. He gave a long shuddering sigh and sank down on to the end of the nearest pew.

"Come here Jonathan," he whispered hoarsly.

Jonathan shuffled forward.

Almost wearily the Vicar grasped hold of his shoulders to pull him face down over his knees and, using the flat of his hand, began to treat the seat of Jonathan's trousers like a very dusty carpet.

Jonathan squirmed free after the fourth or fifth blat.

"I had to go somewhere," he claimed indignantly, thankful that the heavy serge of the uniform trousers had provided some insulation.

Breathing heavily from a combination of emotion and exertion, the Vicar waved a dismissive hand.

He was rather late arriving at the reception at the village hall; presumably he had used the time to empty and refill the font, thereby avoiding a somewhat unusual Christening for the Margoles baby.

The fun of the wedding was followed, almost immediately, by sadness at home.

Poor old Jeb had been failing for some time. Jonathan's grandfather had observed it, but, not being used to evaluating an animal's daily performance, Jonathan himself had not noticed the old dog's unusual lethargy. There came the morning when Jeb stayed on his bed, even when his Master reached up for his twelve bore, an action that usually had him wild with ecstasy.

"Can't Mr Kemp make him better Grandad?" Jonathan asked urgently.

"He's fifteen years old," said his grandfather. "That's a very good age."

"Does that mean Mr Kemp will have to put him down," he asked, feeling a lump in his throat.

"Come you here," his grandfather commanded, "and I'll show you."

With his fingers, guided by his grandfather's, Jonathan could feel the fleshy knot just under Jeb's chest, and observed the old dog wince under even gentle pressure.

"Ted Kemp will say that's kinder to put him out of his pain," the old man said. "And when the day come, either Ted Perriman or Ted Limmer will shoot him."

"Shoot him!" Jonathan heard his own voice crack. "What do you mean *shoot* him?"

His grandfather took one look at his stricken face and lifted him up to sit him on the cattle feed box, while he faced him and explained.

"That would be the easiest thing in the world for me to just let Ted Kemp take him away," he said. "But how would that old dog feel, being taken away in a car to a strange place.

He paused, trying to find the right words.

"What happen is this," he said. "We take old Jeb up into the wood on one of his good days, and he follow me through and I maybe shoot a rabbit for him to fetch, and then, just when he's enjoying himself, doing what he likes doing best, that Ted Perriman shoot him clean in the head. That's all over in a flash, no pain, the last sound in his ears the sound a gun dog likes to hear – the sound of a gunshot."

He paused and looked at Jonathan intently.

"Now wouldn't you say that if old Jeb knew what was going on, he'd take that as a choice rather than be shut up in a box, with that old chloroform wafting up his nose?"

"Why Ted Perriman?" Jonathan wanted to know.

"Fact is," his grandfather smiled wryly, "I haven't got the guts to do it myself. Neither have Ted Perriman, or Ted Limmer, or for that matter Ted Kemp. We shoot each others' dogs. That way old Jeb have me in front of him, not behind him, when the time comes."

Jonathan wondered if, in the brief moment of time when the shot hit him, Jeb would feel betrayed.

When he arrived home from school two days later, Jeb had gone and his grandparents were silent and sad faced.

"We buried him up near the top field, where he used to like to retrieve me a pheasant," his grandfather told him.

A few days later Ted Perriman leaned over the yard gate.

"Don't rush into getting another dog Will," he said. "The Squire want to have a word with you."

"The fact is Cooper," said the Squire, next day, "farmers and gamekeepers around here are so damned sticky about trying anything new. My friend Major Anfield, over at Swaffam, is trying to popularise his breed, and if someone like yourself could be persuaded to try one, at a reduced purchase price of course, the others would very quickly follow suit."

"He breed them ginger dogs don't he?"

"Yellow Labradors Cooper," said the Squire. "Yellow Labradors."

"Why don't you have one if you're all that keen?"

"I'd like to see how you fare," said the Squire. "I might get a bitch later on from another strain. Then, in return for getting you this one at a reduced price, I would expect you to waive stud fees if we breed from them both."

About six weeks later Ted Perriman asked Jonathan's grandfather to attend at the Hall, the folllowing evening, when the Squire would present him with the new puppy.

Chapter Nine

Following lengthy discussion they had decided to name the new puppy Scott, after the Antarctic explorer whose adventures had been related to Jonathan at school. His grandfather said that a dog's name was unimportant unless he was to be registered for showing; the essential requirement, for any working dog, was a name that could be barked as a command, and Jonathan's choice fitted the bill.

He had been building himself up to a fever pitch of excitement in anticipation of the new arrival, especially as his grandfather had agreed that he could be responsible for caring for the pup during the early stages.

"Granny," he began hesitantly, as he and his grandfather were getting ready to go up to the Hall to collect Scott, "when we get him back here, don't you think it best if for the first few nights he slept –"

But she was ahead of him and blocked him ruthlessly.

"You are not having it up in your bedroom," she snapped. "That dog start as we mean to go on. He sleep in the scullery with Snip."

"But Granny –"

"There's no ifs or buts," she glared at him. "I could see that's been on your mind this past week. And the answer is no! You are not having him upstairs and that's the end of the matter."

His grandfather suddenly started to chuckle.

"I remember this same argument about twenty five years ago," he said.

His grandmother glared at him again.

"Your mother was about the same age as you," she said, "when we had a pup given us. A little cross Cairn that was. I told her the same, and what does she do but sneak down in the night and take it up to her room. I go to wake her in the morning for school, and there's the dratted pup in bed with her!"

"What did you do?" Jonathan wanted to know.

"What did I do? Why I give her a good thrashing of course!"

Not only was it gratifying to learn that his mother had received the same treatment that she had, from time to time, meted out to him, but it also gave the lie to her oft repeated assertions that she had been a model child of impeccable behaviour.

His excitement grew as they reached the tradesman's entrance to the Hall. His grandfather had to meet the Squire in the butler's pantry, but he took Jonathan to the kitchen first.

"I don't reckon that's a good idea for you to see that butler Fulton," he grinned. "So you can go and talk to Mrs Musgrove."

Mrs Musgrove and Elsie made him welcome, and after he had given himself the enjoyable experience of scrubbing a block of salt through a fine wire mesh seive into a big wooden box, Mrs Musgrove sat him down at the table with a large helping of gooseberry fool.

"Now how about a drink?" she asked kindly. "Lemonade or cider?"

He secretly felt that Norfolk cider was not a patch on the West Country brew, but accepted a bottle anyway. Miss Nagele, the Governess, came in to see Mrs Musgrove while he was drinking it.

"Could I please to have a tray with some coffee and cheese biscuits sent up to my room?" she asked in her heavy Austrian accent.

She paused and looked at Jonathan.

"Who have we here?" she asked with some curiosity.

"That's Eliza Cooper's grandson," explained Mrs Musgrove. "Her daughter Edith's boy."

"What a pretty little boy," said Miss Nagele, and then recoiled from the twin barrels of hate Jonathan levelled at her over the rim of the cider glass.

Perhaps it was her Austrian way of expressing a compliment, but he loathed her with a dark intensity from that moment on.

His grandfather, who had followed her into the kitchen, stood aside to let her out and then winked at Mrs Musgrove.

"That's a turn up for the book," he chuckled. "So he's a pretty little boy now is he?"

Jonathan glared at him savagely, but then forgot it as he realised his grandfather had finished his business with the Squire.

"Where's the puppy?" he asked, looking around the floor.

"The groom's got it round in the stables for us to collect," his grandfather told him. "Come you on, we'll get it now."

Jonathan had been round to the stables once before, and loved the clean horse smell that sweetened the nostrils as one entered. Normally he would have greeted the horses; but today he only had eyes for the little yellow bundle, that blinked nervously up at him and licked his nose, as he lifted it out of the straw.

"The Squire brought him back yesterday," said the groom. "Proper noisy little devil in the night he were."

Jonathan insisted on carrying the pup, although it weighed a ton, but it rewarded him by going to sleep in the crook of his arm. He had prepared a bed in Jeb's old corner, and Snip, although surprised, seemed affable. Bed time was delayed by nearly an hour because Jonathan had to get Scott settled, and let out to spend a penny 'just one more time'.

It was predictable that Scott would wake him up in the middle of the night; his grandfather had forseen it, and said that the pup must be left alone to get used to it. But listening to his grandparents' comfortable snores not quite drowning the pathetic whimpering from below, Jonathan soon reached a stage where he had to do something. He crept through his grandparents' room to go down and comfort the pup, but then, feeling the little body pressed close to his own, the little heart beating like a steam hammer, he suddenly decided he would have to smuggle him up to his bed. He could guess what his grandmother's reaction would be, but he was always up before her and counted on being able to smuggle Scott back down first thing in the morning. He had a bit of a fright when his grandmother turned over in bed just as he was passing back through their bedroom, and another when Scott fell off his bed while he was trying to get him to settle on the foot of it. In the end the pup insisted on sleeping with his whole body pressed against Jonathan's ear, and it seemed no time at all before he awoke to the sound of his grandfather pulling on his trousers. Grabbing the still sleeping pup, he thrust him under his nightshirt and slid past the end of his grandparents' bed.

His grandfather looked surprised.

"I'm going down to see to the pup," Jonathan explained, truthfully, and scurried downstairs to let Scott out of the back door.

"Now leave him be," his grandfather had followed him down. "That pup's not to be used as an excuse for not doing your jobs before you go to school."

Normally Jonathan would not have gone back up to his bedroom once he had left it, as all his clothes were downstairs. Recalling however that he had left his handkerchief under his pillow, he shot up to retrieve it before putting his boots on.

It was as well he did.

In his haste to scramble out of bed and get the pup downstairs, he had not noticed the neat little sausage of puppy excreta which lay on the coverlet.

As he stood, wondering what to do about it, he heard his grandmother mount the stairs on her way to make the beds, her first job after breakfast. He was panicked therefore into doing the first thing that came into his head. Scooping the incriminating evidence up in his handkerchief, he thrust it into the pocket of his shorts. The brown pattern of the coverlet disguised the faint residue clinging to the fabric.

"Let me see if you have a clean handkerchief to take to school," demanded his grandmother suspiciously.

He offered up a little prayer and briefly released one corner of the handksrchief to show her before scuttling downstairs. On the way to school he stopped and shook the contents out into the hedgerow, but by this time,

128

possibly because of his body heat, it no longer took the form of a neat sausage; it had resolved itself into a gooey disgusting mess. He could have thrown the handkerchief away, but his grandmother always checked to make sure he still had one at the end of the day, and imposed dire penalties if he had not.

"Handkerchiefs cost money," she would grumble, and of course, she was right. Very few children carried handkerchiefs, but made do with bits of rag or just their fingers or sleeve.

Folding it up sides to middle, he made a mental note not to use it, but halfway through the morning he forgot, and drew it out. Fortunately he remembered in time, and hastily stuffed it back into his pocket, but Melanie Wright, sitting next to him, wrinkled her nose in disgust and shot her hand in the air.

"Please Miss I think Jonathan has messed his trousers," she said primly, so he punched her in the mouth and spent the rest of the lesson snivelling in the corner, his legs smarting from the application of Miss Burket's hand. She carefully checked to make sure there was no truth in the allegation before risking contact with that area of his anatomy however.

His troubles were not over; at lunch time Melanie's brother James approached him. Normally they were friendly, but James' manner was now aggressive.

"You hit my sister," he said grasping Jonathan's shirt front. "I'm going to –"

Something, as they say, snapped.

It was probably a combination of several aggravating factors. The nervous tension engendered by breaking the rules about having the pup in bed with him in the first place; the further tension of dealing with the pup's lavatorial offering; the awareness that he had yet to convincingly explain the state of his handkerchief; and Melanie's accusation that he had filled his trousers. All had combined to make him feel resentful and hostile to the world, so he kneed James in the groin.

Mrs Morven, watching from her window, made further application to the backs of his legs, and he spent another period snivelling in the corner, while poor James sat shivering and nursing his testicles in front of the fire.

Their sniffs alternated in the quiet of the classroom as the rest of the children got on with their drawing.

They had both recovered by the end of the day, but Jonathan squared up to James, who approached him as he walked down the road towards home.

"Don't worry," James said ingratiatingly. "I'm not mad at you; I'm going to do you a favour."

It appeared that he and Melanie had fallen out during playtime.

"I'm going to let you hit her again," he said generously.

Jonathan declined his offer, whereupon he became more ingratiating.

"I want you to hit her," he said. "I'll give you some of my crisps," he added.

"Why don't you hit her yourself?" Jonathan asked

"Because my dad'll belt me if I do," said James.

"I'm not hitting her either," said Jonathan. "I'll only get into more trouble if I do."

James' manner became threatening.

"If you don't hit her I'll hit you," he said.

But having reduced him to a shambles once, Jonathan felt confident of his ability to do it again. Anyway, Colin and David were close by, taking an interest, so he felt secure. He shuffled his feet as though preparing for a repetition of the earlier attack, at which point James hurriedly backed off.

Melanie, who had been walking two paces behind them, listening to their conversation without any evident concern, tossed her head, stuck her nose in the air, and continued indifferently on her way.

Later that night Jonathan's grandmother held out, at arms length, the handkerchief she had taken out of his shorts pocket.

"What happen to this?" she yelled. "What you been using this for?"

"There was no paper in the school lavys," he lied.

He cuddled Scott before he went to bed.

"You haven't half got me into some trouble today," he whispered. "You're going to have to stay down here tonight. I can't go through all that again."

James Wright approached Jonathan with gloom the next morning.

"You know what that little cow did?" he said indignantly. "That cut on her lip where you hit her; she told my dad it was me as did it and I got a strapping."

Arms around shoulders, they commiserated with each other on the perfidy of the female sex.

Jonathan's troubles were still not over.

"So that Governess up at the Hall think you're a pretty little boy does she?" his grandmother chuckled as she washed him ready for bed.

"Who told you?" he demanded indignantly.

"That Mrs Musgrove," his grandmother told him. "And she didn't think you seemed best pleased."

"I hate that Miss Nagele," he said bitterly.

After a few minutes of thought he began to feel uneasy.

If Colin or David should get to hear about this, his life would not be worth living.

"Granny," he said cautiously. "I want you to promise me something."

"What's that then?" she whisked his nightshirt over his head.

"I want you to promise me you won't ever tell anyone what that old bitch said."

"That's enough of that language!" she cuffed him angrily. "We don't use that word talking about a lady."

"Well promise me then," he said urgently.

She paused and looked thoughtfuly into his eyes for a few moments.

"Yes," she said, half to herself, "I do believe you're beginning to grow up."

"Promise," he demanded. "I'll clean the geese and the ducks out," he added recklessly. "I'll do any jobs you want."

He lived on the edge of his nerves for a few days, but as nothing more was said – by anyone – he presumed she had kept her promise.

The discussion reminded him of something that had puzzled him for a while.

"Why does the Squire have a Governess?" he asked. "He doesn't have any children."

"Yes he does," said his grandmother. "He have a grown daughter, Dorothea. That so happen she's what's known as a simpleton; she have the mind of a child although she's a lot older than your mother. She still have to be looked after like a child, and that Miss Nagele was kept on to do the job."

She looked reflectively into the fire.

"I often wonder if we do the right thing by these people," she said. "That poor creature just sit in her bedroom up at the Hall, all day and every day, except for maybe a little walk in the grounds – and then only when none of the estate workers are around to see her. The Squire being insistant on that because he's ashamed of her do you see."

She shook her head sadly, lost in reverie for several minutes before suddenly sweeping him off towards bed.

"Likely there'll be a letter from your mother in the morning," she said. "I'm right curious to know how she get on with them Salvationists."

In fact Jonathan's mother had been both disappointed and puzzled by the contents of the letter from the Salvation Army Missing Person's Bureau. It said simply that they could not continue with the enquiry, but that an explanation would be offered if she wished to call again.

Once more she climbed the shabby stairs to the Bureau.

"Our records show that we undertook enquiries into your brother's whereabouts, on behalf of another relative, some four years ago," the kindly Captain told her. "We don't feel further enquiry will be any more productive; we exhausted all possible leads then."

"What happened four -" she began, but he stopped her.

"I'm sorry, I'm not allowed to give you any details," he told her. "All I can say is that the person who sought our help, four years ago, was your brother's wife."

Jonathan's mother was absolutely astounded.

"I can't give you her address," the Captain went on, "in case that would be against her wishes. But I can write to her – if you agree – giving her yours. She can then contact you if she feels disposed to."

He hesitated.

"Actually, I think she would have done so before this if she had really wanted to," he said. "She only lives in Norwich; within easy reach of your parents."

She thought quickly.

"I've a better idea," she said. "If you'll agree?"

"Go on," said the Captain.

"Let me write to her," she said. "I can explain that it was not indifference that kept me from acknowledging her letter nine years ago. It simply arrived too late. Perhaps I can persuade her to meet me. I'll send the letter to you, in a stamped envelope, and you can address it."

"Provided I can read it first", said the Captain. "I dare not risk sending her something she may find distressing."

As she left, her mind a whirl of questions without answers, she had the satisfaction of having an extra shot in her locker should the Salvation Army Officer's help fail to produce a response. Working with consultants over the years, she had acquired a rudimentary skill in reading a patient's notes upside down, and had applied this skill to the Officer's file as it lay before him on his desk. She had not been able to decipher the number, but she knew that Arthur's wife lived in a street just off the bottom end of one of the shabbiest areas of the City; an area noted for poverty verging on squalor, with a population struggling to survive against a background of damp housing and inadequate sanitation.

It occurred to her that a few enquiries around the neighborhood might be appropriate, but they would have to be discreet; Arthur could have returned in the intervening four years, and may resent his sister's interference.

Her brother Bert was unresponsive to the point of hostility however, when she telephoned him next day.

"I'm certainly not going knocking on doors asking for her down that end," he said angrily. "I told you I want nothing more to do with it. That's a mucky area anyway; she can't be up to much if she live down there."

"You might be a little more helpful," she was also angry. "He is our brother."

"I'm not doing it and that's flat," he said. "And if you've any sense you'll forget the whole thing."

By chance however he found he had to pass through that part of the City, while on official business, the following Saturday.

He hesitated as he passed the end of the street where, his sister had told him, his brother's wife had certainly been living four years ago, and might still be. Curious, he turned and sauntered along, noting the peeling paintwork, bits of sacking substituting for curtains, and dirty nosed ragged children playing in the gutter. He turned and walked back, and then, as he paused and glanced into an alleyway, he beheld that which came close to giving him a heart attack.

"That were like walking into a Public House and seeing the Kaiser sitting there taking a drink," he said later.

"Boy Jonathan!" he roared. "What the hell are you doing down here on your own?"

Later that day, as Jonathan sat at the kitchen table, with tears running down his cheeks, his Uncle Bert described what had happened, while his grandfather sat listening, and watching him intently.

"My God he were quick," said Uncle Bert. "He take one look at me, and turned and took off like a shot out of a cannon. I took off after him, and I can usually catch the little bugger, having a fair turn of speed, but next thing I know, he dive through a hole in the wall so small a ferret would a thought twice about it, and by the time I get round the other side he'd vanished into thin air."

"But I keep telling you as I wasn't in Norwich," Jonathan yelled. "I been playing with Colin and David in the village all morning. I never been to Norwich on my own in my whole life."

"He's lying dammit," said Uncle Bert. "I see him with my own eyes. I near as anything have a hold of his trousers as he went through that hole."

There was a long pause while the old man continued to stare at Jonathan.

"I think he's telling the truth," he said at last. "I think you saw another kiddy as looked like him."

"I was as close to him as I am to you," Uncle Bert began to shout in his excitement and frustration. "Do you think I'd bike all this way out here this afternoon unless I were sure?"

"Colin and David were with me all day," Jonathan said. "And Aunty Mavis gave me my dinner at twelve o'clock."

"You'll have to talk to them Bert," said his grandfather.

"They'd lie to back him up," said Uncle Bert.

"Mavis?" Jonathan's grandfather looked at him as though he were mad.

"Not Mavis," said Uncle Bert, "but he could a got back for his dinner there."

"Don't be daft. You say you saw him at half past eleven. Now how the hell is he going to get up from that side of town to Castle Meadow, and on to a bus, and out to the village by twelve o'clock.?"

Uncle Bert began to look frustrated.

"Did any other grown ups see you in the village about half past eleven?" he demanded, sounding less sure of his ground.

"Mrs Froggett," Jonathan said promptly. "She gave us a penny between us for carrying her shopping home. And that were as the Church clock were striking eleven."

"I'll ask Mrs Froggett mind," he said warningly.

Jonathan felt reasonably comfortable as his Uncle Bert left, looking defeated, but experienced all the frustration of the occasional liar who is not believed when he does tell the truth.

A week later his mother felt a rising sense of excitement as she walked along the corridor of the Nurse's home to her room. Firmly closing the door, so that she would not be interrupted, she opened the letter she had found in her box that morning. She looked first at the signature, which confirmed her guess that the letter was from the sister-in-law she had never seen.

'Dear Edith,'

the letter began.

'I read your letter with some misgiving. I had really come to believe that Arthur's family had decided they wanted nothing to do with me. There have been times over the years when I have been tempted to ask your mother for help, but I suppose I always feared a rebuff. I would rather we met, as you suggested, than try to explain everything here.'

The letter concluded by detailing arrangements to meet for tea in Jarrolds on the Saturday afternoon, adding:

'Arthur left an old photo with you on, so I should be able to recognise you. I would rather meet out than invite you here, as neither the house nor the area are at all pleasant; in fact I would be ashamed to entertain you here. Unfortunately it is all I can afford.'

Jonathan's mother read the letter with mixed feelings of anxiety, frustration and irritation; it told her very little and left a great deal to speculation. His grandmother wanted to know more of course, and wrote a long list of questions to his mother, with instructions to provide the answers as soon as she had concluded her meeting.

For someone who had originally been opposed to the whole exercise, she was remarkably interested in the outcome, as Jonathan was able to witness – being present when his mother had described the meeting with his Aunty Polly.

Arriving at Norwich Thorpe at three o'clock, she had window shopped around the Market Square before slipping into Jarrolds at the appointed time. She found an empty table and hoped that Polly would recognise her from the old photograph.

Then she had a shock!

The tall, pleasant, albeit careworn looking woman approaching the table, was not alone.

"I really thought I'd gone crazy," she told Jonathan's grandmother. "There's me expecting to meet a woman who none of the family had barely heard of, let alone met. What do you imagine I felt when I see her leading my own son by the hand?"

As they advanced towards her, her mind had raced to the conclusion that Polly must have been out to the farm earlier in the day, introduced herself, and then brought Jonathan in with her. It was the only possible explanation.

"I just gawped at him," she told his grandmother, "and asked him what he was doing here, and he just looked at me as though he were half cut."

Polly had also looked puzzled.

"I'm just surprised to see boy Jonathan with you," his mother told her.

"Who's Jonathan?" asked Polly.

Jonathan's mother just gaped at her again, and then at the boy, and wondered if she were losing her grip on reality.

"This is boy Nicholas," said Polly. "Say hello to your Aunty Edith, Nicky."

"Of course," his mother had continued, "when Polly said that, I looked more closely and I could see that it was not boy Jonathan. But the likeness is really incredible. They could be identical twins. Nicky is perhaps a little fuller in the face, but – the same build – the same grey pullover and shorts – I bet you couldn't have told the difference."

As an icebreaker, for what could have been a strange and difficult meeting to handle, the situation could not have been bettered. By the time they had sorted it all out, they were firm friends, finding they had much in common having both been left to cope alone with a child, albeit for different reasons.

All the way through tea her gaze continually wandered towards Polly's boy, and she found herself marvelling that a trick of nature should determine that her son, and her brother's son, born within two days of each other, should inherit such incredibly similar physical characteristics.

She had a sudden thought.

"I hear you were chased by a policeman a couple of weeks ago," she told Nicky.

He blushed and looked sideways at his mother, who was obviously hearing of this for the first time.

"I weren't doing nothing wrong," he bleated. "I'm just walking down the alley and this big copper starts chasing me for no reason."

"Don't worry," she said, seeing the anxious look on Polly's face. "It was my brother Bert. Your Uncle Bert," she told Nicky.

Then she dissolved into giggles.

"Poor Bert," she spluttered. "He was convinced he'd chased Jonathan down your road. Most upset because nobody would believe him."

"I'm not too sure I like the idea of having an uncle what's a policeman," said Nicky dubiously.

Polly's story was a sad one, and Jonathan's mother found her anger towards her brother Arthur growing, as she listened to a story of betrayal and callous indifference towards his wife and child.

"I suppose I loved him," said Polly, tears beginning to gather in her eyes. "But how I would feel about him now, if he came back, I don't know."

She rummaged in her bag for a book to keep Nicky occupied while she talked.

"My father had left me a little money when he died; enough for Arthur and me to marry and pay our fare to Canada where he had a house and a job lined up – or so he said."

A month after they were married, nearly all the money had been spent on entertaining Arthur's dubious friends, so he had persuaded her to let him take what was left and go on ahead to Canada to establish himself. He would send for her, he said, when he had saved enough out of his wages to pay her fare over.

His first letter had been full of promises, but no more, and, she later discovered, he had left no money to pay the rent. She had to leave her flat and throw herself on the mercy of a disapproving and infirm aunt in Bury.

Six weeks after he had left, her suspicion that she was pregnant had been confirmed. She wrote in desperation to him, begging him to get her out somehow, but his reply did nothing to ease her anxiety; rather it increased it. He suggested that they wait until after the baby was born, by which time he would have everything organised.

"The next year was sheer hell," Polly said. "My aunt in Bury barely tolerated my being there, and was even less welcoming after Nicky was born."

Arthur had written, about a week after Nicky's birth, saying that he was moving to Quebec, and would send for her as soon as he had a job and somewhere for them to live.

The Aunt in Bury suddenly died, and although there was a small legacy, the house was sold over Polly's head to pay the other bequests. Through an aquaintance she managed to rent the damp seedy house in Norwich, believing it would only be for a short while, then wrote to Arthur stating her intention of using the Aunt's legacy, as soon as the lawyers had released it to her, to pay her fare over.

He promptly replied to the effect that if she sent the money to him, he could buy himself in to a lucrative business and would send for her and Nicky within six months.

"I hope to God you didn't send it," Jonathan's mother broke in at this point.

Polly hung her head.

"I really felt I had no choice," she said. "I believed he would want to see his son; that he would genuinely want us both out there."

The next Christmas, by which time Nicky was a year old, Polly's letters to Arthur began to come back to her marked 'no trace of addressee'.

"My luck changed a little at this time," said Polly. "Having pawned all I had, including the jewelry my mother left me, I was now really desperate. Then a nice gentleman from the Chapel heard of my plight, and came to see me. He ended up finding me a job in the shoe factory that had just opened in Norwich. Another Chapel lady offered to take care of Nicky while I was at work, and I began to pick up some kind of decent life again."

She found herself strangely unaffected when, after nearly a year with no word at all, a letter from Arthur arrived. Postmarked Montreal, with no return address,it simply said that, having given it a lot of thought, he felt she and Nicky would be better off without him, and that they should go their separate ways.

"It came almost as a relief," she said. "Once I knew there was no hope, I was able to accept that I had to get on and fend for myself and Nicky. But I decided on one last try. That's when I contacted the Salvation Army. When they could not trace him, I finally turned my back on him and determined to manage on my own. If it hadn't have been for the Depression, and having to take a cut in wages in order to keep my job, I might even have found a better place to live."

"Why didn't you contact us?" asked Jonathan's mother.

"Knowing Arthur, it seems ridiculous, now, that I believed all his stories about how awful his family were and how badly you had all treated him," said Polly. "But I had the strong impression that none of you would be interested; that I would only be inviting humiliation by asking any of you for help. When you didn't reply to my first letter, Arthur said that if you were not interested then the rest of your family would cetainly not be, and that we should forget the lot of you."

It was as they were about to conclude, Polly having been persuaded to visit the farm as soon as it could be arranged, that she dropped her bombshell.

"I just wonder if it was fate that brought us together at this time," she said hesitantly. "I have to go into hospital for three weeks, and I have no one to have boy Nicholas while I'm in. I had reached the conclusion that I would have to put him into a Home, but do you think any of the family could have him for just that short while?"

Chapter Ten

Jonathan's mother lost no time in calling a family conference.

He fully expected to be excluded, but to his surprise she said, that as he would be involved, he should be allowed to know what was going on. His Uncle Jack from Thetford could not get across at such short notice, but Uncle Bert and Aunty Eliza turned up. Jonathan sat on the settee, wide eyed at the family interaction he observed.

"I can't have the boy," said Uncle Bert. "I'd have to get permission off the Police Authority, and I know that would be refused even though he is a relative."

"Jack can't have him," said Jonathan's grandmother. "He only have two bedrooms, and that would not be right to put the boy in with those two girls."

"The logical thing is for him to come here for those three weeks," said Jonathan's mother briskly. "Boy Jonathan's bed is big enough for both of them, and they would be company for each other. Keep each other out of mischief."

Uncle Bert gave a hoot of derision.

"You're a comedian and no mistake Edie," he said. "What I see of that little varmint he's no stranger to mischief. The way he took off when he saw me, that's not the first time he ran away from a policeman. Which is not surprising being in that area," he added.

In the end she won the day.

Jonathan's grandmother would not hear of the 'poor little mite' going into a home.

His Uncle Bert rather nastily reminded everybody who Nicky's father was, and gloomily forecast problems. But Aunty Eliza told him he was talking nonsense and to give the boy a chance before condemning him.

His grandfather, who had maintained a total silence up to this point, looked across at Jonathan.

"What does the little ol' boy have to say about all this?" he asked, fixing him with discerning eyes.

There was no doubt whatsoever in Jonathan's mind.

He did not want to share either his bed, or his toys, or his grandparents, with another boy; especially one who looked so much like him that even his own mother mixed them up.

"I don't know," he said, falling back on his standard response when he knew that what he wanted to say would not be well received, or understood, by adults.

His grandfather looked at him for a long time; Jonathan had the feeling that the old man knew exactly what was in his mind.

"I want to meet Polly and the boy before I make my mind up," his grandmother said cautiously.

"I've already invited Polly over for next Sunday" said his mother. "I shan't be here of course, but I'm sure you'll like her. She's certainly too good for the likes of my dear brother Arthur."

"You took a lot on youself didn't you?" said Jonathan's grandfather. "Inviting her over before we'd a chance to talk about it?"

"They both need feeding up," she said, ignoring the comment. "So I told her to come early; to be here in time for Sunday dinner."

Naturally Colin, Terry and David, were mystified and excited by the news of a hitherto unknown cousin living in Norwich, and pumped Jonathan for all the information they could get. For his own part he found himself reluctant to talk about it too much; his curiosity having been satisfied by his mother's disclosures, he had, to some extent, lost interest. Not only that but he now found himself regretting the fact that his persistance, in pushing the issue of his 'missing' uncle, was leading rapidly to a disruption of the lifestyle he was enjoying. Having to be prepared to accommodate himself to another boy in the house filled him with disquiet and resentment.

He was, however, able to push it into the back of his mind for the most part. Quite a number of exciting events were pending, including the invitation, as a choir, to sing in Norwich Cathedral.

The boys of certain Parish Church or School choirs were invited to 'fill in' when the Cathedral Choristers were unavailable, and they had been selected to cover for one Service. Only a week before they were due to sing however, Mr Price brought them bad news.

"Somebody's slipped up," he said. "They've double booked."

Due to an administrative error at the Cathedral office, Lanbury, a nearby public school, had been given the same date, and it began to look as though one of them would have to withdraw. At the last minute however, Mr Price was able to negotiate a solution.

"We're both small choirs," he said, "so we're going to double up."

"What about joint rehearsals?" asked the Vicar.

"No time," said Mr Price. "But I've had a word with their Music Master, who has asked me to conduct, and I shall be going up to the school to take their choir through the programme."

James Wright's elder brother was acting up as head choirboy, because Terry was off with tonsilitis. They all subsequently agreed that the debacle which ultimately ensued was directly attributable to Terry's absence. They liked Steve when he was an ordinary choirboy like them; he seemed to suffer some change whenever he was temporarily promoted however, and tended to make erratic decisions.

Jonathan had been to the Cathedral before of course, though never in the Song School area which was normally inaccessable to the public. They were all a little overawed by their surroundings, and a little unnerved by the blase air of sophistication with which the other choir walked in a few minutes later. Some of the Lanbury boys began looking in their direction, and making comments in very posh public school accents.

"I've heard they're not bad for mere village oiks," said their Head Chorister in a loud voice to one of the others, his voice and manner reminding Jonathan of the Squire.

Steve froze in the act of pulling his cassock on, and stared with narrowed eyes at the boy, who promptly began the contest.

"What are you staring at oik?" he wanted to know.

"I was looking to see if you were going to drop that plum out of your mouth before you start singing," said Steve, thereby throwing down the gauntlet.

"We'll see you lot after the Service," said another plummy voice.

"You won't have far to look 'cause we'll be waiting for you," said Steve.

David did a quick head count.

"There's nearly twice as many of them as there are of us," he said nervously. "Do you reckon that's a good idea?"

"They're public school types," said Steve, who had won a Scholarship to the Grammar School. "Soft as butter and thick as two short planks."

Jonathan reflected soberly that the Squire was a 'public school type', and, although he detested the man, he had to acknowledge that winning medals for his willingness to tackle the notoriously fiery Pathan tribesmen, on the North West Frontier, hardly qualified him for Steve's blanket description. Besides, some of the boys opposite had a distinctly hard look about them.

Halfway through the first anthem it became obvious that they were deliberately trying to outsing the Parish Church boys. Steve's whispered instructions to respond were passed down the line, creating a marvellous effect with nearly thirty boys singing at the top of their voices and earning warm comments from the congregation later.

As they launched into Wesley's beautiful anthem 'Blessed be the God and Father', Steve, who was singing the solo, surreptitiously passed down a note he had written on the torn out page of a hymn book. It travelled down the line slowly, arriving with Jonathan just as Steve reached his liquid treble contribution:

"Love one another with a pure heart fervently"

he sang, as Jonathan read: 'We are going to kick shit out of the Lanbury lot after. Are you on?'

"See that ye love one another"

the rest of them responded, as they nodded assent.

The problem of arranging a venue away from the adults was solved while they were unrobing, and in due course they scurried through the South door to a point about a hundred yards away. The opposition ranks had swollen; obviously Lanbury had drawn additional manpower from their supporters in the congregation; something the Parish could not do because they had not got any. The extra Lanbury boys had, in fact, turned up in the role of spectators, but the Parish were not to know that.

"I wish my brother was here," muttered Colin.

The battle was brief and inglorious, culminating in the Parish boys' ignominious flight from the scene, hotly pursued by the whooping jubilant Lanbury lot.

Unfortunately, being the smallest, Jonathan was left behind and even overtaken by their leaders; this created the impression, for a few seconds, that he was one of the pursuers rather than the pursued. Only when the Lanbury boys realised what had happened did they think to converge, and wedge him into a corner between St.Luke's and the Regimental Chapel. He cowered in terror as they all gathered round to inspect him, but he took time off to observe that – far from mounting a rescue operation as he had wildly hoped – Steve and the others were sitting on the grass, getting their breath back, and watching with interest.

The first discovery he had made that afternoon was that public school boys were not 'softies', as Steve had suggested.

The other discovery was all about 'fair play' and how it worked.

Instead of descending upon him in a pack and tearing him limb from limb, as would have happened if the situation had been reversed, their leader called them to order.

"It's got to be a fair fight," he said. "So it's got to be one to one, and it's got to be someone the same size."

He pointed imperiously to a fair haired boy only marginally bigger than Jonathan.

"You'll do Maitland," he said. "Go on, get it over with."

It was only a little reassuring for Jonathan to realise that the fair haired boy was no more enthusiastic than he was, as they rather hesitantly edged forward, clenching their fists and squaring up to each other like old fashioned prize fighters. Suddenly Jonathan thought he saw an escape route; the ranks of Lanbury supporters had opened up behind the fair haired boy, leaving a gap he thought he could nip through if he could get the other boy out of the way.

Without giving it further thought he took off like a whippet, sweeping his arm round to push his adversary aside, and heading for the gap. He felt his elbow make contact with something soft, but then realised the gap had quickly closed and their leader was standing in front of him.

Jonathan was lucky; the fair haired boy was one of those people who can't stand the sight of blood, especially when it is their own. He was sitting on the grass, looking with shock at the hand with which he had experimentally dabbed the lip Jonathan had caught with his elbow.

"I say, I'm bleeding," he said, a tremor in his voice.

Jonathan envisaged the whole group bent on avenging the drawing of blood.

"I'm sorry, I didn't mean to hurt you," he said, hoping that some expression of regret might go some way towards reducing the level of violence towards him.

"Oh that's alright," said the fair haired boy, his voice still tremulous.

Their leader stood aside.

"Alright, you can go now," he said. "It was a fair fight and you won."

He glared disgustedly at the fair haired boy who, Jonathan felt, was going to come in for some unjust critisism later on. He suddenly experienced, despite his own fright, a feeling of warmth towards the other boy, coupled with a strong feeling of guilt.

"I was trying to run away because I was scared of him," he told their leader, "and he got in the way."

For some reason this made them all, including the fair haired boy, look uncomfortable.

"That was good," said Colin excitedly as Jonathan rejoined his compatriots. "You won him good, and he was older than you, even if he wasn't much bigger."

"That was a good one you gave him," exulted Steve. "One up for us and down with Lanbury!"

Jonathan felt rage boiling up inside him, and hit Colin – who happened to be standing nearest to him – in the face as hard as he could. Colin was so surprised he didn't even try to hit him back.

"You're a rotten stinking lot," Jonathan yelled. "You left me on my own and I'm never going to get into one of your fights again."

He sulked for the rest of the afternoon, trailed fifty yards behind as they walked back to the bus – snarling at anyone who dropped back to offer the olive branch – and refused to let anyone sit next to him on the journey home. When they reached the village he ran straight into the Church to hang up his choir robes, and trudged off home without a word to anyone.

He noticed that Colin had sustained more damage from his punch than he had from the fight with the Lanbury boys.

The next morning, by which time his petulance had evaporated, Colin was waiting for him at the school gate.

"I'm going to let you off hitting me," he said magnanimously. "Our Terry says it was daft of Steve to get us into a fight with more of them than there was of us."

An Inquest had been held – presided over by Terry – and Steve, a choirboy on each limb, had been bumped six times on the hard flagstones of the Church porch. Like many Generals, whom history has sunk without trace, Steve discovered, the hard way, the fate of the leaders of the defeated.

The incident left Jonathan with some discomfort however; the feeling that he was in some way to blame for what had happened. He was still brooding about it the next evening when he joined his grandfather at the yard gate.

"You know something," his grandfather said pensively, gesturing towards the open fields in front of them, the distant wood providing the backdrop to his pastureland, "I a stood here looking at this view, hardly missing a day, for nigh on sixty years. As did my father before me and his father before him."

Jonathan climbed up as usual, and sat on the top bar, leaning back against his grandfather'chest.

"Now you look over that same view from the top door of the barn," the old man went on, "and you can just see Limmer's new Dutch barn over the tres, all red and bright, and on a clear day you can see them pylons taking that electricity across the County. But from down here you can't see any of that. Now that mean that what you see from this gate haven't changed, not one bit, for more than a hundred years."

He paused and added:

"Both my father and my grandfather – and for all I know my great-grandfather and great-great grandfather too – used to stand at this same gate looking at that same view."

He paused again.

"That make you think don't it?" he said. "The number of people, now dead and gone, who a stood looking at what we're looking at now, and the people – yet to be born – who'll stand here long after I'm dead and gone."

Jonathan felt tears smarting his eyes.

"I don't want you to die Grandad," he said. "I want you to go on for ever and ever and ever and ever and -"

"Alright, alright," his grandfather chuckled. "I'll have that in mind if ever I feel like moving on to the Churchyard."

Sampson suddenly snorted and moved around in his stall, and he jerked a thumb in his direction.

"Take horses," he said. "I've had his mother, grandmother, great grandfather and great great grandmother in that stall over the years. And he have half brothers and sisters scattered between here and Yorkshire. But I wonder if that'll count for anything in fifty years time."

"You always told me the best horses come down in the stallions line," Jonathan said. "Is it the same for all animals?"

"I'd certainly want to be sure I'd got the right bull if I wanted my whole herd serviced," his grandfather said. "Otherwise I'd have six mistakes instead of one."

Jonathan thought of the Lanbury boys and their similarity to the Squire.

"What about people?" he asked.

His grandfather rumbled his deep belly laugh.

"I suppose the gentry as have ancestors going back to Norman times would lay claim to that," he said.

"Like the Squire and the boys at Lanbury?" Jonathan asked.

But his grandfather shook his head.

"That don't follow," he said. "I never learned no history; I wasn't at school long enough. But I do know of famous men whose fathers were very ordinary people. Likewise some out and out villains who've come from what is thought to be the upper crust."

"Like the Squire?" Jonathan asked.

Again he shook his head.

"He can be right nasty that's true," he said. "But that don't make him a villain. I don't like the man, but if it weren't for him working hard to keep the estate going there'd be a lot of men in this village without a job and a wage. Like all the Tory landowners he think he's a cut above the rest of us, but that's not his fault; that's the way he's been brought up to think – right from when he was a boy at a place like Lanbury. And that's why he get so nasty tempered with his men when they don't toe his line, because he's been brought up to believe he is always right, and his word have to be law."

Little did Jonathan know, but he was very shortly to experience the Squire's nasty temper at first hand.

The following afternoon was set aside for the Cub ramble through Burrell's wood, so they duly presented themselves, smart and uniformed, to Mrs Morven in the school playground. She hoped to interest them in the natural history of the area, and although they were seeking to make an adventure of it, they found her explanation of various phenomena quite fascinating.

Having examined some interesting fossils they had found, Colin and David ran on ahead. Chasing after them, Jonathan rounded a corner in time to see them vanishing into a culvert that ran under a gateway leading into the wood.

"We're going to jump out and scare them as they come through the gate," David explained.

Scarcely had Jonathan squeezed in behind them, when the drumming of hooves terminated in the snorting and blowing of a well exercised horse immediately over their heads. Curious, he peeped over the edge of the culvert and found himself staring straight into the eyes of the Squire.

Jonathan had seen him before of course, both in Church and on those occasions when business with his grandfather required a visit to the farm. He had never spoken to Jonathan, however, or even acknowledged his presence.

"What the devil are you doing here?" the Squire snapped.

His eyes popped even further as Colin and David, also curious, pushed Jonathan aside to squeeze out of the culvert.

"What is this?" he roared. "Who gave you boys permission to come into my wood?"

Jonathan felt frightened, but also indignant.

"We've got a right to be here,"he said. "We're just walking."

"Right? What right? Get off at once, do you hear me?"

"We're not doing any harm," he protested. "We're only looking at stones and plants –"

He stopped, terrified by the sudden eruption into violence as the Squire rowelled his horse into a sideways shuffle, raising his riding crop as he did so. David and Colin, equally terrified, vanished back into the culvert, while Jonathan dived under the horse's belly and out the other side.

The threat with the riding crop was probably only a gesture; had the Squire really intended to hit Jonathan he would have been unlikely to have missed. He had, after all, been a Cavalry Officer, wielding his sword against Pathan tribesmen who had a reputation for not giving you a second chance if you missed the first time.

The horse, unnerved by the manouvre, executed a little dance and began evacuating over the edge of the culvert.

"Your horse is shitting on my cousins," Jonathan told him, giggling at Colin and David's obvious discomfiture.

Then Mrs Morven and the rest of the Cubs came round the corner.

"What the devil –" the Squires face went an even deeper shade of purple.

He remembered however, despite his wrath, to touch his riding crop to the peak of his cap in deference to Mrs Morven's sex.

"Obviously they are in your charge, so I shall not complain," he said. "but I would have preferred to be informed of your intention to bring them through my wood."

Mrs Morven flushed.

"I beg your pardon Squire," she said, indignation apparent in her own voice. "I asked you two or three weeks ago – don't you remember? – as you were coming out of Church."

"Dammit!" The Squire allowed himself to betray a slight embarrassment. "I remember now. But I must confess I understood you to mean that same day."

His Adam's apple pumped up and down in his scrawny neck, while his broomstick thin thighs gripped the flanks of his restive horse as he strove to maintain both physical and emotional equilibrium.

"I discussed it with Mr Perriman, who assured me it would be alright now that the young birds were all on the other side," said Mrs Morven, her face still red with annoyance.

"Then it seems I owe you an apology," said the Squire.

He made it sound as though he were doing her a favour.

He suddenly caught sight of Jonathan again, and pointed at him with his riding crop.

"That boy there," he said. "That's Cooper's grandson isn't it?"

Jonathan dived behind Mrs Morven, standing as close to her as he could, peering round at the Squire from behind her protective back.

"That's right," she said. "That's boy Jonathan."

"He's impertinant," snapped the Squire. "Needs to be taught his manners. Kindly see to it."

"What did you say to him?" Mrs Morven demanded, after he had touched the peak of his cap again and cantered off.

"He just said we'd got a right to -" began David defensively, but Mrs Morven shut him up.

"I'll hear it from boy Jonathan if you don't mind boy David," she said. "Now –"

"He only told him we was looking at stones and plants –" began Colin.

"Be quiet boy Colin!" snapped Mrs Morven. "I want boy Jon-" she suddenly stopped and peered closely at Colin. "What's that on your jersey?" she wanted to know.

"The Squire's horse shat on him," said Jonathan, and got his legs smacked for his pains.

"We do not use words like that," she said crossly. "Now I'm going to suggest we forget this unpleasant incident, and go on and enjoy ourselves."

Jonathan's grandfather thought it was hilariously funny.

"That'll teach you to stay out of his way," he rumbled his belly laugh.

The Sunday of his Aunty Polly's first visit dawned, and Jonathan went straight home from Sunday school, having been forbidden to stay in the village to play with Colin and David.

There being no bus on a Sunday, Mrs Limmer had volunteered to fetch Polly and Nicky from Norwich, so they were already there when Jonathan arrived.

He found that his grandparents had, as his mother had predicted, 'taken to' Polly and Nicky. He too liked his Aunty Polly, who went through the same experience, when she beheld him for the first time, as his mother had when she first saw Nicky.

They were made to stand side by side while all three of the adults scrutinised them and marvelled. Then they looked at each other in the mirror.

Jonathan could see why his Uncle Bert and his mother had been fooled. But there were some slight differences when they were seen together; Nicky was a fraction taller, thinner in the face, and his hair was a shade lighter. The stronger similarities were of build – they were both wiry – and mannerism, and in the way they carried themselves.

"Given the layer of grime and muck that boys seem to be covered with by halfway through every day," said their grandmother, "no one's going to be able to tell which is which."

They were both a little shy at first, largely because the adults were making so much of their likeness, but the ice was broken when Jonathan told Nicky he must be quick on his feet to have got away from Uncle Bert.

"I've never managed it once," he told him admiringly. "You must go like a hare."

"Not really," said Nicky modestly. "It was just that I was scared stiff when I hear this big copper shouting at me, and see him charging up the alley."

Jonathan felt any residual resentment fading as the day wore on. He allowed Nicky to play with his toys, but was not yet ready to show him his secret hiding places; they were far too personal and private.

They were both disappointed when the time came for Mrs Limmer to take Nicky and his mother back to Norwich. As they waved to each other through the back window of the car, Jonathan felt a hand on his shoulder.

"I get the feeling you're quite happy about him staying now," said his grandfather, his eyes crinkling at the corners.

"Your Aunty Polly go into hospital next Saturday," his grandmother said. "And Mrs Limmer is going to take me over to pick her up and take her in, then we'll bring Nicky back here."

"You'll miss the choir outing to Ely Cathedral," said Jonathan. "You said you wanted to come with us."

"I'll have to give it a miss this time," she said. "There'll always be another year."

153

In fact the choir outing was a bit of a washout because it rained heavily all day, but the Cathedral accoustics did wonders for their singing.

Because the charabanc was late getting them back to the village, Uncle Percy agreed to run Jonathan home on the crossbar of his bike. Colin and David wanted him to get out his coal lorry so that they could come too, and satisfy their curiosity by meeting Nicky. This was vetoed because of the lateness of the hour, and as it was getting dark Jonathan said he would run down the lane to save Uncle Percy bumping his bike over the rutted surface. Out of breath therefore, he burst in at the back door to find his grandmother holding her finger to her lips.

"Nicky's in bed and asleep," she said. "So let's have no noise."

"Why didn't you let him stay up," he complained. "I wanted to talk to him."

He was disappointed because he had built himself up to give Nicky a glowing account of the choir outing and to give him the messy remains of the Mars bar he had bought specially for him, and only eaten slightly more than half of on the way home.

"Plenty of time for that," she said. "You have three weeks to do all the talking you want."

She drew him over to the settee.

"Now listen," she said. "You remember how upset you were that first night after your mother left you here? Well Nicky's upset too, because his mother's gone into hospital and have to be put to sleep like you was when you had your tonsils out."

She held the candle while Jonathan climbed into bed beside Nicky's sleeping form, and noticed his puffy eyes and tear stained cheeks. He felt a twinge of sympathy; he recalled how he had felt, nearly a year ago now, when he had felt himself to be abandoned to complete strangers.

The following weeks, however, had to be counted as among the happiest of his life.

It was school holidays, it was harvest time, and he had what he had sorely missed since he had left Gloucestershire; a companion of his own age to share all the adventures of time and place. He had friends in the village in addition to Colin and David, but his grandparents' restrictions on travelling distance, and time of arrival home, precluded close involvement in their activities.

Not that Nicky and he agreed all the time of course; they frequently quarrelled and bickered and fought, and nearly drove their grandmother mad with frequent demands for arbitration in disputes. But they developed an almost emotional dependance on each other which was similar to the relationship between Colin and David.

"They're a bit like the Cumberworth twins," Uncle Silas had chuckled of them, referring to the strip cartoon in the Eastern Evening News which featured the activities of twin small boys.

"That Cumberworth wouldn't dare put in some of the things they get up to," said their grandmother grimly, having just had to mollify Mrs Brown, at the shop, after they had placed a dead rat just inside her door.

One of the advantages of living on an isolated farm was that most of their mischief went unobserved and therefore undetected. Only in the village were they at risk, and that could be reduced by trying to ensure that they knew where Uncle Bert was most of the time.

Although they often quarrelled, they gave up fighting after the first week; they were too evenly matched for any battle to be conclusive. Naturally they both wanted to be the leader; neither of them would accept a subordinate role; but somehow, without spelling it out, probably without a conscious awareness of what was happening, they found a formula based on compromise.

They took it in turns to ride and lead Sampson, as he pulled the sail binder cutting the corn, and allowed the sun to burn their skinny bodies as they worked in the harvest fields, following on and standing up the sheaves. Together they sat in the hedgerow at 'fourses' time, eating their grandmother's pies, and listening to the men reminiscing about the "ol' days afore the Jarman War," and horses they had known and loved, and whose names they could remember after thirty years or more.

Their visits to Uncle Silas were joint, and they would sit at his feet and listen to his wonderful stories of the Norfolk Regiment in South Africa.

The other children in the village took to Nicky immediately, especially Colin and David. In the early stages they were able to play tricks on other children, and on adults, by exploiting their likeness and pretending to be each other.

"He's Nicholas, I'm Jonathan," Nicky would say firmly to a flummoxed Mrs Brown in the shop.

Jonathan ended this game after he had been cuffed, by Uncle Bert, for something Nicky had done.

At the end of an exhausting day, and every day was an exhausting one, they would snuggle down in the big feather bed and sleep like logs.

Both being an 'only child' they had to learn to share, and their grandfather had a prominant role in overseeing this. He had tightened up on discipline since Nicky's arrival and was less inclined to overlook mild delinquencies. He treated them both alike, with no favouritism, and insisted on Nicky taking a share of some of the routine jobs, especially cleaning up the yard.

Jonathan no longer sat on his knee to listen to his stories, there was not room, even on his big frame, for two of them. They sat instead on either side of the big brass fender, in their nightshirts, taking it in turns, on alternate evenings, to sit on the side nearest to him.

Quite early on Jonathan had made the decision to share his secret hiding places.

Nicky looked around in awe at the little den Jonathan had created under the barn eaves. They found they both fitted in quite comfortably, at opposite ends with their knees overlapping. Jonathan felt himself go red however as Nicky picked up the faithful Teddy bear from his place of honour in the corner.

"You can't share that," Jonathan said, snatching it away, expecting Nicky to pour scorn on him for still needing a Teddy.

To Jonathan's surprise he suddenly scrambled out of the hide.

"I'll be back in a minute," he said.

When he returned, five minutes later, he was clutching a Teddy of his own, rescued from his suitcase where he had kept it hidden from Jonathan since his arrival.

He could not help a blush as he propped it beside Jonathan's.

"They can keep each other company when we're not here," he said.

There were some things they could not share of course; Nicky could not accompany him to choir and Cubs, and he could not go with Nicky when their grandmother took him to the hospital to see his mother. Aunty Polly had come through her operation, and was soon making plans for resuming a normal life, but Nicky looked gloomy as the time drew near for him to return home.

"I wish I could go on living here," he said. "I don't want to go back to living in Norwich."

"I'm trying to persuade your mother to come here for a week or two after she come out," his grandmother told him. "She need convalescence."

But Polly would hear none of it.

"I shall only fret if I'm not in my own place," she said. "I've been away from it too long already."

Both Nicky and Jonathan looked crestfallen.

"It would be helpful if you could keep Nicky for a week or two longer though," she added, twinkling at them.

They both brightened up.

It was not often that Jonathan was caught unawares by the activities of the adults nearest to him, having developed mechanisms designed to give him advance warning of any that could affect his personal well being. It must have been his pre-occupation with Nicky's company that blunted his awareness that a 'plot' was being hatched. The final link in the chain was being forged.

His mother's visits suddenly increased, which surprised him because she always complained bitterly about the cost of railway travel. She was often in a huddle with their grandmother between flying cycle trips to the village. She did not even complain about having to sleep on the settee because Nicky was, of course, sharing Jonathan's bed.

One Saturday, when Polly had been out of hospital for three weeks, she came up to the farm and the three of them – Jonathan's mother, their grandmother and Polly herself – all trudged off to the village.

They all three looked very cheerful and self satisfied as the two boys ran to meet them on their return.

Polly took hold of Nicky by the arm.

"Tell me," she said. "How would you like to live around here, and go to school with Jonathan and Colin and David?"

Nicky's face was a mixture of delight and disbelief.

"Live here with Granny and Grandad?" he really sounded disbelieving.

"No," she said. "In the village."

Due largely to Jonathan's mother, whose idea it was to solve two problems at the same time, an arrangement had been agreed. In return for a roof over her head, Polly would go to live with Uncle Silas as his housekeeper. She would keep her job of course, and would have to cycle in to Norwich on the three days a week when there was no bus.

"Boy Nicholas can come out here and play," their grandmother told both boys, "and stay the night sometimes. And boy Jonathan can stay in the village and share Nicky's bed when Cubs or choir practice goes on late."

Jonathan experienced that feeling of joy which comes when life seems to be full of promise .

It was perhaps as well that neither of the boys could see into the future.

Chapter Eleven

One morning, as they were both crammed into the secret hiding place under the barn eaves, Nicky began sifting through their pile of bits and pieces. He came across the photograph which Jonathan had found in the lumber room, and looked puzzled.

"That's your dad when he was a boy," Jonathan told him, pointing.

Nicky was silent for a while, gazing at it.

"My dad was a thief," he said casually, his tone expressing neither approval nor condemnation.

"He was a bit bad," said Jonathan cautiously. "But I don't think he ever stole anything."

"He did", said Nicky. "Mum told me, the last time I saw her in hospital."

Jonathan waited, feeling a little uncomfortable.

"Did you know him and Uncle Bert had a fight?" asked Nicky

"I knew that," Jonathan told him. "But I don't know what it was about."

"It was because he stole money off Grandad and Uncle Silas," said Nicky. "That happened a long time ago. Before you and me was even born."

During his visit, in nineteen twenty one, when he had talked his mother out of money from her egg and chicken sales, Arthur had seized an opportunity to slip upstairs unnoticed. He remembered his father used to keep all his money in a tin box under the bed, and guessed he still did. He had only taken half the contents, about a hundred pounds, believing his father would not go to the box before Market Day, by which time he, himself, would be on the ship to Canada.

His plan may have worked but for his own greed; intent on raising even more, he had persuaded old Silas to lend him twenty five pounds out of his compensation. Later, regretting his generous gesture, Silas had discussed it with Bert, who had been incensed to hear of the transaction.

"Poor old Silas will never see that money again," Bert said to his father, to whom he had gone in the hope of finding his brother at the farm.

His father's response had been immediate.

"I'll give you the twenty five now to take to Silas," he had said, mounting the stairs to the bedroom. "I'm not having him out of pocket through that rogue."

That was when he discovered there was only a hundred pounds left in the box.

"I'll get the bugger arrested," said Bert, heading for the door.

"No you won't," said his father. "I have my pride. I'm not about to let the whole world know I brought up a thief."

He had insisted on Bert taking the twenty five pounds to Silas, even though it meant he would have to sell livestock at a loss, instead of buying in heifers at a good price as he had intended.

First going home to take off his uniform, Bert had cycled into Norwich and combed the City lodging houses until he found Arthur. He demanded all the money back, but was told it had been posted off to the Shipping Company in payment for his ticket to Cananda. This was probably untrue, but Bert, realising he was not going to get the money, had risked his job by beating his brother senseless.

Jonathan was puzzled by Nicky's almost casual attitude to his father's behaviour, as he filled in the only remaining gap in his knowledge of the family scandal.

"Don't you sometimes wish your dad would come back from Canada?" he asked, remembering his own sometimes wistful envy of other boys who had fathers.

But Nicky's early environment had differed from Jonathan's.

"Not likely!" he said. "All the kids where I lived in Norwich had dads that get drunk, and come home and knock them about."

He suddenly changed the subject.

"Let's make ourselves Blood Brothers," he said, the expression on his face clearly indicating his discovery of something else to be enthusiastic about.

"What does that mean?" Jonathan asked cautiously, having learned from bitter experience that Nicky's ideas, implemented without too much thinking through, usually got him into trouble.

"I read it somewhere," Nicky waved a vague hand. "In olden days when a Knight met another Knight, or a Red Indian, and they wanted to be specially friendly, and never tell on each other, and always help if the other one got into a fight, they'd make themselves into Blood Brothers."

Jonathan began to express the opinion that Red Indians hadn't been invented when Knights were around, but Nicky was uninterruptable when in full flow.

"They'd cut each other with their sword or dagger, and then rub the cuts together to mingle the blood, and at the same time they'd take an oath," he went on.

"Couldn't we do it with spit?" Jonathan asked, not relishing the prospect of deliberately allowing pain to be inflicted upon himself.

"It's got to be blood," said Nicky firmly, producing his penknife.

"You're not cutting me with that!" said Jonathan shrinking back against the brickwork.

In the end Nicky managed to convince him that it would only be a slight prick with the point, which would produce no more than a pinhead spot of blood, so he screwed up his face and clenched his teeth while Nicky made several innefectual stabs with the knife at the ball of his thumb.

"The point's' too blunt," said Nicky at last, changing his technique to employ a sawing motion.

"Pack that in," Jonathan yelled, snatching his hand away.

The act of suddenly withdrawing his hand achieved the objective Nicky had been aiming for, and opened up a livid gash a quarter of an inch long, and almost half as deep.

"Don't be such a cry baby," Nicky said contemptuously, as Jonathan first squealed and then whimpered as he attempted to staunch the flow of blood with a very grubby handkerchief. "Thats only a – little – bit –".

His voice tailed off and he turned white as he observed the volume of blood seeping through the handkerchief.

"Let me go and do it to you then," yelled Jonathan, snatching the knife away from him.

"Alright," said Nicky holding out his hand, and attempting to sound nonchalant, but he was obviously a little unnerved. As Jonathan made one or two exploratory jabs, he turned a little more white and pulled his hand away.

"Maybe that's not such a good idea," he said. "Perhaps we should think of something else to do."

Jonathan was engulfed by a surge of rage at the idea that Nicky should abandon the project at the point at which he was to be on the receiving end. He tried to punch Nicky on the nose, forgetting, in the heat of the moment, that he was still holding the knife.

Fortunately Nicky threw his own hand up in time, and then it was his turn to squeal and weep as he found an equally grubby handkerchief to staunch the flow from his wrist.

Violent aggression seemed to be the only solution, but the battle was brief – not only were they too evenly matched, but there was not room in the secret hiding place – so they descended to the barn floor and stood glaring at each other in frustration.

"We may as well do it now," Nicky said eventually, "seeing as how we got the cuts. Otherwise we'll have to go through it all again."

It never occurred to Jonathan to challenge the assumption behind this statement.

"Alright," he said sulkily. "But get a move on. I want to get Granny to put a bandage on."

As, both wincing, they rubbed the cuts together, Nicky realised they had not ritualised the proceedings.

"We have to say the magic words," he said.

"Go on then," said Jonathan impatiently.

Nicky thought for a moment.

"I've forgotten them," he said.

"Make some up then," said Jonathan heatedly. "And don't take all day about it."

In the end Nicky came up with 'I Swear A Roath of Royalty', which did not sound quite right, but Jonathan was too fed up to argue; he wanted some urgent repair work to his thumb, even though it meant some of that horrible stinging iodine his grandmother was so fond of.

He had to reflect that seldom could a pact of undying friendship and loyalty have been made in such an atmosphere of mutual hostility. But the antagonism did not last for long; there is nothing like shared adversity to reduce differences, and this was provided by their grandmother cuffing them mightily about the ears after she had bandaged them up and confiscated the knife.

Loyalty to each other grew naturally, without the need to ritualise it; the night of the 'Blackout' provided the best example of this.

On the night of the seventh of August they had an Air Exercise over the Eastern Counties, one of the objectives being to test the effectiveness of a blackout of all lights. Everyone had to cover all windows, or extinguish all lights, between the hours of one o'clock and three o'clock in the morning. The Royal Air Force would be flying over during those hours to assess whether, in the event of the war which was now beginning to look inevitable, the German bombers would be denied guiding lights to pinpoint their position. Most people would be in bed of course, and the only affect at the farm would be the absence, for one night, of the lantern that hung outside the back door for emergency visits to the petty, or to the barn if an animal needed attention.

There was so much talk about it at school, and so much excitement generated, that Jonathan and Nicky decided to remain awake to see what happened. It was difficult because they kept dozing off, but at last they heard – over their grandparents' snores – the downstairs clock chime the hour of one. Almost immediately the Church clock in the village faintly followed suit. The barn, from their bedroom window, looked totally unfamiliar without the friendly lantern light; in fact it took on an unearthly eeriness, silhouetted against the faint starlight. There was no moon, but it was just possible to discern the pasture and the wood beyond.

Nothing exciting happened; the planes were at too high an altitude for them to hear more than a faint hum as they passed overhead at intervals.

Then Nicky produced a box of matches he had stolen from the drawer downstairs.

"We'll see if they can see a lighted match," he said, striking one out of the window. "Maybe they'll fly low to see what it is and we'll be able to see the plane."

Jonathan tried to stop him.

"Grandad threatened to take his belt to me if he ever caught me playing with matches again," he told him. "And likely he'd do the same to you."

Nicky persisted however, and got a bit nasty when Jonathan tried physical restraint.

The newspapers, a day or so later, wrote it up as 'a highly successful exercise' so, obviously, a lighted match was unlikely to bring the Luftwaffe to the farm.

Three days later, their grandmother – shaking a duster out of their bedroom window – saw all the spent matches in the guttering.

"I want to know which one of you took the matches and played with them in the bedroom," said their grandfather that evening, taking off his belt and laying it on the kitchen table as they stood nervously in front of him.

Jonathan saw Nicky open his mouth and knew he was going to confess, having discovered, the hard way, that there was no mileage in lying to their grandfather.

"It was both of us," he said quickly, although he could not have explained why he did so.

Nicky's startled look towards him was not lost on their grandfather.

"So I have to strap the both on you do I?" he looked coldly from one to the other of them.

"We weren't striking them in the room," Jonathan told him. "Only outside the window, to see if the planes on the exercise would see them and come down to see what was going on".

"He didn't strike any," said Nicky urgently. "I struck them all. He even tried to stop me."

There was an agonising pause.

Then their grandfather replaced his belt round his waist.

"They can both have their supper and straight to bed," he decided, looking at the clock which showed the little hand only just coming up to half past seven.

"You was daft," said Nicky as they lay in bed gazing up at the ceiling. "You should a kept your mouth shut, then you wouldn't a got sent to bed."

"Shut up," Jonathan told him crossly, thumping him.

"Shut up youself," said Nicky, thumping him back.

The following evening their grandfather looked thoughtful.

"They say that when that old war come, they'll have to close down the brickyard at Rockland," he said. "On account of how the glow from the furnaces can be seen from the air, and there's no way of preventing it. Them old Germans see that, they'd know right away where they were at."

Their grandmother began to put pressure on him to complete Polly's move, delayed because of his pre-occupation with harvest.

"That's time them two little varmints was kept apart for a while," she told him. "That business with the matches , and slicing each other with knives, that's a full time job watching one let alone two."

When their grandfather eventually made time to complete the move, he hitched Sampson to the big Suffolk waggon, and took both boys with him.

Jonathan had never seen Nicky's house, so he gazed around in curiosity as they lumbered down the narrow street, and Nicky pointed out the alley where Uncle Bert had chased him in the mistaken belief he was chasing Jonathan. The house was pathetically small; every room in it, including the upstairs, could have been fitted into the kitchen at the farm, and there would have been space left over. Patches of damp and fungus on the wall gave it an air of seedy dilapidation despite Polly's efforts to disguise them with wallpaper and paint.

As they trundled away, with his mother's furniture piled high on the waggon, Nicky looked back over his shoulder just once. He seemed relieved, rather than regretful, at leaving what had been his home for most of his formative years.

Sampson took up the load without apparent effort, eating up the miles at a steady plod. After they had unloaded, their grandfather took Uncle Silas down to the King's Head, while Polly straightened things out, aired Nicky's bed, and left both boys to sort out the toys which had come up in a big cardboard box. Then it was time to go, and Jonathan had to face up to the fact that his close companion of the last few weeks was no longer immediately available. He found it difficult to get to sleep that night, conscious of the empty space in the bed beside him.

His grandfather was unsympathetic.

"Blame yourselves," he grunted. "Happen if you hadn't been so intent on leading each other into mischief, Granny might a put up with having the pair of you together for a bit longer."

His lack of sympathy was partly induced by bad temper; his best young heifer had caught her tongue in a rabbit snare, set in his field by a poacher, and Mr Kemp became almost a daily visitor until she recovered.

Jonathan enjoyed the more frequent contact with Mr Kemp, who had noted his interest in stories about the Civil War.

"These parts saw a lot of action in Cromwell's day," Mr Kemp told him. "Did you know that a group of young girls in Norwich raised a lot of money to buy horses for the Roundheads?"

"That was called the Maiden's troop from then on," his grandfather put in. "And a lot of local men joined Cromwell's Ironsides."

He turned to Mr Kemp.

"Do you reckon there's any truth in the stories about our barn here?" he asked him.

Mr Kemp, an authority on most matters of local history, nodded.

Jonathan listned in wonderment as, between them, they unfolded the story of a troop of Cromwell's men bivouacking in the barn, it was believed, one stormy Summer night.

"It was definately round here," said Mr Kemp. "The question has always been – was it this barn or was it Limmer's old barn, which stand behind the new one?"

"The Roundheads was here in sixteen forty three," said his grandfather "That say in the Parish records as that was when they camped for the night. But we don't know for sure that our barn had been built then, whereas we do know that Limmer's had been built in sixteen thirty eight."

"On the other hand," said Mr. Kemp, "we do know your grandad's barn was mentioned in the Parish records, as a wool store, only two years after the Roundheads had been. So my guess is that it had in fact been built before their visit to the area."

"If it had been built, then it's more likely to a been this barn," said Jonathan's grandfather.

"Why?" Jonathan wondered why they were so sure.

"Because Limmer's barn stood on land owned by the Lord of the Manor, who was a Royalist," said Mr Kemp. "They'd hardly bivouack there, if they were weary and wanted to rest rather than fight."

"Whereas this barn stood on the Canfields land," said his grandfather. "And they were Cromwell's men."

This came as a disappointment; Jonathan had always espoused the Commonwealth cause in his fantasies, and had always assumed that someone as arrogant as the Squire would have had a Royalist ancestry.

He toyed briefly with the idea of changing sides.

"Let's be fair Will," Mr Kemp chuckled. "The Canfields changed politics as often as they changed their shirts! They made damn sure they were always with the winners."

A few days later, as storm clouds gathered and flickers of distant lightning split the humid air of the late Autumn evening, Jonathan reflected that it could have been on such a night as this that the Roundhead troop, eager to settle into shelter before the storm broke, would ride thankfully up to their barn and dismount. After ridding themselves of their accoutrements, and ensuring the horses were unsaddled and made comfortable, they would light a fire to cook their meal.

As he sat in his secret hiding place, looking down through the gap in the masonry, he peopled the barn floor with the characters of his imagination. He heard the rough laughter, and the clash of metal as swords and muskets were propped against the wall, and sentries were posted.

His fantasy took on a dream like quality; indeed he may have dozed and continued his fantasy in a dream.

He suddenly jerked awake with a sense of forboding; his heart began to race and he felt his throat constrict.

As he looked down into the darkening interior of the barn he could see nothing there. But he was filled with an awful premonition that, in a moment, there would be. That something he could not see *was* there, and would materialise in the form of flesh and blood. Not ghosts but real people.

He whimpered with fright as a crash of thunder broke overhead. Scrambling along his escape route under the eaves, rather than descend into the interior of the barn, he dropped onto an old pile of hay at the end, sneezing as the dust attacked his nostrils, and ran into the house with his heart still thumping.

"You look as white as a sheet," his grandmother complained. "You'll have to start going to bed earlier. Or else you need a dose of syrup of figs."

For months thereafter he would not stay in the barn once dusk had fallen.

He managed to see quite a lot of Nicky; a new routine evolved whereby he stayed the night on Cub and choir practice nights, sharing Nicky's bed and thus saving someone the job of getting him home. Nicky, in turn, would stay most of the weekend at the farm, sharing Jonathan's bed. They played with Colin and David after school, and Nicky joined the Cubs as soon as he was officially a resident of the village. But membership of the choir took rather more organising.

"He can't sing," Mrs Morven told Terry, when he tried to do the organising.

For some reason Nicky had not developed the technique of singing treble, but croaked like a rusty frog. He claimed he did not know how to get up into treble.

He was also shy and self conscious about singing in public.

Terry, who had now made Nicky's entry into the choir a personal crusade, solved both problems by the simple expedient of pinning him up against the school wall, and threatening to thump him unless he sang, loud and clear, in treble.

Then he produced a third problem.

"I'm Chapel, not Church," he said.

"I'm beginning to think you don't want to be in the choir," said Terry suspiciously.

"I want to be in the choir," said Nicky. "It's just that I don't like singing."

It turned out however that Nicky's birth had preceded his mother's transfer to Methodism; he had in fact been baptised into the Anglican faith, and only needed her agreement to transfer back.

Uncle Percy, pressured by Terry, had called round to see her but had not found her easy to persuade.

"When I was in dire trouble," Polly told him, "with boy Nicholas a baby, and Arthur having abandoned us, I got nothing but words from the Church. At the Chapel I found real friendship, a lot of pracical help, and people willing to do all they could without being patronising about it. It wouldn't be right to throw that back in their teeth by going back to the Church now that things are going right. Besides," she added frankly, "I don't like the Vicar."

"None of us do all that much," conceded Uncle Percy, equally frankly. "But he's all we've got so we're stuck with him."

In the end she agreed, so Nicky was fully integrated into all their activities, and both he and his mother became accepted members of the village community.

It was shortly after this problem had been solved that another one arose.

Jonathan was standing by the barnyard gate one morning when he saw the Squire's gaunt figure riding across the top field. As he cantered towards him, Jonathan opened the gate to let him to ride through; if he remembered their previous encounter up at Burrell's Wood he gave no sign, but brusquely ordered Jonathan to fetch his grandfather from the barn where he was cutting chaff for cattle feed.

"I want a word with you Cooper," he said coldly.

"At your service Squire," said Jonathan's grandfather easily.

"I understand you have moved your daughter-in-law and her child in with Bews?" said the Squire.

Jonathan's grandfather scratched his bristly chin.

"That's not quite the way I'd put it," he said. "That was an arrangement, come to by the women folk, that seemed like a good idea – "

"Do you not think I should have been consulted first?" snapped the Squire. "After all I am the landlord. It is my cottage."

Jonathan's grandfather was seldom caught wrong footed, but he cursed inwardly as he realised that the necessary involvement of the Squire had been overlooked in the excitement of getting Polly and Silas together.

"Dammit Squire, you're right of course," he conceded. "That's something we should a thought on."

"I shall be having a word with Bews of course," the Squire went on. "But I felt it appropriate to have a word with you first. She is your daughter-in-law, and your family have been instrumental in bringing about the arrangement."

"Now let's get this right," his voice had gone as cold as the Squire's "Are you saying as you object to it and want her out?"

"I object to my permission not being sought," snapped the Squire. "As to her getting out – well – that may not be necessary at the moment. But I may as well be frank with you. I had not anticipated that Bews would require that cottage for much longer; he is after all nearly seventy, and not in the best of health. I intend to sell that cottage as soon as he – as soon as he no longer has a use for it. Your daughter-in-law will certainly have to leave then."

Jonathan's grandfather said nothing, but his face was set hard.

"There's another thing," the Squire sounded forceful. "You may not be aware of this, but in deference to Bews' condition, and the fact that the accident happened on my land during one of my shoots, I have not increased the rent on that cottage. I have in fact been accepting the same rent for the past thirty years."

"Is that a fact," the old man's voice was edged, "that can't have been an easy thing for you to do."

"I have no intention of subsidising your daughter- in-law as well," the Squire went on, apparently oblivious to the sarcasm. "So I shall be raising the rent to thirteen shillings a week to bring it into line with the others."

"You know something?" Jonathan's grandfather thumped the top bar of the gate with his fist as the Squire cantered away. "If something nasty ever happen to that man one dark night, your Uncle Bert's going to have a lot of people to choose from when he have to find out who did it."

Jonathan's mother came – her last visit before Christmas – and brought good news.

"I've written to Jim and Gwen in Wallsend," she said. "They will be coming for Christmas."

Both Uncle Jack's and Uncle Bert's families would be with them; but not Uncle Silas, who had opted to spend it with his new daughter-in-law and her father at the gamekeeper's cottage. They even hoped that Sergeant Bews might get leave.

"That's going to be quite a party," said Jonathan's grandmother. "Who's going to do all the work I'd like to know?"

But she was obviously relishing the prospect.

Christmas day was on the Sunday, so, having broken up from school a whole week before, they had plenty of time for the preparations. It was just as well; the Thursday before Christmas saw the heaviest snowfall for twenty six years, and this had been preceded on the Tuesday by eighteen degrees of frost. His grandfather had to keep all the livestock in the barn, having first lit the old forge fire in the end of it. His grandmother had even put the paraffin heater in the big chicken house, sending Jonathan out every ten minutes to make sure the stupid birds were not knocking it over and setting fire to themselves. She did not have to worry about the geese or ducks; every one had been killed for someone's oven.

Jonathan was let off his jobs; even his grandfather could not break the ice on the water butt, and the manure on the yard had first frozen like concrete and had then gathered a foot of snow on top. Reports of the railways grinding to a halt caused anxiety, and doubt; they wondered whether his mother or Uncle Jim and family would get through. The Church was so bitterly cold, during the Advent Service, that the candles the choirboys clutched kept going out because they could not stop shivering.

The sleeping arrangements had to be very complicated; Jonathan's and Nicky's mothers shivered together in the draughty cleared out lumber room, while the two boys shared of course. Uncle Jim and his family took over Uncle Silas' cottage, he having moved in temporarily with Ted Perriman. Uncle Jack and his family were only staying for two nights, so they crammed in with Uncle Bert, the police house being quite large.

Somehow they were all together on Christmas Eve, and as the roads were just passable the old man surprised them all by wrapping Sampson's feet in sacking, covering him with horse blankets, and hitching him to the Suffolk waggon for the journey into to the village for the Midnight Service. The three uncles opted to walk in front, carrying the lanterns, their laughter and barely heard snatches of conversation echoing back over the soughing of the frosty wind. There was no heating in Church, but the choirboys all had about three pullovers on under their cassocks. Even the Vicar was unusually benevolent towards them while they were robing in the vestry, although Jonathan's grandmother had a less than charitable explanation for that.

"He been at the brandy bottle," she claimed.

They all sang in accord with the spirit of the occasion; even Nicky forgot his shyness at singing and yelled with the rest of them in their attempt to drown the congregation with the descants.

Finally it was Adeste Fidelis, sung in Latin, and they were free to enjoy Christmas.

Sampson, who had been stabled at the King's Head during the two hour Service, made fast time home to get out of the bitter East wind. Jonathan and Nicky, almost too tired to stand, tumbled onto the feather mattress clutching their oven hot bricks and stone hot water bottles.

Everybody was up early; their grandfather had to milk of course, and both boys helped. Every fire in the house was lit, and no less than four huge geese were distributed between the ovens. The boys were banished to the barn, to keep out them out of everyone's way, and to avoid them getting a preview of the presents. These, by tradition, were not opened until after Christmas Dinner.

The rest of the family arrived at midday.

Thus it was that seventeen of them sat down around the huge kitchen table which – together with the sideboard – creaked under the weight of the geese, hams, a side of beef and a dish of spare ribs, a joint of pork and enough vegetables to feed an army.

Jonathan looked round the table and marvelled that they were all one family.

He had never met Uncle Jim's family before of course, and was intrigued by their 'Geordie' dialect. Uncle Jim himself seemed, in some odd way, to fall exactly between Uncle Jack and Uncle Bert in personality and mannerism. Not so stiff and formal as Uncle Bert, but not so jocular and relaxed as Uncle Jack. All his cousins except Nicky were girls, and he expected them to be as priggish as Daphne, but in fact they were all good sports, especially Uncle Jack's two, who had tomboy reputations.

They were all fascinated by Polly and Nicky of course, and the story of their discovery had to be told all over again, with frequent and embarrassing references to Jonathan's part in it.

"So nobody know where Arthur is?" asked Uncle Jim at the conclusion.

Aunty Polly took a deep breath, and glanced apprehensively at Nicky as she spoke.

"To be honest," she said, "I can't believe he will still be alive. It's almost seven years since anything at all has been heard of him. I'm sure he would have been in some kind if contact if he had been able."

In the silence that followed, Uncle Bert cleared his throat.

"I was going to keep quiet about this," he said. "But I bent the rules a bit, and had a few feelers put out by a chap at County who owed me a favour."

He looked a little embarrassed at having to confess to even a mild deviation from the rule book.

"One thing I can say," he went on, "if he is still around, he's been leading an honest life; he hasn't got himself a police record, either in Canada or in this country."

Aunty Polly again glanced nervously at Nicky, but he merely looked curious, as though everybody were talking about someone completely unconnected with him.

"But that's a funny country out there," Uncle Bert continued. "They tell me that in some parts, especially those that aren't properly policed yet, a man can die and get buried without them as has to do it even knowing who he is. And not able to register it because they don't know."

He looked towards Aunty Polly.

"I also found out," he said carefully, "as they have about two hundred every year like that, across the whole of the country."

Jonathan looked at his grandfather, sitting at the head of the table, benevolently dominating the gathering with his quiet authority; his square face, iron grey hair and moustache lit by the flickering wood from the kitchen range.

Jonathan decided that God must look a bit like his grandfather.

"Wherever he is," said the old man, "I wish him no harm. In fact I wish him well, in spite of all the hard things I've said about him in the past."

He smiled wryly at the surprise on every face.

"He did us a good turn, even if he didn't mean to," he explained. "He left me and your mother with a daughter-in-law and a grandson we didn't know we had, and which we wouldn't now be without."

Then he turned to Jonathan.

"And while we're at it, let's not forget that if it hadn't been for the little ol' boy here, pestering the life out of everybody, and making a damn nuisance of himself, we wouldn't a got to know about Polly and Nicky."

Jonathan felt himself go red as they all grinned at him.

Later, with everybody crammed into the parlour, and with presents distributed and opened, his grandfather called for silence and ensured all had charged glasses.

"Nineteen twenty four," he said pensively. "That's fourteen Christmasses ago. The last time as I recall the whole of the Cooper family, as it was then, being all under one roof at the same time. So I'm giving a toast to 'The Family'.

"The Family" intoned everybody solemnly, and suddenly they all seemd to break into laughter and conversation at the same time.

The children all played hide and seek, and Jonathan even began to entertain warmer feelings towards Daphne, who was finding less to be toffee nosed about as it was Christmas. Then they went out to the barn and Jonathan and Nicky challenged the girls to find them in one of their secret hiding places.

Late in the afternoon his grandfather suddenly disappeared upstairs, and emerged after a few minutes clad once again in his working clothes.

"I just wonder if I have to do the evening milking myself," he said, "or whether them idle good for nothing sons of mine will come and help."

The next half hour was funny, especially as Uncle Jim had not milked a cow for ten years. Even Uncle Bert relaxed his dignity a little and started larking around, pushing his brothers into the feed store and shutting the door on them.

"That'll do now," said Jonathan's grandfather with mock severity. "Or I'll have to take my belt to the three of you."

Jonathan and Nicky collapsed into hysterical giggling at the picture this conjured up.

Then, as dusk fell, the milking all done and cleared away, the six of them stood in silence at the barnyard gate, and Jonathan saw that which was to remain imprinted upon his memory for all time; his grandfather, flanked by his three sons, breath frosting on the air, gazing out over his snow covered Norfolk acres.

Jonathan suddenly knew that he was sublimely happy; happier than he could ever remember being in his whole life. As the others drifted indoors, leaving just his grandfather and himself standing in the dusk, he climbed up on to the top bar of the gate and hugged his grandfather nearly hard enough to strangle him.

Chapter Twelve

Empty larders, the aftermath of Christmas, always saw an upsurge in poaching and a consequent increase in work for Ted Perriman and Jonathan's Uncle Bert. His Uncle Jack over at Thetford was also kept busy, so it was not just a local phenomenon.

Although his grandfather did not wholly support their oppressive atittudes, he still simmered over the pain and suffering caused to one of his heifers back in the Autumn.

"I mind no one lifting the odd rabbit off my field," he said. "And God knows, there's more than enough to go round; we're just about overrun with them. In fact, I'd even look the other way if I knew it was someone hard up to feed his family. But a man, born and bred in the country, as sets his snares in a field of cattle, is either a fool or a rogue."

He looked sideways at Bert.

"But you and your brothers did enough poaching when you was boys," he said. "So you don't have a lot of room to shout."

Uncle Bert had the grace to look uncomfortable.

The old man remembered, with anger, an incident from his own youth, when a labourer on a neighbouring estate had refused to stand on being challenged by the gamekeeper, and had tried to run away. Not only had the keeper shot him in the back, but had boasted about it later. In the end the Chief Constable had reluctantly bowed to public opinion, and brought a prosecution for manslaughter. A jury of landowners and farmers had found the keeper 'not guilty', and the Judge had made the position of the Court quite clear.

"It is unfortunate that the man should have lost his life," he said. "But he was breaking the law at the time. It is however wrong, in my view, that a loyal and conscientious servant, discharging his bounden duty to his master, should be placed in jeopardy of losing his liberty."

"I'm not disagreeing with you on that particular case, Father," Uncle Jack had said. "But don't forget that happen at a time when a keeper as wasn't hard on poachers could get the sack. And that could still happen now."

The war between keepers and poachers in the early part of the century was bitter and sometimes bloody, with the loser losing all. The penalty for the keeper, for losing against a successful poacher, was loss of job and tied cottage and the lifetime of reasonable security that went with them. For the poacher the penalty was, at best, a prison sentence. At worst he could be maimed or crippled for life by a keeper violently desperate to preserve his own livelihood.

The Squire supported this system.

"If you want to hold on to your job Perriman," he had told Ted in his early days, "you'll find ways of keeping poachers off my land."

Uncle Silas had been a renowned poacher in his youth, but mostly for the sport of outwitting both the quarry and the keeper.

"Sam Sharpe's grandfather was the Old Squire's keeper in them days," chuckled Jonathan's grandfather. "Many's the night he'd lie in wait all night for Silas, but never see hide nor hair of him. Then, when he get back to the keeper's cottage, he'd find a hare or a brace of pheasants lying on his doorstep. He were the happiest man in this village when Silas went off to join the Army."

Uncle Silas had to face up to making a big decision before the Christmas festivities were barely over.

"There's a message from Uncle Silas for you to give to Grandad," Nicky told Jonathan at school one morning. "He need to see him urgent like."

His grandfather cycled in, wondering what it was all about.

"I've had a visit from one of them lawyer fellows," Uncle Silas told him. "I could do with your advice, Will."

The Solicitor had been friendly, but his message had been quite clear. It seemed that the shoot guest responsible for the accident had died, leaving no provision in his will for the continuation of the monthly payment of the compensation.

"But –" the Solicitor held up a reassuring hand as Uncle Silas went white, " – do not worry. The family feel under a moral obligation to ensure you are not disadvantaged."

The problem was administrative; the continuation of the payment on a monthly basis created difficulties for the trustees of the esate, and these could best be solved by a once and for all payment of five hundred pounds.

"Properly invested you could probably live off the interest," said the Solicitor. "You would be well advised to accept the offer."

Uncle Silas had opted to take the money.

"That'll give me the chance to put Jim and Enid on their feet," he said. "They could do with some help right now, what with the baby and all. My worry is the rent. Polly and me put our money together and we get by, but what happen after I've gone to meet my Maker? Will the Squire let her stay on? And if he do, can she afford thirteen shillings a week?"

He paused, and then came to the point which had been exercising his mind.

"Suppose I offer to buy this cottage off the Squire," he said. "You told me yourself he was planning to sell it after I'd gone. Only thing is, that'll leave me nothing to live on when what's left of the money run out. I'd have to go on the Parish, and that mean I'd have to sell the cottage again because you can't go on the Parish if you own property. And that mean that Polly would have nowhere to live."

"I have an idea," Jonathan's grandfather told him. "But give me a day or two to think it over. I have to talk to Eliza and Bert first."

Two days later he went to see Uncle Silas again.

"I've a proposition for you," he told him.

For some time he had been putting aside money to buy back the field he had sold to Mr Limmer, some fifteen years earlier, when times had been hard and he had needed the money badly.

"There's neither Bert, Jim nor Jack will want the farm when I'm gone," he said. "So that seem a bit daft paying Land Tax and fees and Stamp Duty to make the farm bigger, and me getting too creaky to take on the extra work anyway."

He paused and looked at both Uncle Silas and Aunty Polly.

"I'm thinking I'll put the money into buying this cottage from the Squire," he said. "I won't charge you any rent at all –" he held up his hand as Uncle Silas began to protest. " – All I ask is that you keep a roof over the heads of Polly and the boy, and use a little bit of your money to repair the roof and sort out the damp bits at the back. Then, when me and you's both pushing up the daisies, Polly and the boy will be alright."

The Squire showed no surprise when Jonathan's grandfather went to see him.

"I expected you to come up with the idea long before this," he said briskly. "Especially after our last conversation on the subject. You can have the cottage, freehold, for two hundred and fifty pounds."

Jonathan's grandfather was surprised; he had expected to have to try to beat the Squire down from a much higher sum.

"Provided," the Squire went on, looking at him speculatively, "I can reset the hedge and take thirty yards off the end of the garden to incorporate into my field."

For Jonathan's grandfather it was not really a good deal; but it brought the cost of the cottage into his price range, and the Squire probably knew it.

"I'll shake hands on that," he said.

A few weeks later he called in to see how Uncle Silas was getting on.

"This came in the post today," Aunty Polly gave him an oficial looking envelope. "That was sent to you by name at this address."

"The Deeds," he said, after a brief glance at the contents. "That's all settled. You neither of you need to worry about it any more."

Immediately after Christmas the weather took a turn for the worse; eighteen degrees of frost played havoc with Jonathan's chilblains, and he needed two stone hot water bottles and a house brick, left in the oven and wrapped in a pullover, to keep him warm in bed.

He marvelled at his grandfather; the only concession the old man made to the freezing weather was a pair of socks, with the toes cut off, over his hands, and a fisherman's oilskin over the moleskin waistcoat to reduce the wind chill effect. At night he disdained a hot water bottle, but grudgingly acknowledged the need for bedsocks.

Despite the cold, Polly took Nicky and Jonathan to the Haymarket Cinema to see Warner Baxter and Freddie Bartholomew in 'Kidnapped', which changed their fantasy adventure play from Cowboys and Indians for the next few weeks. Jonathan had only been to the cinema once since he had come to live with his grandparents, and that had been to see a Shirley Temple film. He had fallen for Shirley Temple at the time. But she was soon ousted in favour of Princess Margaret Rose, who he had seen in her Brownie uniform on their Cub visit to Sandringham. This did not last either, because of his anti-Royalist tendencies, nurtured by his having identified with the Commonwealth cause when reading stories about the Civil War.

Mid February brought a change for the better in the weather after the bitter cold of January. It also brought Jonathan and Nicky into serious conflict with their Uncle Bert.

Long standing tradition determined that the Wolf Cubs, Brownies, Girl Guides and Scouts used St. Valentine's Day to run money raising events. These included a collection to purchase equipment and to fund the annual outing, for which purpose the Church collecting boxes were borrowed; heavy oval wooden objects with a handle running from the base, they looked rather like table tennis bats with depth.

Jonathan wanted to man the coconut shy in the hope that he could filch one at some point, but Mrs Morvern firmly directed Nicky and himself with one box, and Colin and David with the other, to start at opposite ends of the village and work inwards. Before ten minutes were up they realised Colin and David were cheating by going through the village ahead of them; nearly every person they stopped had already donated. A brief skirmish ensued when, having caught up with them, Jonathan tried to surreptitiously swap boxes. But their box was so much heavier that he could not run very fast, and Colin easily caught him and tripped him up, while David sat on Nicky's head to stop him coming to Jonathan's assistance.

"This is no good," said Nicky grumpily, "we haven't hardly got nothing."

Then Jonathan had his bright idea.

"Let's sneak on to the bus," he said excitedly, "and go in to the City and collect round the Market. There'll be millions of people."

"Somebody will see us on the bus," Nicky said, but he was not really arguing against the idea.

"We'll tell them Mrs Morven said we could," said Jonathan "They're not really likely to ask her."

They needed fourpence for the bus but only had threepence between them.

"It'll be alright to take it out of the box," said Nicky, producing his knife, "seeing as how its going to get a lot more put in it than it would have done."

One or two people who knew them, including the driver, looked them over suspiciously, but nothing was said.

The harvest exceeded their wildest expectations; obviously the cheery beery farmers thought there was something highly amusing about a couple of Wolf Cubs wandering around with Church collecting boxes, and donated without hesitation. Jonathan kept a wary eye out for his grandfather because he did not think it would be a good idea to let him see them. Nicky felt, too, that they should avoid policemen.

"They ask too many questions," he said, "and we han't got all day to hang around answering them."

Their box was full to the brim in no time, and Nicky took of his pullover and used it as an impromptu sling, so that they could carry it between them. They walked out of the City, to pick up the bus on the outskirts, hoping thereby to reduce suspicion. By this time however, they were footsore and weary; also they were hot and thirsty.

'Tizer' said the advertisement in a small grocer's window, showing an enthusiastic child pouring himself a glass.

"We've no money," said Jonathan as they gazed longingly through the window at the crates of bottles in the dim recesses of the shop.

"The way I see it," said Nicky, "there's far more money in the box than we would have got ordinarily."

They dived into a small alleyway and Nicky got busy with his knife again.

They took it in turns to carry the box while the other swigged from the bottle, and then paused outside a baker's shop to gaze at the cream buns and pastries therein.

"I'm hungry," said Jonathan.

Ten minutes later they stuffed the remains of the cream buns into their pockets as the bus came round the corner.

"If we get off before we get to the village," Jonathan suggested, "we can just walk in and no one will know where we've been."

The same bus driver looked at them suspiciously, especially when they dismounted a good mile before their destination, but again said nothing.

"I reckon Mrs Morven will be right pleased with us," Jonathan said. "I bet we got more in our box than all the others put together."

Then, as they rounded the final bend, they came virtually face to face with Uncle Bert, his helmet pushed on to the back of his head to cool his brow. He was not very happy as he dismounted from his bicycle; neither for that matter were Nicky and Jonathan; quite apart from the encumbrance of the collecting box there was nowhere to run to.

"I've had half the village out looking for you these past two hours," Uncle Bert raged. "It were only that bus driver as stopped me calling out the police force to find you!"

"We only went to collect money in the City" protested Nicky.

"And we'll have got more than anyone else," Jonathan added. "I reckon you ought to be glad."

"Glad!" Uncle Bert looked as though he were going to swell up and burst, his moustache bristling, his face purple, and the turkey wattles standing out on his neck. "I'll give you glad! There's the Vicar, Mrs Morven, your Uncle Percy and as many men as I could raise, scouring the County for half a mile around looking for you."

Suddenly he pointed to the incriminating evidence.

"Where did you get that Tizer?"

He plucked the remains of the cream buns from their pockets.

"Where'd you get the money to buy these?"

But it was a rhetorical question because his eyes were already scrabbling over the tell tale scratches around the slit of the collecting box.

"Right!"

He threw the remains of their alfresco lunch, including the Tizer, over the hedge.

"I'll deal with this now," he said as he took off his trouser clips and walked over to prop his bike against a tree.

"I hope he don't put our names in his little book," Jonathan whispered to Nicky.

"I'd rather that than him tell Grandad and he give us a good hiding," said Nicky nervously.

"No you wouldn't," said Jonathan. "I knew a kid back in Gloucester as ended up in a Reformatory after he got his name put in the little book."

But Uncle Bert had no intention of involving their grandfather, or putting their names in his little book. Unhooking his handcuffs and truncheon, he removed his belt, folded it in two, grabbed hold of Jonathan and pulled him down over his thigh as he knelt on one knee.

Every lash, Jonathan lost count of how many, stung his rear end like a thousand wasps.

Nicky, standing by the roadside, shivered in anticipation and winced every time the supple leather descended on to the seat of Jonathan's shorts. As Uncle Bert finished with Jonathan, and reached out for him, he made a futile escape bid. Uncle Bert simply hooked an enormous hand under the snake belt holding up his shorts, and lifted him off his feet.

They huddled together, snivelling, in the roots of the tree, while Uncle Bert replaced his equipment and his trouser clips.

"I don't know if that's done you any good," he said. "But that's certain as anything made me feel a lot better."

As they dolefully trudged into the village, carrying the box, with Uncle Bert bringing up the rear, they were met by a reception committee which included an anxious Mrs Morven, the Vicar, Uncle Percy, Aunty Polly, their grandmother and most of the Cubs including an awed looking Colin and David.

That they were in disgrace there was no doubt, although Mrs Morven did keep saying, in a loud voice, how heavy the box was and that some account needed to be taken of the fact that their intentions had been good.

The Vicar looked angry.

"Both suspended from Cubs until further notice," he announced.

He was about to say more, but was interrupted by Uncle Bert, who always seemed far less in awe of the Vicar than everybody else.

"Before you make free with dishing out the penalties," he said, looking as nastily at the Vicar as he had looked at Jonathan and Nicky, "you should have note of two things. Firstly these two boys have already been thrashed, by me, and that should be punishment enough. Secondly –"

"The question of how much punishment is my –" the Vicar began, but was again interrupted.

"Secondly," repeated Uncle Bert, in a louder voice, looking at the Vicar with an even nastier expression, "it is quite clear that the Law has been broken by the adults responsible for organising this event, by reason of children under the age of twelve years being used to collect money unsupervised."

There was a long silence.

"Too much more said about it, and I'll have to consider whether I need to take any more action," said Uncle Bert as he cocked his leg over the bar of his bike and rode away.

No further reference was made to their suspensison from Cubs.

Later that evening Nicky and Jonathan compared bums in the petty, and disagreed over who had the most weals. They also discovered that the expression 'not able to sit down for a week' was not an adult exaggeration; it was at least that before either of them could sit, or even lie down comfortably. Colin and David demanded to be allowed to inspect the weals, and shuddered and affirmed their intentions of keeping out of Uncle Bert's clutches – indeed they were both noticably well behaved over the next several weeks. At least until the choir outing, when it was their turn to blot their copy book.

The combined visit and outing of the choir to Lowestoft and Yarmouth always took place at Easter, concluding with the singing of Easter hymns and anthems in one of the larger Churches.

It did not start too well, although the boys enjoyed the discomfiture of the adults when the char-a-banc broke down twice on the way there. In the end it limped into Yarmouth with the driver promising to get it fixed, so they went off to enjoy themselves without worrying too much about how they were to get home. None of them had swimming costumes so they found a secluded spot and bathed in the nude, despite the cold, until discovered by the Vicar and Mrs Morven who descended upon them in anger. Before they caught up with them they had combined their efforts to try to teach Nicky how to swim, but after they had come within a hairsbreadth of drowning him they abandoned the attempt. Each of them had been given a florin from the choir fund, and Jonathan used his to buy yet another Toby jug for his grandmother's collection.

The Paddle Steamer trip to Lowestoft was funded from the same source, so after watching the Punch and Judy show on the beach, they set off for the quay.

The sea was choppy, causing most of the adults to be seasick, so the Vicar, who suffered the worst, made the decision to return to Yarmouth by bus. The boys were quite peeved about this because they had enjoyed the battle with the elements.

It was too early in the season for all of the amusements to be open, and David and Colin expressed some dissatisfaction. Together with Nicky and Jonathan they had been put under the supervision of Cecily and Joan, David's elder sisters. So intent were the two girls upon keeping a rigid eye on Nicky and Jonathan – having been strongly warned to do so by Mrs Morven – that David and Colin were able to give them the slip quite easily. When they didn't turn up to catch the bus, Cecily and Joan were harangued by Mrs Morven and left to scour Lowestoft for them, and bring them straight to the Church in Yarmouth where the choir was singing.

Uncle Percy sat rubbing his hands and fondling his belt throughout the whole of the bus journey.

"Just you wait till I get a hold of them," he was muttering. "I'll give them the hiding of their lives, you see if I don't."

They were quite surprised to find them, looking the picture of injured innocence, waiting for the rest of the choir at the Church. It transpired that they had simply tacked themselves on to a family who were boarding the Paddle Steamer, and were halfway back to Yarmouth before it was discovered that they had not got tickets. The family to whom they had attached themselves suffered the embarrassement of not being believed when they denied all knowledge, and ended up having to pay for their tickets. David and Colin glibly justified the exercise by claiming they were only motivated by a burning desire to be sure of getting to the Church on time, so Uncle Percy was persuaded to suspend punishment.

To everybody's consternation however, they vanished somewhere betwen the Church door and the vestry, and the Service took place without them. It turned out that they had observed, sitting in the front row of the Congregation, the very family who had had to accept responsibility for them on the Paddle steamer. They felt, therefore, that it would be wiser to sneak out of a side door and engage with some other project for an hour. Uncle Percy, urged on by the Vicar and Mrs Morven, took them off to a secluded part of the Churchyard, removing his belt as he did so. They were further chastised the following day by Cecily and Joan, who somehow got overlooked and had to make their own way home from Lowestoft.

The char-a-banc coughed again before they were halfway home, and finally died at the side of the road. A friendly Inkeeper allowed them to sit in his parlour while the Vicar made desperate efforts on the telephone to find alternative transport. He finally returned with the news that Sam Sharpe was going to turn out with his Carrier's cart, and would be with them in about four hours.

"We can't all get on that," said Uncle Percy. "I'll borrow a bike and go home and come back with my coal lorry."

The men, and those of the older boys who could be trusted not to deliberately get their clothes dirty, piled on to the lorry while the rest of them waited for the Carrier's cart.

"This is like the old days," said Mrs Morven cheerfully, climbing up beside Sam.

It was the old type Carriers cart, pulled by two horses, where the passengers sat round the outside facing inwards, and as Sam had thoughtfully put some straw into the well of the cart, the boys burrowed into it and curled up like puppies. Some of the adults started a sing song, and they all began to enjoy the novel experience, although they were dog tired. The steady clip clop of the horses, the rumble of the wheels, the clouds scudding across the starlit sky and the twin lanterns casting a warm glow on to the road in front of them, combined to produce a romantic atmosphere which they all enjoyed.

Some of the boys started larking around, causing Mrs Morven to utter threats. After they had been cuffed by the adults they decided to burrow further into the straw and go to sleep. Then at some point Nicky put his boot in Jonathan's face, so Jonathan punched him in the back, then Nicky punched Jonathan, and in the flailing around some of the adults got their shins kicked.

"I'm going to have to sort them out," said Mrs Morven, but Sam, after looking round, told her not to bother.

"Mrs Frogget's dealt with it," he said.

Mrs Frogget, whose shins had taken the brunt of the punishment, had grasped a handful of Jonathan's hair and a handful of Nicky's and brought their heads together with a resounding thunk which nearly knocked them cold.

"I been wanting to do that to them two little devils all night," she said. "Now maybe we'll get some peace."

A period of relative calm followed the choir outing, especially as Nicky and Jonathan were extra careful to ensure that Uncle Bert did not observe them up to any mischief.

Uncle Silas told them about their three uncles one evening as they sat listening to his marvellous stories.

Both Bert and Jim had enlisted in Regular Battalions of the Norfolks long before the War started.

"Bert were in Ireland in nineteen fourteen," said Uncle Silas. "In the First Battalion. He went to France right at the beginning, so the poor devil have it right the way through until they went to Italy in nineteen seventeen."

Jim had been with the Second Battalion in India when the War began, and had ended up in Mesopotamia. He had missed the dreadful seige of Kut because he had been ill with dysentry when his Battalion marched, and could not accompany them.

"Like as not we wouldn't a seen him again otherwise," said Uncle Silas.

Uncle Jack had been with the Territorials, the Fifth Battalion, and had stayed in England until they went to Gallipoli in nineteen fifteen.

"That were a nasty thing happen out there with them Turks," said Uncle Silas. "Not that your Uncle Jack were in that or we wouldn't a seen him again either."

The Sandringham Company of the Norfolks had disappeared in it's entirety after charging the enemy, and only four years after the war did a War Graves Unit find a hundred and fifty bodies, of whom a hundred and twenty two were Norfolks, all in one grave.

"They had all been shot through the head," said Uncle Silas. "Which point to them being shot *after* they had been taken prisoner. But by that time our politicians had other fish to fry in that area; they didn't want to upset the Turks by making a fuss, so they let it slide."

Uncle Silas spat his contempt for politicians on to the hot bars of the fire grate, and then paused reflectively.

"You look at that War Memorial next time you walk past," he said, "and read through all the names and think on it. There was thirty five young men went into Kitchener's Army from this village, and only sixteen came back. Your Uncle Bert had six boys in the same class as him at school, all the same age as him. And he was the only one of those six to come back from France."

They learned another interesting fact about their Uncle Bert.

It was the recognised policy of the Norfolk County Constabulary to avoid posting a man as village 'bobby' to his own village, or even to his own part of the County, in case he should be biased for or against men with whom he had shared boyhood indescretions. Uncle Bert agreed with this policy, and had, in fact, not wanted to be posted to the village. He was not only happy where he was, but his promotion prospects could well be inhibited by a posting to a comparative backwater.

"There had been problems for years," said Uncle Silas. "The place had hardly been policed at all during and right after the War; poaching, violence and even stealing of livestock out of the fields was rife."

A crisis point was reached when the Squire, using his authority as a Magistrate, had to ride his horse into a near riot outside the King's Head one night, restoring order by laying about him with his horsewhip, while the elderly village Constable stood helplessly by.

"The Squire went to see the Chief Constable," said Uncle Silas, "and told him as the village needed a man who was known and trusted. That so happen that most of the village men had been under your Uncle Bert in the trenches in France; he'd been their Platoon Sergeant, so they already had a respect – maybe even a bit of fear for him."

He paused and grinned at them.

"I know you two little varmints might have other ideas," he chuckled. "But the fact is he's a damned good policeman. The best this village have ever had."

"You only say that because he give you a bottle of rum sometimes," said Nicky cheekily.

Uncle Silas chuckled again.

"Your Uncle Bert know I'm partial to a drop o' Lamb's Navy," he said. "Did I ever tell you how I got a taste for it?".

While he was a very young soldier, Uncle Silas' platoon had been called out to help the Customs Officers catch some smugglers.

"We had to march all the way to Castle Rising," he said, "because the horses had all gone down with the horse flu. Dog tired when we got there, and by that time the smugglers had scattered, and no sign of them or the rum they'd been running."

He chuckled as he remembered back nearly half a century.

"We caught up with one of them hiding in a barn. We was supposed to hand him over to the Excise Men, but our Sergeant knew him, having been born in the same village, and as our Officer wasn't around we all agreed we'd let the poor devil go, seeing as how they'd a put him in Norwich Jail for ever and a day. So what does he do but tip us off where him and his mates a hid some of the rum, hanging down a well."

His eyes moistened.

"So we get it all up, and the Sergeant make us all take an oath, and we put that rum in our haversacks and that's the last them Excise Men or the smugglers see of it."

As a story teller Uncle Silas had a rival in Ted Perriman, who had also seen service with the Colours in South Africa. If the boys were lucky they would catch them both together and hear them trying to outdo each other with their yarns.

Sadly Jonathan's grandparents had to say farewell to Ted after a friendship which had begun forty years earlier.

He had been planning to retire for some years, the tough physical demands of the job requiring the energy of a young man, and when the opportunity of a part time job as a ratcatcher came up near his widowed sister in Suffolk, with whom he was going to live, he took it.

Apart from an overture – through Jonathan's grandfather – to Uncle Jack in Thetford, the Squire made no effort to replace Ted, and the gamekeeper's cottage was still standing empty well into May.

His foresters were given a twelve bore between them, with instructions to shoot any vermin, and the tenant farmers were requested to protect pheasant eggs where they could. Bert became aware that one or two of the local poachers were having a field day, and after he had nabbed one in the act he went to see the Squire.

"I have my own Police duties to perform sir," he said. "That's one thing to help out a keeper when he ask; that's something else to do the job for him."

"Can't you persuade your brother to take it on?" the Squire had asked. "I would have thought he would have jumped at the chance to move back nearer home."

Bert had judged it wise not to tell the Squire of his brother's response to the suggestion.

"Give up a good job with a good Master to work for that old bugger!" hooted Jack, who thought the idea was funny. "He have another think coming I can tell you that!"

The day after the National Service Act was introduced to Parliament, the Squire had another word with Bert.

"It's as I expected Cooper," he said. "This War is now beginning to look inevitable to me. What's the point of paying a keeper's wages? Everybody will be too busy shooting Germans to shoot pheasants."

Bert was uneasy; he could keep tabs on local poachers, but when word got around the county he could have them travelling from miles around to attack an unguarded estate. He could expect no real support from his colleagues in neighbouring villages; they would even encourage their own poaching fraternity to ply their trade off their own patch.

In the end the Squire called a meeting of his three tenent farmers and invited Jonathan's grandfather and Mr Limmer along. All five would share in the work throughout the nesting season in return for being allowed to shoot pheasants and hares – for their own ovens only – come the Autumn.

Jonathan benefitted from this arrangement because his grandfather used the opportunity to begin Scott's training, and allowed him to be involved. He was fascinated by the interaction between man and dog as his grandfather took Scott through the various manoeuvres required. As with a sheep dog, Scott was helped by an instinct bred into him through generations of gun dogs. By keeping him at a distance initially, but then moving him closer every time, Jonathan's grandfather got him to the point of not even flinching when the twelve bore was discharged.

"A dog as is gun-shy is no use at all," he said. "I've seen a good dog ruined by having a shot blasted off in his ear the very first time out."

Early on he had taught Scott to carry an egg without breaking it.

"He have to have a soft mouth," he said. "No one wants to eat a pheasant as has been chewed up by the dog that's retrieved it."

Jonathan loved to search the Squire's woods for the pheasant's nests, becoming almost as adept as his grandfather at finding them, and carefully packing the best eggs in cotton wool before taking them home for his grandmother to place under a broody hen. The chicks looked cute when they were hatched out, but could not be kept for long as they had to be taken up to the Hall, to be kept in a wire enclosure, before they began to fly.

His one disappointment was that his rambles through the Squire's woods and fields could not be shared by Nicky.

Chapter Thirteen

Without doubt Nicky would have liked nothing better, had he been well enough, than to join in the fun of helping their grandfather 'keep' the Squire's game.

He had been puzzling his playmates for some time.

It was quite out of character for him to decline to come out to play, and even when he did come he seemed to tire of the game quickly and want to play something less strenuous, or even leave early to go home. He seemed quieter and more subdued, giving in very quickly whenever he was in conflict with the others over how they should use their time.

His mother put his lethargy down to Spring Fever at first, but in the end she took him to see Dr Dunbar who talked about 'growing pains' and told her to give him plenty of raw liver to eat to build up iron.

"I don't like raw liver," he complained bitterly, and battled furiously with his mother.

After a while the other boys got used to his absences, although Jonathan missed him more than Colin or David did, especially when Nicky opted out of the occasional week-end at the farm.

His mother took him back to Dr Dunbar when he did not pick up, and when they emerged from the Surgery Nicky was clutching an empty bottle.

"I have to keep spitting in it till it's full," Nicky told them. "And then I have to take it back for him to see if there's anything wrong with it."

"Go on then," said Colin. "Let's see you do it."

"Not likely," said Nicky. "I spit in that, and he find anything wrong with it, he's going to make me take some horrible medicine, or worse, he's going to make me eat that bloody liver again."

He shuddered at the thought.

"You'll have to fill the bottle," said David, "or he'll be mad at you."

"I'm going to get you three to take turns," said Nicky, holding out the bottle. "That way he won't find nothing wrong with it."

Rejoicing in the opportunity to conspire to defeat the adults, they were only too happy to oblige.

"He was pleased I'd filled the bottle so quickly," Nicky told them a few days later. "And he say that's 'clear' whatever that mean."

By early May he was away from school more often than he was there, and also began missing choir practice and Cubs. Came the time when his mother would not let the other three boys in when they called to play with him.

"He's not at all well," she would say. "He's asleep at the moment and he's never going to get better if you three keep waking him up and getting him excited"

"That's best to let him be," Uncle Silas put in. "The sooner he get better the sooner you'll have him back to play with you again."

They trooped disconsolately away and tried again three days later.

"Can't we just go in and see him?" they begged Uncle Silas, who was sitting guard at the door.

His expression softened as he looked at their anxious faces.

"Go you stand under his window," he said. "And I'll ask your Aunty Polly if he can talk to you for a minute."

After what seemed an age, Nicky's head and shoulders appeared.

"She won't let me come down nor you come up," he said. "But I can talk to you from here for a little while."

They were disconcerted by his appearance; his face had a curious pallor, with dark rings under his eyes, and he looked even thinner than they remembered.

"We thought maybe you wanted us to sneak you out over the washouse," Jonathan whispered. "Like we did that time when you got sent to bed early and we'd planned to catch sticklebacks."

Some of the old life came briefly back into Nicky's face.

"You can when I'm a bit better," he whispered back, and then he collapsed into a burst of coughing.

"Back into bed," they heard his mother say, but he resisted long enough to thrust his head out of the window once more.

"I want a Dandy," he called. "I've got a Beano –" the rest of his words were lost in yet another bout of coughing.

"He can have mine," Jonathan said, producing it out of his pocket, having just collected it from Mrs Brown's shop.

Both Polly and Silas looked tired, and somehow crumpled, when they presented themselves at the back door to hand it over.

"Can we come again tomorow?" Jonathan asked.

"Best not," she said. "I'll get word to Granny Cooper when that's alright for you to come again."

"I'm taking you into Norwich first thing in the morning, to get your new wellingtons," his grandmother told Jonathan after tea on the following Friday.

"Can we go a bit earlier?" he asked. "Then there'll be time, before the bus, for me to go and see Nicky."

His grandmother bit off the piece of cotton with which she was sewing on one of his buttons.

"No, we can't do that," she said.

"Why not?" his voice rose in frustration. "I never get chance to see him nowadays."

She sighed, pushed her work back on the kitchen table, and reached to pull him up on to her lap.

"Now you have to listen to me," she said softly, and seemingly groping for the right words. "Nicky's not at all well, and the best thing for him is to go where they can make him better. So first thing in the morning he's going into the Sanatorium at Kelling."

Jonathan felt himself go cold.

"Have he got –" he could not bring himself to say the word.

"He have just a touch of the Consumption," she said. "But you'll see; he'll be as right as rain in a few weeks."

But he had already buried his face in her bosom, weeping copiously. He had suspected it all along, but had refused to accept it. He knew that the mortality rate was high.

"What's the news?" his grandfather came in as he sat on the fender in his nightshirt, ready for bed.

"Polly's in a bad way," she told him. "So's poor old Silas. That's settled that Nicky have to go to Kelling in the morning. Percy have borrowed a car to take them across."

His grandfather was silent for a long time, gazing into the coals, before leaning down and pulling Jonathan up on to his knee.

"I suppose I'll have to tell you a story then," he said, with a forced attempt at jocularity.

"Not tonight Grandad," he said, a catch in his voice.

He was thinking of the fun he and Nicky had been having, only a few months ago, while Aunty Polly was in hospital; of the delighted amazement on Nicky's face when he showed him his secret hiding places; of Nicky's acceptence of his leadership when they were exploring forbidden territory in the Squire's woods; of his own readiness to accept Nicky's when they illicitly ventured into Norwich to try to sneak into the Circus.

When his grandfather next spoke, it was with a strong attempt at reassurance.

"Now don't you take on so," he said. "A lot of people get better from the Consumption."

He paused to push a hot coal back off the fire grate.

"You know young Vic Appleby? Well he have the Consumption as a boy; ten years ago that were. You wouldn't think it, to look at him now would you?"

He stopped and searched Jonathan's face.

"And David's father, your Uncle Bob. He have it as a boy, and he look quite healthy now don't he?"

Jonathan began to feel better.

Although he did not know it, his grandfather could have added that Vic Appleby's little brother and sister had also had it, and were dead within six months.

When Jonathan went to bed, he abandoned his usual practice of gabbling his prayers. While his grandmother stood patiently over him, he asked God to make Nicky better so that they could play together again. He gave an undertaking that he would never quarrel with Nicky, that he would give him all his toys and books, and that if ever Nicky wanted to play a game that he didn't, he would give in and let Nicky have his own way.

He felt even better afterwards.

He believed that everything would be alright now; his grandfather had told him that lots of people with Consumption got better. All God had to do was make sure that Nicky was one of them.

As he lay in bed he heard his grandparents talking down below.

"There's questions to be asked of that Doctor," his grandfather was saying. "That boy should a been in the Sanatorium long since."

"He only seem interested in them as has money," said his grandmother. "If Polly had been able to put her hand in her pocket he'd a visited every day."

Admittedly there was a Panel; everybody who paid sixpence a week was entitled to the services of a Doctor at any time, but it was an acknowledged fact that priority was always given by Dr Dunbar to patients who could pay in full for what they needed. His Junior partner, Dr Lethbridge, held a totally different attitude, but he dealt with patients more towards the City, so they seldom saw him. Even so, those who were able preferred to make the eight mile journey to his Surgery rather than put themselves in the hands of Dr Dunbar.

Within days of Nicky disappearing into Kelling, Jonathan's mother telephoned her brother Bert.

"Tell Mother to take him at once to Dr Lethbridge, not Dr Dunbar," she told him. "Tell her to tell him they've been close, sharing bed, toys – "

Dr Lethbridge examined Jonathan thoroughly.

"He seems fine," he told his grandmother. "But of course you must watch him carefully; any weight loss or listlessness or any unexplained aches or pains – bring him back to me."

"What I want to know is," his grandmother sounded belligerent, "why was that such a long time before Nicky got into the Sanatorium? He was ill for weeks."

"For some reason the standard tests did not reveal the presence of Consumption," said Dr Lethbridge. "Unfortunately that sometimes happens."

He skillfully deflected further questioning.

"I really cannot comment on another Doctor's case Mrs Cooper," he said at last. "You daughter-in-law must take it up with Dr Dunbar if she is disatisfied with any aspect of Nicky's treatment. But I can tell you this – " he too began to sound indignant – "I know the area your daughter-in-law used to live in. T.B. does not always reveal itself immediately, and bad housing, damp, poor sanitation – all these things can have a delayed effect. In my view, all the houses down at that end of Norwich where she used to live, should be razed to the ground."

"He start to get a bit political, him being a Socialist," she told Jonathan's grandfather later. "So I came away."

Jonathan's mother was not entirely satisfied, and began protracted negotiations involving Aunty Doris and Aunty Mavis which resulted, in the end, in arrangements for Colin, David and Jonathan to be examined by a top Specialist at the Hospital where she now worked. As the half promised trips to London had never materialised, this was to be his first visit since he had left Gloucestershire, and he looked forward to it with ever increasing excitement. So did Colin and David, neither of whom had ever been before.

His mother's arrangements had originally involved someone loading them on to the train, at Norwich Thorpe, for her to meet them off it at Liverpool Street.

"Are you mad Edith!" his grandmother had responded. "Them three little heathens on their own on a train, they'd never get there. Lord knows what mischief they'd get up to. Pull that cord thing like as not and get us all fined five pounds."

So his mother had to come to fetch them.

"I'm including a treat," she told them. "Sergeant Bews has been promoted to Colour Sergeant, and I'm taking you to Wellington Barracks to watch him drill the Sentries, but only if you behave yourselves on the journey."

They behaved fairly well, and Jonathan took great delight in pointing out landmarks to an awed Colin and David. They looked at the Houses of Parliament, and went into Westminster Abbey just as the choir were singing.

"They don't sing as good as us," said David pompously and innacurately.

Then came the big moment.

As the clock struck four, they observed the tall figure of Colour Sergeant Bews, wearing a peaked cap instead of his bearskin, and carrying a swagger stick instead of a rifle, marching across the Square at Wellington Barracks to inspect the guard. They watched as he was joined by an Officer, who was wearing a blue uniform and peaked cap with floppy bits hanging from the shoulders. Jonathan didn't think he looked as smart as Sergeant Bews.

A few crisp orders dismissed the sentries back to their guardroom, and Sergeant Bews disappeared back under the clock.

But he winked at them as he passed by where they were standing.

Another train took them to where they were staying overnight with Mrs Bews – although all three boys kept forgetting and calling her Miss Perriman – and they had their first view of the new baby. His name was George, which was Uncle Silas' middle name, and of course Jonathan's mother spent a lot of time making a fuss of him.

They were too tired to misbehave, so gave his mother a peaceful evening. Sergeant Bews was still on Orderly Duty, so they would not see him until he joined them next day when, having a few days leave, he and his wife and baby would be travelling back to Norwich with them to spend a few days with Uncle Silas and Aunty Polly.

Very early next morning they all set off together, and Mrs Bews went off to the Barracks while they made their way to the Hospital. Now that the exciting bit was over, and the boys were faced with the real purpose of their visit, they began to feel a bit nervous.

"Don't worry," Jonathan's mother reassured them. "It's only a Doctor examining you. His name is Dr Watson."

"Like in Sherlock Holmes," Jonathan quipped, having heard the Conan Doyle serial on the wireless.

Colin and David both thought this was hilarious, and giggled, but his mother was annoyed.

"Don't you dare make remarks like that in front of him," she snapped. "He's a very important man, and he's doing this examination as a personal favour to me."

They were all three of them overawed by the seemingly endless white tiled corridors, and smells of disinfectant and ether which, for Jonathan, brought back unpleasant memories of his incarceration in Gloucester Infirmary.

After ushering them into a small ante-room, his mother had to leave them.

"I'm on duty now," she said. "But I have permission to be with you during the examination."

A cheerful young nurse with a brisk manner came and told them to take off all their clothes, which they did with much giggling. She gave them each a blanket to wrap up in while they waited for the Specialist, and then left them by themselves.

After a few minutes they began to get restless, and started larking around trying to deblanket each other, until a door opened and an irate voice demanded to know what all the noise was about. That quietened them for a while; then David opened the door into the corridor and peered out.

"I'm going to find the lavvy," he announced, vanishing.

Jonathan and Colin followed him round several corners before finally getting directions from a startled looking nurse. Once in the toilet David had the idea of squirting water over the other two by holding his thumb on the tap outlet, and succeeded in drenching Colin, who complained bitterly.

"My blanket's all wet," he said. "I'll have yours," he added, fighting David for possession of his.

Jonathan helped, and succeeded in shutting the door on David so that Colin and he escaped with all three blankets, leaving David absolutely naked. They raced along several corridors before they realised they were lost. Not only that, they did not know which room to ask directions to.

The whole situation got out of control after that.

David, they later learned, had remained shivering in the ablutions for a while. Then, venturing out, he had been captured by a passing Doctor who had wrapped him in his white coat, to spare his modesty, before taking him in search of Jonathan's mother. She, in the meantime, had returned to find the room empty and the Specialist wondering where his appointments had got to. Scouring the corridor she had come across the captive David, whose totally biased and exaggerated account of his predicament resolved her to visit Colin and Jonathan with the wrath of God as soon as she caught up with them. This intent was so evident from the expression on her face, as she came face to face with them round a corner, that they immediately took to their heels, shedding their blankets in their haste.

The spectacle of a normally dignified nursing sister chasing two nude small boys down and round the corridors, before finally running them to earth in a linen room, excited comment from all quarters and took Jonathan's mother several weeks to live down.

The broad grin remained on the Specialist's face throughout his very searching and thorough examination.

"I can take it that these red marks on their buttocks are of recent origin and temporary in nature can I," he chuckled, as he inspected Colin and Jonathan.

Jonathan's mother, grim faced, said nothing.

As they dressed, a good hour later, he became serious.

"I'm pretty sure you have nothing to worry about Edith," he told her. "They should be watched of course – the usual monitoring – I don't need to spell it out to you."

She simmered right up to the time Sergeant and Mrs Bews came to collect them for the return trip.

"They've behaved very badly," she concluded her account, "and are to have no treats whatsoever on the way home."

She paused and glared at Sergeant Bews.

"Don't laugh at them Jim," she snapped. "The last thing they need is encouragement."

She had recovered her temper by the time she waved them goodbye at Liverpool Street Station, and as all three of them were very tired they slept for most of the journey, arriving so late that Jonathan stayed the night with Colin rather than have Uncle Percy turn out to take him home.

"Well, did you enjoy yourselves?" his grandmother wanted to know.

"We had a smashing time," he enthused, having resolved not to give her too detailed an account of the adventure.

He discovered that while he had been in London she had been over to Kelling, with his Aunty Polly, to see Nicky.

"He feels very poorly," she told him sombrely, "and that's going to be quite a while before they'll let him come home."

"Why couldn't you wait?" he stormed. "I could have come too."

"That's exactly why I went yesterday," she told him. "While you was out of the way, because I knew you'd want to come. And there'd be no telling you it would be a waste of time, with the Hospital not letting children in because of infection, because you wouldn't listen. And you'd a made a scene just like your making now. So that's why I snuck off while you were out of the way!"

He sulked for a while, but there was nothing he could do about it exept glare at his grandmother from time to time.

The following day there was more bad news.

They knew that Mr Price, their choirmaster, had been summoned to Wales to deal with family business following the death of an elderly relative, but they had always assumed it would only be a matter of time before he came back.

His letter to the Vicar contained the information that he had resigned from his job in Norwich, and was staying in Wales to run the family business.

"This means," the Vicar told Uncle Percy, "that I have to find a new choirmaster. Mrs Morven is not prepared to carry on trying to cope with all the jobs."

Mrs Morven did her best over the next few weeks, but they just went on singing those anthems and hymns they knew well enough to require the minimum of practice; she was not prepared to take them through anything new. The Vicar kept telling everyone he 'had someone in mind' to take over, but it was Steve Wright, with an air of deep gloom, who broke the awful tidings. Having won a scholarship to the Grammar School the previous year, he spoke with first hand knowledge.

"I'm leaving the choir if my dad'll let me," he announced dramatically, as they filed in to the Church. "I've heard today we're getting old Mumford."

"Oh no!" Ted Staple blanched. "He's the reason I decided to leave the Grammar School!"

This was not strictly true – he hadn't decided to leave, he'd been thrown out – but they let it pass for the moment.

"Who is this Mumford?" they wanted to know.

"He teaches history at our school," said Steve. "He's a bastard," he added succinctly.

Mr Mumford also deputised for the Music Master at the Grammar School because he played the piano as a hobby, and knew something about Church choirs. He was hated by the boys because of his excessive discipline, believing in the adage 'spare the rod and spoil the child'. Where other teachers used the cane only to punish bad behaviour, Mr Mumford used it in an attempt to improve academic performance.

"Every lesson he'd pick out the kid with the lowest mark and cane him," said Steve. "Even if he'd tried hard to get it right."

He winced as if at some recent painful memory.

"That meant that someone got the cane at every lesson," Ted broke in. "Worse still, he used to plonk all the exercise books on the desk at the beginning of the lesson, and not say who was going to be caned until just before the end. So you'd be sitting there all the way through, wondering if you were going to be 'it'."

He shivered.

"He was made to stop in the end," Steve said, "because one kid was a bit slow, and he got it all the time until his dad complained. But old Mumford found other ways of making sure someone got caned."

Mr Mumford attended a meeting with the Vicar and the adult members of the choir, during which he told them he wanted permission to use his cane on the choirboys if they did not toe the line. Uncle Percy threatened to withdraw Terry and Colin if he did, and as Terry was the only decent treble solo, the Vicar exercised his veto.

Unfortunately Mr Mumford's arrival coincided with Mrs Morven's absence on a long holiday in France.

"The fact is," they heard her telling the Vicar, "I'm certain there's going to be a war with Germany. If I don't seize the opportunity now I may never get another one."

Not only did her absence contribute to the disasters that followed her departure; everybody agreed that they would not have occurred at all had she been around.

They had their first intimation of trouble on the very first practice night, when Mr Mumford announced that his son, Paul, would be joining the choir. At first they were suspicious, but Paul, who went to school in Norwich, turned out to be so subdued and self effacing that they had not the heart to use him as a butt for their hostility towards his father.

They soon found out why he was subdued.

"You stupid boy!" his father yelled at him, hitting him across the face with the flat of his hand. "Can't you read the notes?"

He faced the rest of the choir, white with passion.

"You boys will soon learn that I'm not to be trifled with," he stormed. "Unless you do as you are told, you will be out of the choir. Now do you understand?"

"I'm leaving anyway as soon as my voice is right broken," said Terry later. "But I'll leave now if he carry on like this. I tell you, he'd better not hit me like he hit Paul."

On Sunday they had evidence that Mr Mumford's punitive attitude towards his son was normal routine. As Paul pulled his cassock over his head, while he was unrobing after the Service, his shirt rode up exposing several weals across his back.

"My dad straps me," he responded to Terry's sympathetic enquiry.

From that point onwards they tried to protect him as much as they could; even taking some of the blame for his mistakes. But that only led to slaps across the face for them.

The only time Mr Mumford restrained himself was when any of the men turned up for practice, which wasn't very often because they did not like him either. Word began to filter back to parents, and Jonathan's grandmother asked, with some curiosity, what was going on.

Jonathan was reserved in his reply; he expected her to assume he had been up to mischief, and deserved to be slapped, so he simply said that none of them liked Mr Mumford.

"That could be because he's doing his job and making you work instead of larking about," she said. "But I'll have a word with Doris and Mavis and see what they think."

At their next practice they were kept outside when they arrived, while raised voices told them that Uncle Percy was with Mr Mumford, and seemed to be having an argument with him. He emerged, looking grimly satisfied, a few minutes later, but Mr Mumford did not look at all happy.

"Some of you have been complaining to your parents about my attempts to make a decent choir of you," he shouted. "Well I'll tell you this. If you don't like the way I run the choir you can get out and make way for boys who want to join."

Uncle Percy's intervention worked however; for the next two weeks Mr Mumford hardly shouted at them at all, and they even began to stop dreading practice nights.

"Mrs Morven will be back the week after next," said Jonathan's grandmother. "She'll get him sorted out."

But the crunch came the following practice night; not only for Jonathan at the sharp end, but for the rest of the choir as well. Unlike Mr Price, who allowed them to learn the Latin as they went along, Mr Mumford expected them to be word perfect before they began to come to grips with the music.

"I expect you to know, and correctly pronounce, every word of the Ave Maria," he had announced. "Any boy who does not know it by next Friday will be in dire trouble."

Jonathan fell into a panic on the following Thursday, as did most of the others, but in the end he memorised the words quite easily, and his grandmother, having been a Catholic, was able to check him and help with the pronunciation. Even so, although he was sure he knew it, he hoped Mr Mumford would not pick on him to recite it.

He was out of luck; he was the very first to be picked upon.

"Come on Jonathan," Mr Mumford snapped. "Let's have it."

As he progressed through it, Jonathan could feel his confidence returning. He knew he was getting it right.

"Ave, Maria, gratia plena, Dominus tecum, et benedictus fructus ventris tui Jesu," he chanted. "Sancta Maria, Mater Dei, ora pro nobis nunc, et in hora mortis nostrae."

He felt satisfied and relieved.

But Mr Mumford was not.

"Have you not forgotten something boy?"

Jonathan racked his brains desperately, but he was sure he had got it right.

Mr Mumford lowered his face to a level with Jonathan's, who found himself focussing on Mr Mumford's yellowing teeth, and savouring his foul breath.

"What – have – you – forgotten?" he yelled, accompanying each word with a stinging slap across the side of Jonathan's head.

Jonathan felt the anger of frustration. He was sure he had got it right.

"Amen – Amen – Amen," Mr Mumford yelled, again accompanying each word with a slap. "You forgot to say Amen."

Jonathan's frustration turned to bitter resentment; his anger to rage.

Of course he hadn't forgotten it; he had simply taken it for granted, as he felt Mr Mumford should have done.

"Don't just stand there you wretched boy," Mr Mumford hissed, again thrusting his face close to Jonathan's. "What have you to say to me?"

"Go and fuck yourself," Jonathan told him.

There was an appalled silence.

The pigeons stopped cooing in the belfry; even the wind stopped soughing round the Church tower.

"Sir," Jonathan added ingratiatingly, making a futile attempt to reverse the inevitable slide into disaster.

Into the continuing silence a boy behind him nervously broke wind, and Jonathan giggled.

Mr Mumford brought the palm of his hand up, almost from floor level, to explode on his cheek with a loud crack, bowling him over like a ninepin – or to be more accurate a domino, because he took a straight line of choirboys down with him.

He was too shocked to cry. He seemed to be hearing sounds strangely muffled, as though under water. He was dimly aware that David and Colin had hauled him to his feet and were standing with protective arms around him, while a white faced Terry was between him and Mr Mumford.

"You hit him again and I'll hit you," Terry was saying.

It was a brave gesture on Terry's part; not that Mr Mumford was a big man – he was barely an inch taller than Terry – but he seemed to have completely lost control of himself, and turned into a dangerous raving lunatic in the space of a few moments. He threw a flailing arm at Terry, which missed by a fraction, whereupon Terry quick wittedly toppled the heavy brass lectern on to him.

"That's it," yelled Terry. "Come on kids – we're all going home."

"Come back at once," screamed Mr Mumford as they all trooped down the aisle. "Get back into the choirstalls, or I'll thrash the lot of you!"

It was not just Terry's forceful leadership that caused everybody to respond, so much as a real fear of remaining in the Church with a man who appeared to be completely deranged and capable of any form of violence. Turning around at the door Jonathan was dimly conscious of one solitary choirboy in the stalls; Paul looking crumpled and vulnerable as he cowered down into the corner of his seat.

Uncle Percy heard them out, but, before he could comment, a hammering on the front door heralded the arrival of several other parents who wanted to know what was happening. Some of them were all for going down to the Church there and then, and taking Mr Mumford apart, but Uncle Percy sounded a note of caution.

"It's a pity Bert Cooper's away," he said. "As it is, I reckon the Vicar will have to sort this lot out."

Jonathan began to feel worried.

So far his own contribution to the evening had not been given a public airing, and he did not particularly want too many questions asked.

His grandfather was up at Limmers, acting as midwife to a Friesian, when he arrived home with Uncle Percy.

His grandmother was aghast.

"For God's sake don't tell your grandfather about this," she told him. "I don't want him going up there and fisting that Mumford man and getting himself into trouble."

The Vicar dropped in a few days later.

"I'm going to suggest we forget the whole unpleasant incident Mrs Cooper," he said. "As it happens Mr Mumford has enough to trouble him. His wife has left him it seems, taking the boy with her. He has been ill-treating the child for years, but nobody dare report it."

The sequel did not become public knowledge until several weeks later.

By a curious stroke of irony, Captain Canfield was sitting on the Bench when Mr Mumford was charged by the N.S.P.C.C with ill-treating his son Paul.

"It seems to me," the Squire had said nastily, "that the moment a man tries to introduce some discipline into his dealings with his children, there are a bunch of 'do-gooders' around to discourage him from doing so. Not Guilty!"

So Mr Mumford continued to teach history to the unfortunate Grammar School Boys, but there was, of course, no question of his resuming his role as choirmaster.

The choir struggled on in the doldrums, with Mrs Morven doing her best. Several attempts were made to find a good choirmaster, but in the end the Vicar had to take over the job himself.

Chapter Fourteen

'Dear Cousin Nicholas,' Jonathan wrote, rather formally.

'We would like you to get better so you can play with us again. We would like to come and see you but they won't let us.'

'Your Loving Cousins, Jonathan, Colin and David.'

The reply came a week later, via Aunty Polly.

'Dear Cousins Jonathan, Colin and David,' it said.

'It is not nice here although the nurses are kind. I want to come home. They will not let you come and see me. I keep asking. Your Loving Cousin, Nicholas.'

The paper on which it was written was crinkled and grey.

"The nurse hold it in front of a steaming kettle," his Aunty Polly explained, "to make sure of killing any germs."

It now being several weeks since Nicky had been taken to Kelling, Jonathan had reached the stage where he was not missing him so much. He was allowed to spend more time in the village now, and played with other children besides Colin and David. He still had occasional days when he fretted for Nicky, but more often than not he would forget him for several days at a time, and would then feel strangely guilty for having done so.

"That's in God's hands now," his grandmother said, when he remembered to ask how Nicky was.

Towards the end of May she gave him firm instructions to stop calling on his Aunty Polly and Uncle Silas. Colin and David were told the same.

"They have too much on their minds just now," she said. "Just leave them in peace for a while."

A temporary distraction was provided by the arrival, once again, of Haysel time. He had really been looking forward to Nicky helping them this year, but once he was sitting up on Sampson, watching out for snags that would jam the knives, he lost himself in the sheer enjoyment of it. Planning on holding less livestock this year, and concentrating on his milkers instead, his grandfather needed less hay for himself. Because of this they carted less to their barn, but turned right instead of left out of the field gate and took it direct to Limmer's. Sampson was removed from the waggon and harnessed to an elevator to take the hay to the top of the Dutch barn. It was the only time Sampson ever objected; he had to walk round in continuous circles to work the gears and he did not like it. He was always coaxed into it in the end, snorting and blowing his disgust, and even laying his ears back.

"He think that's beneath his dignity," Jonathan's grandfather chuckled. "That's usually a pony, or even a donkey that's given that job."

Another distraction was provided by Scott, whose training was coming on by leaps and bounds. Pheasants were out of season, but Jonathan's grandfather shot an old sick bird just to try Scott out with the retrieve, as he had only had the opportunity to test him with rabbits thus far.

Scott's coat seemed to have changed colour a little as he matured, and was now more distinctly yellow than creamy white. His broad forehead, gentle but alert eyes, and well proportioned body clearly marked him as a thoroughbred.

"I have to give due where it belongs," said his grandfather grudgingly. "The Squire did me a big favour getting me this dog. He's one of the best I ever had."

Over these distractions however lay a continuing sense of foreboding; even when Nicky was not being talked about he was somehow in the back of their minds. Jonathan had stopped asking questions about him because he was afraid of the answers.

His mother came again, and used most of her time to go to the Sanatorium with Polly, looking very subdued on her return. Two days later his Uncle Bert suddenly appeared in the lane, bumping his bike over the ruts.

"What have you come for?" Jonathan wanted to know as he ran to meet him.

Uncle Bert's usual response to this question was a brusque command to 'mind your own business,' but this time he reached down and ruffled Jonathan's hair, something he had never done before.

After he had left, about ten minutes later, Jonathan went into the house and climbed on to his grandmother's lap.

"What did Uncle Bert come for?" he asked, but really he knew.

"He come to tell us that Nicky's very ill," said his grandmother.

Jonathan suddenly found difficulty in breathing.

"Is he going to die?" he heard himself asking, aware that his grandmother's cheeks were wet.

"We have to hope and pray –" she began, but his grandfather interrupted.

"No," he said. "That's not the way to do it. That's no use to pull the wool over the boy's eyes. He have to know the truth."

He held out his hands.

"Come you here now, boy Jonathan."

As he stood in front of him, Jonathan looked and saw pain.

"That may happen," his grandfather said. "And you have to know that."

Jonathan nodded, and drifted in a dreamlike state out of the kitchen, across the yard, through the gate and down the lane, slashing at nettles with a switchy stick as he moved along, aware of a dreadful feeling inside himself.

He was not able to cry.

Halfway through the night he awoke and crept into his grandparent's bed, taking comfort from the feel of his grandfather's broad solid back and his grandmother's comforting arms. Still in a dreamlike state he went to school next morning, and found a white faced David waiting for him. Colin and Terry, equally white faced, joined them.

"Our Dad had to take Aunty Polly and our Mum over to the Sanatorium," said Terry. "Uncle Bert had a phone call in the night."

Polly had been with Nicky when he died.

It had taken Percy and Doris nearly two hours to persuade her to leave the Sanatorium, and Doris had to hold her tight all the way home.

"That were awful," said a ravaged looking Percy. "She kept saying that, at bottom, it were all Arthur's fault for leaving them nine years ago, and that she hope his soul rot in Hell."

Strangely enough she seemed to have recovered somewhat by the time they got her home, and was even able to attempt to comfort Silas, who was nearly distraught. Jonathan was collected out of school by his grandparents, and taken to the cottage where the whole family had gathered in support. Polly sat in a corner saying little, but at one point she called Jonathan across and hugged him.

"You'll miss him nearly as much as I will," she said softly.

The next day Mrs Morven came across Colin, David and Jonathan, huddled weeping in a corner of the play ground. Abandoning her class she took them all home, even though it meant a round trip of four miles.

His grandmother was able, in some way, to subordinate her grief to his, recognising that he needed her soft bosom to cry on. But it was to his grandfather that he turned mostly; dogging his footsteps and wrapping his arms around his hips whenever he paused long enough in his work to stand still for a moment.

Four days later, Jonathan, together with Colin, David and the rest of the choir, all in their choir robes, wept openly and unashamedly as they watched the little coffin being lowered into the ground.

Polly stood, seemingly frozen, for what seemed like an eternity before allowing Jonathan's mother and grandmother to lead her gently away. Bert, his face softer than Jonathan had ever seen it, pushed a weeping Silas back to the cottage in his wheelchair.

The day after the funeral Jonathan asked his grandmother:

"Why did God let Nicky die?"

She made no reply, but hugged him.

"Either He's not as strong and mighty as the Vicar say, and couldn't stop it," he said angrily. "Or else He want Nicky to die. If that's so I don't like him anymore."

His grandmother's residual Catholicism surfaced.

"That's nearly blasphemy," she said, crossing herself. "Speak to him Will."

His grandfather shook his head, and said nothing.

But children are resilient.

Only a few days later Colin and Jonathan giggled, with only a slight pang, when they recalled the time Nicky's sandal had disappeared into a foot of mud, and he had gone home in one of Jonathan's in the belief, mistaken as it happened, that Jonathan would be less likely to get a cuffing for losing it.

Only once did they come close to relapsing into grief.

"What's up crybaby?" sneered David, coming across Colin, at choir practice, with tears in his eyes.

"Mrs Morven's fitting out the new kid with Nicky's choir robes," muttered Colin.

David fell silent.

One evening, three weeks after Nicky's funeral, Jonathan's grandparents were visited by Percy and Doris, together with Bob and Mavis.

"The fact is Master," Percy spoke hesitantly, "that Polly's in a bad way. We all spend a lot of time with her, and Silas is a great comfort even though he's full of grief himself. But something have to be done and that's a fact."

Polly appeared to have withdrawn into herself since Nicky's death. She kept the cottage spotlessly clean, and looked after Silas, but she had taken to walking across to the Churchyard four or five times a day to stand for an hour at a time by Nicky's grave. She would stare blankly at people she met in the street, and would only speak if asked a direct question. Then the Vicar, disturbed in the middle of the night, had looked out of his bedroom window and observed her standing by the gaveside in pouring rain. Dr Dunbar had been called in, and the word 'committed' had been bandied around.

"What that come down to Master," Percy had concluded, "is that only you can sign the papers, seeing as there's no closer relative."

Jonathan's grandfather was unequivocal.

"There's no papers being signed by me," he said flatly. "The idea of putting the poor woman into an Asylum because she's grieving for her dead child, is not one that I would countenance."

Both grandparents began to call round more often, but neither his grandmother's "Pull yourself together Polly," nor his grandfather simply sitting ready to listen, were of any avail.

"She dust and clean the boy's room and remake his bed every day," Silas confided to them. "All she say, when I try to get her to see reason, is that the boy will be coming home from the Sanatorium soon, and everything have to be ready for him."

Then came a disturbing time for the whole family when she disappeared for several hours one Sunday, and Bert had a telephone call from the Sanatorium to say she was there, demanding to see Nicky, and refusing to leave. Bert had taken off his uniform, and he and Percy had driven over to fetch her, the doctor having given her something to calm her down.

Jonathan found his own involvement both uncomfortable and even frightening; more than once she addressed him as 'Nicky'. The incident he found particularly unnerving arose from a visit he made after Cubs one evening. A thread had been pulled after a particularly boisterous game, and his jersey had started to run.

"Boy Nicholas! Do you think I have money to burn?" she stormed, cuffing him round the head. "Go you upstairs this instant and take it off. And you can put yourself to bed as a punishment for not taking care of your clothes."

As he stood, gaping, his Uncle Silas had moved his wheelchair closer and gently restrained her.

"Go you on home now boy Jonathan," he had said softly.

It was Mrs Morven who eventually provided an answer to the problem by unearthing the existance of a Church of England Rest Home, somewhere near London, for cases like Polly's.

By putting pressure on the Vicar, and Dr Dunbar, she managed to secure a bed at the Home, and then set about organising fund raising events to pay for it.

Every member of the family contributed of course, but there was an overwhelming response from almost every household in the village. By the time all this had been done Polly's condition had deteriorated to a point where she was scarcely rational, and it took the combined efforts of Jonathan's grandfather, with both Bert and Percy, to get her into the car for the journey.

On the Vicar's and Doctor's advice the cottage was virtually cleared, during her absence, of everything connected with Nicky. His toys and clothes were removed, even his bedding. Even those of his toys which had been left at the farm were included.

"Is that everything?" Jonathan's grandmother demanded, poised over the cardboard box into which it had all been packed. "We don't want her visiting out here and being upset by seeing something of his that remind her."

"There's nothing else," Jonathan said dully, feeling guilty because he knew there was.

Nicky's Teddy Bear was still sitting, next to his own, in the secret hiding place in the barn. He wanted to leave them there, and it was unlikely that his Aunty Polly would ever know.

His mother visited Polly several times at the home, and, with the help of the doctor in charge, told her that the cottage had been stripped of Nicky's things, and why. She did not, however, tell her that they had all been stored in Percy's attic, so that they could be retrieved in the event of the disposal turning out to be a mistake.

After a while Polly accepted the situation, and seemed quite calm when she returned to the village several weeks later. She was still depressed and withdrawn, but she only visited the grave once a day thereafter. Jonathan had resumed his visits to Uncle Silas, and simply carried on. She never again confused him with Nicky, but she would occasionally reach out and touch him, or hold his hand for a moment. After a while he stopped feeling embarrassed or uncomfortable about it.

Most of the village children were rather subdued in the first weeks following Nicky's death; indeed Uncle Bert commented on it.

"I'm not too sure I wouldn't sooner see them up to some mischief," he said wryly. "That seem unnatural to me, them being so quiet."

It was shortly after this that he produced his own momentous news.

"I'm off to King's Lynn," he said. "Transfer on promotion."

Some of the children at school had seen him sporting Sergeant's stripes that morning, but Jonathan had thought they were pulling his leg.

Strangely, the news filled them with gloom.

"He was always fair," said Terry. "And you knew where you was with him. We don't know what the new bloke will be like."

Most of the adults in the village, – even those who had felt his hand on their collar at some time – expressed regret at his departure. Some of the older people, for whom he had always time for a friendly word, were quite upset.

With amazing rapidity a farewell 'do' was arranged, to take place in the Village Hall, and the Squire was prevailed upon to make the presentation of an antique clock.

The Superintendant came from Yarmouth, and made a speech reassuring everybody that the area would continue to be well policed. The Squire, in the process of handing over the clock, thanked Uncle Bert, in his clipped staccato voice, for the work he had done for the village.

Then Bert rose to his feet.

He betrayed some emotion, and he was obviously touched by the evidence of goodwill surrounding him. He spoke hesitantly at first, thanking everybody for their kindness, but struck one slightly bitter note.

"That look to me," he said," as if the job we thought we had finished in nineteen eighteen have to be done all over again. When I think of all the names on that Memorial, names of men who had the right to expect they'd got things sorted out for their sons and grandsons, well I reckon they're turning in their graves right now."

He sat down to applause followed by a rousing chorus of 'for he's a jolly good fellow.'

The move was achieved incredibly quickly, and in full accord with standard Police procedure. One evening Bert was seen on duty in the village High Street, with Eliza fetching in washing off the line at the police house, and no sign of an impending move. The next morning, at breakfast time, a pantechnicon was seen drawing away, having just offloaded the new policeman and his furniture. Ten minutes after that he was on duty in the High Street, while his wife was hanging out *her* washing on the same line.

The other momentous news affected Jonathan even more directly.

His mother, after nearly two years hard labour in the London hospital, had obtained her additional qualifications. But the significance of this had become lost in the trauma and aftermath of Nicky's death.

"Your mother's going up in the world," said his grandmother, waving the letter that had arrived in the morning post, as they played with his snakes and ladders on the hearthrug.

"Never mind that," he said. "It's your go."

"Put that board up on the table," she said irritably. "I'm sure you make me bend down there so you can cheat easier."

"There's no room," he pointed out.

She had covered most of the table with cooling preserving jars, having just made several batches of various jams, including her delicious rasberry and blackcurrent.

She got fed up and let Jonathan win the game, and then referred to the letter again.

"She's going to try for an Assistant Matron's job. But not in London she says."

"Maybe down here," said Jonathan. "Then she could come more often."

He had forgotten this little exchange, but was reminded of it a few weeks later when he arrived home from school to find his grandparents looking solemn.

"There's a letter from your mother," his grandmother said.

"Did she send any money?" he asked, not with a great deal of hope.

Sometimes his mother would fold a sixpence in a wad of paper and include it in the envelope.

"You remember me telling you she was going after a new job?" said his grandmother. "Well, she have got one."

She paused for dramatic effect.

"Can you guess where it is?" she asked.

Jonathan shook his head, only half interested.

"In Gloucestershire!" his grandmother said. "Back at the place she was at before she brought you here."

"Gosh," he said. "Perhaps I'll be able to go and see her, and see all the kids I used to play with."

"I think she have a bit more than that in mind," his grandfather said casually. "She's thinking of having you back to live with her."

Jonathan chuckled.

"I live here now," he said. "I can't live in two places."

He munched contentedly at a slice of bread and jam.

He suddenly became aware that they were still looking at him with the same solemnity, but with an added wariness.

"You have to now listen to me," said his grandmother sharply. "Your mother is saying she have been given a flat in that Convalescent Home just so that she can have you to live with her."

"She want to take you back to Gloucestershire for good," his grandfather said. "To go back to live there, and go to school there, just like you did before. You wouldn't be living here with us any more."

Jonathan felt his mouth go dry, his head begin to swim, and his bowels turn to water.

Almost as if he were watching himself from outside of himself, he saw himself throw a temper tantrum. He stamped his feet and screamed at the top of his voice. "I won't go – I won't go – she can't make me – I won't go – "

He became aware that his grandmother was trying to restrain him.

"Do something Will," she gasped. "I can't hold him. He'll have a fit or something."

"Just let him be," said his grandfather, who had not moved out of his chair. "He'll work himself out of it."

Five minutes later he lay shivering and exhausted on the hearthrug. Only when he had virtually immobilised himself did his grandfather speak.

"Come you here," he said quietly.

Jonathan climbed shakily to his feet, drooping from sheer fatigue, as his grandfather leaned forward, grasping his shoulders, to stare straight into his eyes.

"Now I want you to understand what I'm saying," he said slowly and distinctly. "What I'm saying is this."

He paused for several seconds to make sure Jonathan was hearing him.

"If you don't want to go to Gloucester, then you don't go to Gloucester," he said.

He paused again, and put it another way, determined to leave Jonathan in no doubt.

"If you want to stay here living with us, then you stay here living with us."

Jonathan heard what he said, but was too emotionally drained to feel anything, even relief. He tossed and turned all that night, and was aware, at one point, of his grandmother standing by his bed holding a candle.

The next morning he was tired and listless, but more able to feel reassured when his grandfather pulled him up on to his knee after breakfast.

"Granny's writing to your mother telling her you're staying here," he said.

He was still a bit subdued when he arrived at school, and Mrs Morven spotted it.

"My mum want's to take me away from Granny and Grandad," he told her, in response to her searching questions. "And I don't want to go."

She looked pensive for a moment.

"Tell Granny I'll be out to see her tonight," she said.

His mother was staggered by the volume of mail she received a few days later.

Her mother wrote an impassioned epistle, implying that her father would disown her if she took Jonathan away from them. Mrs Morven wrote a three page letter outlining his progress, and claiming that his education would suffer disasterously if he were moved. Doris and Mavis, probably prompted by Colin and David, wrote in support of his remaining, and so did Uncle Silas.

His Aunty Polly wrote:

'I know you'll think I want to keep him around because he reminds me so much of Nicky, and there may be a lot of truth in that. But I feel it would be wrong to take him away from the family now. Please leave him be Edith.'

Mr Kemp wrote:

'Your father needs the boy around to give him a purpose in life.'

But perhaps the most surprising correspondent was her brother Bert.

'You'd be making a bad mistake Edie,' he wrote on Norfolk Constabulary headed paper.

'He's no angel, that's true. But he's a king to the little varmint he was when you first brought him. Our father have him straightened out, and you could undo all that by taking him away. Our Jack say the same.'

In the teeth of so much opposition, his mother capitulated.

'Tell boy Jonathan I'll not take him away from you,' she wrote to her mother, 'but I'll keep the flat on so that he can come and stay during the holidays'.

Gradually Jonathan lost his fear, and began to resume a fairly normal life, at least until she came on her next visit. As the taxi appeared, lurching down the lane, he went and hid in his secret hiding place and refused to come out. When hunger finally drove him indoors, he greeted her with sullen reserve.

"Granny's told you I'm not taking you away," she said. "So why are you being so awkward?"

He knew why, but could not find the words to explain. He drew back his foot and kicked her hard on the shin bone.

"God!" she gasped, hopping about on one leg and frantically massaging the other.

His grandfather, grasping a big handful of Jonathan's shirt and jersey with one hand, lifted him off his feet and carried him into the scullery while removing his own belt with the other.

Then, his anger subsiding, he put his belt back on.

"I know I've threatened," he said. "But I've never once used this on you in the whole of the two years you been here, and I'm damned if I'm going to start now."

They both listened to Jonathan's mother's bad language coming from the kitchen.

"Go you in now and tell her you're sorry," his grandfather said.

"No," he said.

Apart from that first day, two years ago, he had never defied his grandfather.

There was a long heavy pause.

"I'm not telling you to," said his grandfather. "I'm asking you to – as a favour to me."

There was another long pause.

"Alright," said Jonathan.

His grandfather cocked an ear towards the kitchen.

"I've never heard your mother cuss like that before," he said wonderingly. "I never knew she knew the words."

Jonathan and his mother made it up with a bedtime cuddle of course, and they were back on their old terms by the time she left two days later.

"I'm coming back here for a few days after I've moved to Gloucester," she told him. "How about coming back there with me for a couple of weeks as it's school holidays? You can see all your old friends, and I'll have time to take you places."

He thought for a moment.

"I don't really want to come just yet," he said. "I've got the Choir outing, and the Cub weekend, and then I'll be helping with the harvest."

"You could be back for those," she said. "Think about it anyway."

"You know," his grandfather said, as they were leaning on the barnyard gate a week or so later, "your mother must be feeling a bit peeved at all the fuss you made about her wanting to take you to Gloucester. Happen she might just feel a bit better if you went and had a couple of weeks with her."

"She might not let me come back," Jonathan said, expressing the real fear that had been lurking ever since his mother had first raised the idea of a holiday.

"I already thought of that," his grandfather told him. "And when she asked me to try to talk you into it I made her promise, come what may, she'll bring you back after two weeks."

"Promises are like pie crusts – " Jonathan began.

" – Easily broken," his grandfather grinned.

"Now you be sure and have a good time," his grandmother said, the following week, buttoning up his coat and brushing him down, while his mother and grandfather carried the cases out to the gate.

His anxiety about leaving his grandparents, if only for two weeks, was forgotten in the excitement of preparing for the journey, and anticipating the revisiting of old haunts. Earlier, while his mother was packing, he remembered he had left some of his soldiers and horse brasses in his secret hiding place, and scuttled across to climb up to retrieve them. Once inside he had second thoughts; there was nothing he really needed, and they would all be there waiting for him when he got back in two weeks time.

He did wonder about his Teddy; he had not played with him for nearly a year now, but was unsure about leaving him behind.

"No," he finally decided, brushing the dust off both his and Nicky's Teddy. "You can keep each other company while I'm gone."

Sam Sharpe had come to collect them, as he was delivering in that direction, but only taking them to the village. After a brief call on his Uncle Silas and Aunty Polly, they would have to go into Norwich by bus. Thus it was that they left the farm as they had arrived two years before – in Sam Sharpe's trap, with the same grating wheel, and the same motheaten pony in command.

His grandfather, leaning on the barnyard gate, with Sampson behind him and Scott and Snip at his feet, stood silhouetted against the morning sun, raising his arm briefly in response to Jonathan's final wave.

Then, as their progress round the bend began to take him from their view, Jonathan watched him resume his familiar stance; hands on hips, legs apart, sniffing the wind, and feeding his soul on the sight of his Friesians grazing contentedly in his pasture.

Chapter Fifteen

Everything semed strange, almost unreal, as he snuggled down in an unfamiliar bed and found he could not get to sleep. For a while he longed for his own bed back at the farm, and the comforting movements of his grandparents in the big kitchen below.

When he awoke he felt at a loss; his morning routine should have been taking him scurrying out to the cowshed to do his jobs, and he wondered if his grandparents were missing him as much as he missed them.

"All your old friends are expecting you," his mother told him, as he made preparations for venturing forth. "But P.C.Pogmore has been transfered to Painswick, and the new policeman isn't as soft as he was, so don't get up to any mischief."

He felt shy, even nervous, as he turned out of the drive to walk down to the village; he was not sure how he would be received by his old friends and playmates after an absence of two years. Perhaps he would be classed as an outsider, and have to prove his worth before he could be accepted back into the gang.

He need not have worried; they were actually on their way up to collect him, and charged up the hill with Red Indian war cries as soon as they saw him. Within an hour it was almost as if the two year absence had never happened, except that at an early point his Norfolk dialect caught their attention.

"You don't half talk funny," said Terry Nesbit, so he immediately demonstrated his versatility by mimicking them, and reverting to passable West Country. In fact he became almost bilingual, in terms of dialect, over the next few days; talking to his mother in pure Norfolk and to his playmates in West Country.

There had been remarkably few changes since he had left, indeed only one of real significance. This was the arrival of a new family to the village, the Hewitts, and there was something about Jimmy Hewitt, who he had met as a fully fledged member of the gang on that first morning, that strongly reminded him of Colin and David back in Norfolk. It transpired that Jimmy's father, who was the new village policeman, was acceptable to the gang as a whole; he was stricter than P.C.Pogmore but in a parental rather than an official sense.

The two weeks flew past; barely had he adjusted to his changed lifestyle than it was time to make preparation for the return journey.

"Couldn't you take me back the next week end?" he asked his mother. "Then I could have another week with you."

But her duty times were not flexible enough to permit a change of plan; neither would she agree to putting him on the train in Gloucester and having him met the other end. She had visions of him vanishing forever somewhere between Paddington and Liverpool Street.

She produced an alternative solution the following day however.

"I've had a word with Matron," she said. "And I could have the week-end after off. But that would mean you staying another two weeks, and you would miss out on both Choir and Cubs outings."

"That's no use," he grumbled. "This lot have their own Cub camp in the Forest of Dean the week after next, so I'd be here with no one to play with during the second week."

"That's settled then," she told him. "We will stick to the original arrangements, and take you back this Saturday."

Jimmy Hewitt hammered excitedly on the side door later that evening.

"Akela says that as you're a Cub you can come on our camp with us," he said. "We all said we wanted you to come, and she's got a spare jersey and cap."

Unwittingly Jonathan had arrived at one of life's seemingly innocuous crossroads; he simply had to decide between two courses of action, neither of which seemed to hold any potential for long term effect.

His mother did not try to influence him, having no strong feelings either way. He was beginning to feel homesick for his grandparents, but it would only be a two week delay before he saw them again, and the compensation would be lots of fun with the Cubs in the Forest of Dean.

She rang his Aunty Polly at work in Norwich, and asked her to get word to his grandparents that he would be staying another two weeks.

"Your father won't be best pleased," Polly told her. "I saw him last night, and he was saying how much he was looking forward to having the little ol' boy back home again."

The weather was perfect during the first week of the extension, and they swam in the canal, and fished, and ranged freely over familiar country while they eagerly anticipated Cub camp the following week.

Disaster struck on the Thursday.

"We're having to cancel the Cub camp," Akela told his mother. "Little Terry Nesbit has gone down with diphtheria, and Jimmy Hewitt has a suspiciously sore throat."

By Saturday morning the whole village was plunged into gloom and despondency. Two little girls had also succumbed, and had joined Terry and Jimmy in Standish Isolation Hospital. Jonathan felt an awful sense of foreboding; he had become almost as close to Jimmy as he had been to Nicky, and was filled with an agony of suspense lest another of his friends should be taken away from him.

The mortality rate from diphtheria, among children in the nineteen thirties, was appallingly high.

On Wedneday morning he awoke feeling thoroughly wretched, with a sore throat and aches in his head and limbs.

His mother went as white as a sheet as the doctor confirmed her worst fears.

His memories of the Isolation Hospital were blurred and vague during the early days; he remembered a darkened room and hearing a child's persistant crying and only later realised it was himself he was listening to. He remembered a doctor, kind, who sucked mucous from his throat with a tube into his own mouth, spitting it out into a bowl. He recalled Jimmy Hewitt sitting up in the next bed, and saying something he could not understand and could not be bothered to try to anyway.

And then suddenly it was alright again, except that Terry Nesbit had gone from the next bed but one, and Jimmy and he did not feel it fair that Terry should be allowed home before them.

"He's not gone home," said Mrs Hewitt, her eyes moistening. "He's gone to live with Jesus."

"I'm sorry to say little Terry died last night," his mother was less euphemistic.

Both Jimmy and he were allowed outside in the Autumn sunshine when they were a little better, but the nursing staff were a bit peeved when they wandered off and were missing for about four hours. Dr Cuthberts, who had sucked mucous from his throat, spent a lot of time with them, teaching them to play cricket and making jokes. One day the two boys were having a mock wrestling match on the damp grass, and were caught in the act by the Staff Nurse.

"You are very bad boys," she scolded, but Dr Cuthberts laid a restraining hand on her arm.

"It's a good sign they're getting better," he said. "It won't do them any harm."

Two weeks after their release from the hospital his mother called him into the kitchen.

"Jimmy is going back to school on Monday," she said. "What are you going to do?"

He was conscious of conflicting feelings.

"I suppose I'll have to go back to Norfolk now," he said.

"No," she said firmly. "I want to keep an eye on you for a while, until you are completely over this thing. But you can't hang around here not going to school or I shall have the Attendance Officer on to me. So I'm going to suggest you go to this school for a week or two, and then I'll get you back to Granny and Grandad."

Over the next two weeks he found himself wistfully longing for Colin and David's company, but most of all he missed the end of the school day with the long walk home past familiar landmarks, and the dogs rushing out to greet him. Then wading through chickens, ducks and guinea fowl, and dodging belligerent geese to get in the back door. Then, boots off and the warmth of the great kitchen range, and his grandmother hugging him and telling him off for scuffed boots, lost handkerchiefs, ripped shorts and general scruffiness; cuffing him in simulated wrath, and then hugging him again.

He recalled the restful evenings, reading the Eastern Evening News to his grandfather. His grandmother sitting him up on the draining board to wash his knees ready for bed. Then sitting on his grandfather's knee, or on the hearth at his feet, to be told stories. Being chased by his grandmother to sink into the enveloping feather mattress while the wind gusted round the eaves of the old house, and becoming drowsy while listening to the rise and fall of his grandparent's conversation in the kitchen below.

"I want to go back to Granny and Grandad," he told his mother.

"Two weeks today," she said. "That's the earliest I can take time off to take you. But I'll write to Granny tonight."

He felt better once the decision was made, although he realised he would have to prepare himself for the wrench of parting from her and from his playmates.

Pre-occupied as he had been with his own problems, he had not taken too much notice of events in the outside world; they were brought rather forcibly to his notice on the following Sunday morning however. Arriving home from a solitary exploration of the wood, he found his mother glued to the wireless and holding up a warning finger for him to be quiet.

"I have to tell you now," said the rather reedy and somehow unconvincing voice of Mr Neville Chamberlain, "that no such undertaking has been received, and that consequently this country is at war with Germany."

There was a strange atmosphere in the village over the next few days; outwardly nothing had changed, but there seemed, somehow, to be a purposeful attitude in the way people walked briskly around without sauntering, and groups formed on bends in the road, and outside shops, to talk about the war.

Then young men in uniform began to appear, and a convoy of army trucks drove through the village on the way South. The older men, crowding into the village pub, relived their First World War experiences for the benefit of the younger men who were preparing to enlist.

Strangers, carrying their authority in their bowler hats and rolled umberellas, appeared and went away again. Rumours of spies and parachutists abounded, and an unfortunate Scotsman with a speech defect, who had merely paused in the village to purchase cigarettes, was forcibly detained in the grocers shop for nearly an hour.

Jonathan's mother seemed pre-occupied.

"Constable Hewitt wants to see you," she told him, on the Wednesday before she was due to take him back to Norfolk.

"I haven't done nothing," he responded, immediately on the defensive.

"Nobody says you have," she said. "He just wants to talk to you."

He discovered later that she had asked Jimmy's father to talk to him; she felt his arguments would carry more persuasive authority than her own.

"Come here both of you," he said to Jonathan and Jimmy, leading them through into the little cubby hole that seemed to be standard 'office' accommodation in all police houses.

He produced a large map of Europe and asked if they could identify the various countries. Jimmy did better at it, geography being his strong point.

"Now look at England," his father said. "And show me where Norfolk is."

Jonathan pointed immediately, and was even able to indicate Norwich and the village.

"Now," said Jimmy's father, stabbing his finger first on France and then on Holland and Belgium. "They're a bit close to Norfolk aren't they? Them Germans move into them places and send their old aeroplanes across with them bombs on, where's the first place they're going to drop them?"

He puffed at his pipe while Jonathan considered this.

"Fact is old son," he went on, "your mum isn't all that keen on you going back there, seeing as how that's likely to be the first place to be bombed."

Jimmy may or may not have been primed by his dad, but he came in right on cue.

"I don't want you to go back to Norfolk, Johnny," he said. "I want you to stay here."

"What I should do if I was you," said Jimmy's father, "is wait a bit until we've knocked them Germans out. Everybody says it will only take a few weeks, you mark my words. Your mother will be happy then, and you can go back to your Granny and Grandad when it's all over."

* * * * * *

A bright but rather showery May evening, some two and a half years later, saw Jimmy Hewitt and Jonathan, their Grammar School uniforms still new enough for them to feel self-concious about them, pausing every now and then to stamp in puddles to splash each other as they made their way homewards.

Jimmy's father, minus his helmet and with his uniform tunic unbuttoned, was waiting by his front gate.

"The 'phones up at the hospital are out," he told Jonathan. "So scoot on up there's a good lad, and tell your mother to 'phone your Uncle Bert back when she can. She can come down here if she can't use the hospital 'phone."

He hesitated.

"Sergeant Cooper from Kings Lynn Police," he said. "I've got it right? He is your uncle?"

Jonathan nodded.

Jimmy's father paused again, seeking his words carefully.

"It's your Grandad Johnny," he said. "I'm afraid he's very poorly."

Jonathan's heart was thumping, not only from exertion, as he ran all the way home to tell his mother, who had only just finished bullying the telephone engineer into putting the telephone back on.

She rang P.C.Hewitt first, to find out how much more he knew.

"It was a bad line," he told her. "All I got was that your father was caught in last night's air raid and has two broken ribs, and that the family are worried about him."

She eventually got through to Uncle Bert, who tried to be reassuring.

"We were going to tell you to come," he said. "But I've just left him, and he seem to have improved a bit."

"What happened?" Jonathan's mother was trying to compensate for the bad line by speaking slowly and distinctly.

"He was on his way home from a meeting in Trowse last night," said Uncle Bert. "Farmer's Union business. An unexploded land mine went off as he passed by."

Following the R.A.F. raids on Keil, the Germans had launched 'reprisal' raids on Norwich. She knew about the one on 27th April, but did not know there had been another one two nights later.

Jonathan's grandfather had taken to riding his bicycle during daylight, but preferred to walk and push it after dark, being unable to cope with the tiny slit of bicycle lamp light permitted under the Air Raid Precautions. Coming across an unmanned barricade, isolating an unexploded German land mine, he had opted to push through it rather than try to find his way around it in the dark. He was actually well past it when it went off, but the blast had knocked him off his feet, and he had fallen awkwardly, the handlebars of his cycle driving up into his ribs.

He had managed to walk the remaining eight miles home, but had felt too ill to climb up to bed. Poking the fire into a blaze he had spent the night in his chair rather than disturb Jonathan's grandmother, who thought the air raid had kept him in Trowse. Early in the morning he had forced himself to do the milking and feed the livestock, even though he was coughing blood by this time.

Only then would he admit defeat.

Dr Dunbar looked ill himself, having been up all night dealing with air raid casualties.

"He has two broken ribs," he said. "One of them has damaged a lung. Thankfully it is not actually piercing it, but we have to keep him absolutely still in case it does."

After strapping the old man up, he stood back and weighed up his prospects.

"I must emphasise the need to avoid movement as far as possible," he said. "We cannot even risk moving him into hospital – the journey would finish him."

Sitting up against half a dozen pillows, in the big brass knobbed bed, Jonathan's grandfather had briefed Ted Limmer's man on the jobs that needed completing around the farm. He insisted that the dogs be allowed upstairs, briefly, so that he could reassure them he was still around.

As his mother relayed all this to him, Jonathan tried to come to terms with his feelings about his grandparents, who he had not seen now for over two years.

A great deal had happened to him in that time; not the least being the transition from small boy to young boy; a transition which – nurtured by the wartime climate – had been accelerated by the acquiring of responsibilities. He had, for example, been selected as one of the Boy Scouts to act as runner for the Home Guard. During exercises he was allowed to ride his bike as fast as he liked in order to deliver important looking packages, wrapped in yellow oilskin, to various units.

Not being particularly enthusiastic about academic work he had been lucky to get into Grammar School; reports, probably exaggerated, of children being machine – gunned on their way to and from school by low flying German planes, had determined some parents to decline the offer of a place, so he got in almost by default.

He and his mother had been kept well informed, by his grandmother's weekly letters, of events back in Norfolk. At first they had been somewhat bitter in tone:

'Your father believe you never had no intent to bring the little ol' boy back to us,' she wrote, 'but that you had it planned all along to get him to Gloucester and then keep him there.'

In similarly acrimonious vein she later wrote:

'We heard about the bombing around Bristol and Avonmouth, and that's more than we've had here, so you saying you kept the boy because of the German bombs won't wash with your father, and anyway he would not have got that dipthery if you had brought him back when you should have and would have been safely back here before that old war start'

Jonathan's mother was quite upset by these unfair charges, and wrote back protesting quite strongly.

It seemed though, that venting her spleen in the first few paragraphs gave his grandmother the emotional release she needed, because she would then go on to be chattily informative about life back in the village and the activities of relatives.

Poor old Silas had died a year after Jonathan had left, and Polly, now left quite alone, had sunk into a depression which worried everybody. Then, when Boulton and Paul's factory in Norwich came under threat from German bombers, and children who lived in the vicinity were evacuated out to surrounding villages, she was persuaded to take three of them into her cottage. Her maternal instincts thus re-awakened, her friends and relatives were gratified to observe a marked change for the better.

One letter from his grandmother, just after Dunkirk, upset Jonathan and his mother considerably.

> 'Jim Bews was badly wounded in France. In some ways that's as well poor old Silas is departed at least he's been spared that.'

Thankfully, the next letter from Enid Bews was more cheerful.

> 'He's lost an arm, and he's no longer fit for active service. But he put up such an argument to the Medical Board that they have agreed he can be posted to a Prisoner of War camp in Scotland, as Sergeant Major, and baby George and I can live close to the Camp'.

Another letter from Jonathan's grandmother informed them that the Squire had died as an indirect result of the war; a combination of enemy action and military requirments had resulted in his being stranded on a remote railway station in the middle of the night. At his age, even his leathery frame could not withstand the rigours of a bitter wartime English winter, and the resultant chill had turned to pleurisy. The Hall had been taken over by the Army, and the Trustees had appointed an Agent to manage the farm and woodland, as Lady Mary had retired to the family house at Herne Bay.

As far as Jonathan's grandparents were concerned the war had made very little difference to their lives. Like most farmers they had a guaranteed market for their livestock, and rationing was not a burden because they lived off their own produce as they always had done. His grandfather had learned to tolerate the constant 'interference' from Ministry officials, who bumped their cars down the lane to 'advise' him how to manage his land. He would listen courteously to them, and then do it his own way.

For his own part, caught up in events and new relationships over the two year period, Jonathan had somehow distanced himself from all that had happened to him between nineteen thirty six and nineteen thirty nine. His friends and relatives in Norfolk, even his grandparents, had become strangely unreal; like characters in a film seen long ago with the plot barely remembered. There were times, it was true, especially during the first months, when the sight of a distant farm worker, dressed like his grandfather, would cause an ache in his throat.

At these times he would recall events and incidents, and experience again the feelings that they evoked. He could remember, clearly, his last Christmas in Norfolk; the benevolent control with which his grandfather had presided over the family gathering, and his own sudden and absolute conviction that God must look a bit like his grandfather.

Equally clearly he could remember how, later that same day, he and Nicky had stood with their grandfather, and their three uncles, gazing over the snowbound pasture from the barnyard gate; not knowing that it would be the last time that the old man would stand by that gate with his three sons and two grandsons; the last time that the whole Cooper family would be together under the same roof. Neither could Jonathan have known that it would be the last real Christmas of his childhood; the next six would be overshadowed by the shortages and pre-occupations of war, and after that he would no longer be a child.

These feelings were resurrected later that week when his mother came along the passage from her office one evening, after a long telephone conversation with his Uncle Bert.

"I'm afraid Grandad is much worse," she said, hugging him, "and I think you should know that he may not recover."

His grandfather died the following day.

In the early afternoon he had become suddenly lucid after hours of rambling. He had known he was going to die, and had said so, weakly lifting a restraining hand when Bert and Jack, who had been summonned to his bedside, tried to reassure him.

"I'll be on my way in a bit," he said, as if he were just going out to milk the cows. "And I never did get round to making one of them Will and Testament things, so you'll have to sort it all out Bert. Make sure your mother and sister are alright. I know none of you want the farm, so you'll be selling up."

He suddenly found a stronger voice.

"That horse go to Ted Limmer," he said. "Not sold – that's my gift to him. I know he'll give him a good home. Jack, you'll take the dogs. I know they'll be alright with you."

He seemed to shrink, exhausted by the effort.

After a while he remembered Jonathan.

"I'd like to a seen the little ol' boy again afore I went," he said.

An hour later he began to wander again, and seemed to be living in the past.

"Tell Silas to walk up and see me," he said. "I haven't set eyes on him in weeks."

Then came an eerie and unnerving moment, which caused the hairs to rise up on the backs of his son's necks, as he peered into a darkening corner of the room.

"Is that boy Nicholas or boy Jonathan waiting there for me?" he said. "I can't hardly tell them apart."

He said no more but quietly slept away.

Jonathan's mother insisted that they travel to Norfolk for the funeral, but he secretly wished they were not going. He hated the sadness of funerals, and had always dreaded the sight of the coffin being lowered into the grave even when, as a choirboy, he was there as part of the Service and did not know the deceased all that well.

Not only that, but his memories of his two years with his grandparents were fixed and comfortable. They included scenes in which both of them were present, and he wanted to retain those memories as they were. He wanted to continue in a land of make believe, where, imprisoned in some sort of time capsule, the farm, Sampson, the dogs, chickens, cows and above all his grandparents, remained for ever.

Or at least for as long as he needed them to.

He did not want those memories overlaid by another one of his grandmother on her own, and all the relatives sitting around the big kitchen talking about his grandfather not being there any more, and all the livestock gone from the barn and cowshed and pasture.

With the aid of the telephone his mother evolved complicated plans for getting them to the funeral and back again in the minimum of time. As she had now been promoted to Matron she did not want to be away from the Hospital for too long.

Her plans did not work out of course.

A combination of Air Raid warnings, bomb damaged stations and tracks, and trains diverted for 'Military Purposes' resulted in their arrival at Norwich Thorpe long after the time scheduled for the funeral. The taxi booked to meet them had long departed, but they were lucky enough to get another after his mother had found some financial incentive to enthuse a porter.

"We'll go straight to the farm," she said. "They will all have left the Church now, and we can pay our respects at the graveside tomorrow morning on our way back to Norwich Thorpe."

Most of the guests had left before they arrived at the farm, including Colin and David – although Jonathan would see them later as he would be sharing Colin's bed for one night. The three Teds were still there; Ted Perriman, having creaked his rhuematic bones up from Suffolk, was arguing with Ted Limmer and Ted Kemp about the respctive merits of alternative remedies for ticks, and quoting Jonathan's grandfather as his authority.

His grandmother hugged him, and commented on how much he had grown; she seemed surprisingly cheerful and 'normal', as did his three uncles, who seemed pleased to see him; his Uncle Bert even shook his hand as though he were a grown up. They were talking about the new Vicar, and how he had managed to strike just the right note in his address to a packed Church.

"Everybody," he had said, "in their passage through this life, influences and even changes the lives of others to a greater or lesser degree. Such a man was our departed Brother William. Many of you could testify to having had your lives changed for the better by his very presence here on earth."

"He never spoke a truer word," said Mr Kemp. "As you of all people should know, boy Jonathan."

"I can't get over how many was there, at the Church," said Jonathan's grandmother. "I stopped counting after about two hundred."

"I reckon there was just about every farmer this side of Norwich," said Uncle Jack, "and a good many from other parts of the County."

"Well," said Ted Limmer, "I don't know how far that'd hold now, but certainly twenty years ago if you had walked from here to Norwich and stopped every man as you met on the way, and asked them if they knew Will Cooper, the answer would have come pat. And they'd a like as not had some story to tell about him."

When the guests had dwindled to only the immediate family, Uncle Bert, who had just seen off Ted Kemp, made an announcement.

"The way that's shaping up," he said, "the land is going to be sold. Some to Ted Limmer, some to the Trustees of the Squire's estate, and the rest, with these buildings and the barn, is down for compulsory purchase for the Military. Although what they want it for the Lord alone knows."

"Granny is coming to live with me in Uncle Silas' old house," Aunty Polly told Jonathan. "And we want you to promise to come and stay with us for a while just as soon as this nasty old war is over."

It was getting too wet to wander around outside; in any event there was nothing to see. All the livestock, including Sampson, had gone to Limmers, and the dogs had already been taken to Thetford.

But Jonathan wanted to pay a visit to his secret hiding place, and seized an opportunity while everyone else seemed pre-occupied. Scooting into the barn, and climbing up to the eaves, he had a momentary anxiety when he thought he was too big to squeeze through the gap; he had grown in two and a half years. Once inside he found what he wanted. They were exactly where he had left them; his horse brasses, special soldiers, Norfolk

Regiment Badge and the faded photograph of Arthur, which he had shown to Nicky when they had sat together in this very space.

Stuffing everything into his pockets, he turned his attention to the thickly cobwebbed corner and lifted out the two Teddies, his and Nicky's. Both were remarkably well preserved; probably because foraging insects had been kept at bay by the spiders. Then he remembered that Aunty Polly was still in the house, and that the sight of Nicky's Teddy, even after three years, could be upsetting for her.

He hesitated a long moment before gently returning them both to the corner, covering them up again with the cobwebs.

The whole family looked surprised when he put on his raincoat.

"I'm going to see Grandad's grave," he said. "On my own," he added firmly, and shot out before anybody could object.

The wet drizzle accompanied him all the way to the village, and stayed with him as he walked slowly through the deserted Churchyard towards the mound of soil, piled by the still open grave, which awaited the arrival of the Sexton to fill it in. He was affected with a strange feeling as he looked around. He had known every square inch of the Churchyard, but it was as though he were seeing it for the first time, and remembering someone else, not himself, playing hide and seek between the gravestones after choir practice.

Some loose earth, additional to that thrown on by the Vicar, had crumbled and fallen on to the coffin lid; but the brass plate was still clearly visible.

William Robert Cooper
Born September 3rd 1870
Died May 5th 1942
R.I.P.

He gazed down, and tried to recall his grandfather's bulky frame, grey white moustache and stern face, lying only a few feet from him under the coffin lid but never again to be seen by him or by anyone else.

He thought he ought to be sad, and there was a little guilt because there was no sadness. He tried, and failed, to recapture some of the emotion within himself on that day when they had stood together by the yard gate;

the day that he had told his grandfather that he did not want him to die, ever. It was as though it were another boy who had sat on the old man's knee and listened to his stories; walked around his pasture with him, and endured the hardness in his eyes when he had earned a reproof. He felt tears ought to come, but they wouldn't.

He stood, a solitary figure by the graveside, his raincoat collar turned up and the increasing drizzle plastering his hair over his forehead, as he took off his cap and twisted it in his hands. Feeling self conscious, and hearing the embarrassment in his own voice, he said to the coffin lid:

"Bye bye Grandad."

As he turned to walk away he had to avoid a small mound right alongside his grandfathers grave. He suddenly realised where he was, but stooped to confirm it by reading the inscription on the little headstone at the top of the small mound.

Nicholas James Cooper
Aged 8 years
Died 12th June 1939
"Suffer Little Children"

Then the sadness came; a sadness which touched him gently with the awareness that a way of life, of which his grandfather and Nicky had both been a part, had come to an end.

As had his childhood.